Sifting Through Static

Ben Tyler Elliott

SIFTING THROUGH STATIC

Copyright © 2015 by Ben Tyler Elliott

Contronym Press
P.O. Box 14392
San Francisco, CA 94114

For the latest on Ben, visit:
www.BenTylerElliott.com

Production assistance and supplemental editing by Ryan Willard
www.RyanWillard.com

Cover art and design by Sara Wood
www.Sara-Wood.com

ISBN-13:   978-0-692-44385-9
ISBN-10:   0-692-44385-1

Library of Congress Control Number: 2015907981
Contronym Press, San Francisco, CA

FOR DAN

One less thing.

19 FEBRUARY 1968

I'm sorry, boys—

If this is the letter that finds you, then I'm sorry. He won.

I hope that it doesn't. I hope that this isn't the message you're reading.

I've written you two: this one, which a friend swore she'd send if I don't signal by Easter, and another, which I'll drop in some faraway mailbox just as soon as I'm safe. I hope it's the latter you're holding. I'm hoping that this one will burn, still sealed and unstamped.

If this is the note you've received, please know I'm not aiming for pain. I intend to bring peace. But they're transposable concepts. Peace. Pain. In time you'll discover that those words are the same.

I need you three to know that should the worst happen—and I suppose that it has—I have my affairs all in order, less a few final things. Some things left to say. To him, I mean. It will be quick, our encounter, and it will not be calm. But he'll hear me. I've left him no other option.

I've found a great weight dangled far from his fulcrum, and that leverage will last independent of me. Please know this. There are things in his cellar. There are bones in his well.

1

I know I sound vague. I know. My other note skins him completely, but I won't do so here. This letter means that I've died, and that's burden enough.

Boys, I need you to know that I wanted to live, so please do not think I steered into him blind or that I sought to be martyred. I love each of you greatly, but altruism never could meet all my needs—I showed him my hand so that he would not seek me. There was no other reason. I love each of you greatly, but I had plans past Colorado.

Please use what I next proffer to leave and move past him. Please break from his shadow, unburdened by me.

Aside from his secret, I've hung a deadfall above him. Had I lived, he would have muzzled himself on account of my blackmail. Because I have died, I must see that he's muzzled in the other way.

Before I sign off, I will share a few facts. I hope they will cultivate closure:

• I died on a Wednesday. Next Wednesday, in fact, because the next morning I'm gone.
• I will be confronting him late, after Mother's asleep. I had planned on leaving before dawn.
• I died in my favorite dress, and I was barefoot by choice.
• If I know him at all, then it didn't go quickly. It hurt. He used his boots. He used his hands.
• My body will not be found. He won't let that happen.
• He'll place me somewhere pleasant, beneath the sun and the stars. He'll sit with me all through what's left of the night.
• If there is an investigation, then justice won't find him.
• Your father did this to me, but I'm not who you think.
• He did this to me, but he's not what you are.

Roy: I am gone, but I am not gone. To you I leave my dear copy of Homer, so that you may remember Bellerophon. Hold him in your heart. Remember what he did, and remember why he fell. The book is buried along eastbound I-70 west of Denver, beneath the mile marker of our favorite number.

Conrad: I am dead, but I am not dead. To you I leave nothing, so that you may remember what you need. Your brothers and I—our yoke is not easy. We are brambly, burdensome things that you'll be tempted to tow, but shelve us instead along the less-traveled hallways of your mind. Retreat through those hallways when the world gets too loud. Do this, and you will cope well.

Wayne: I am you, but I am not you. I left on my terms, so please live on yours. Please place me a stone on that hilltop we liked, beneath the oak, when you're able. That marker will be as thorn in your world, yes, but that's just my intention. Better a thorn on our hill than a thorn in your shoe. Please place it. And leave this place. Wherever you are, that's where I will be.

And of course I expect that you'll see the rest through. I've mailed you this letter. You know what to do.

All: I miss you, and I love you, and I am so sorry.

-H.
Colorado

This is simpler when you assume there's no recorder.

—Hm?

Never mind. You were saying?

Oh—. Well I was gonna say how that's one of my fonder memories of Wayne, actually, that whole day when he nearly killed me.

Right. Go on.

—So it's August, '62. I don't remember the date. But it's afternoon, and we're out across town, way farther than we're allowed to go, and I remember it was hot. Thick hot. Sticky hot so it feels like someone's always touching your face, and all three of us—me, your uncle Con and your pops—we were way out across town, past the boundary, with some Cokes Wayne bought us because of the heat, because he said he wanted to buy us Cokes from this market he liked, but mostly I think he wanted to rope ol' Big Brother Con into a plan that'd make him squirm between disobeying the Man and weenieing out of one of these rarer times when we all three of us boys'd actually hang out.

And did he?

Did who?

Conrad.

Mm. We broke one of the capital-R Rules, the three of us, and wouldn't you know it—the heavens did not crumble.

But on the way back with our Cokes, walking back through streets we didn't know—or at least I didn't know, but maybe Wayne did since he's the middle kid, right, so he's ignored enough that he's got the time to wander everywhere—we happened upon this wooden spool in a dirt lot, or maybe Wayne walked us there without telling, I don't know. But it was huge, this spool, big as a Fiat, but it was made almost entirely of particle board save for the metal cross-braces across the flanges of the thing, and the core of it was that industrial cardboard shit you can drive a screw into, so it was reasonably light. Con's guess was that it must've been used to transport telephone wire, and I'd buy that. Thing had to be five feet wide, flanges probly seven in diameter, but the axle—the axle's a cozy hollow, just about the size of a bent-up little boy—.

—**Big enough for you, Roy?**

Heard this one, have you?

I know you've always been small.

Have I? Hadn't noticed.

You know what I mean.

Hmp. But yeah, the three of us were just standin' there around that spool, all thinking the same thing, and eventually it's Con who speaks our mind: *Oh look, Roy, it's just big enough for a gimp*, and I smacked him in the back of the neck with my crutch and he shoved me down.

But he was right. It was just big enough for a gimp. So we pushed it back toward Main Street, back toward town, and—

Why?

And—. Okay, so there's this block of Main Street over by the elementary school that's a nothing but a huge hill. Like, huge-huge. Like, fuck it if you're gonna drive that block without chains when the winter asphalt goes to ice and the plows can't pull the grade.

Ah.

So you can see where this is going, then. Or maybe Wayne told you this one. Or—

Assume he's never told me anything.

Yeah, well, then we've already got lots in common.

More than you know, probably.

Hmp.

So it took us all day to get it back to town, this spool, and then a few attempts to get it up the hill's steepness. It wasn't the heaviest thing, but neither was it a feather, so we were doing our best Tantalus there for a while, awkwarding it uphill until, inevitably, the spool would free itself and blast downrange and we'd go back for it, determined.

I think you mean Sysiphus.

Which one is he again?

Tantalus could never quite reach the fruit above him or sip the water he stood in.

Oh. Well, anyway, it wasn't until Wayne took one of my crutches and wedged it beneath one of the flanges while we took our breaks that we made it to the top with our—well, I guess you could call it a vehicle. The school had some proper basketball courts and some dudes stopped their shirts-and-skins to watch, one of them pointing at us from all the way down there.

So we're finally at the top and Con says *Get in, Crips*, prodding me between the shoulder blades, and I remember I told Wayne I wasn't so sure anymore after seeing how fast the thing had hauled ass down the hill when we lost it those times before and that wasn't even all the way up where we were, but he told me, Don't worry, I'm pretty sure I can aim you, but I was still worried, and he could tell. He could always tell.

Listen, he said, *Listen*, you'll scoot right by that tree when I aim you and then it's flat and straight for blocks so you'll just roll to a stop. Here, pack one of your crutches and drag it on the ground either on your head side or your feet side depending on which way you want to turn if you're so worried. But don't worry about turning. I can aim you.

So I got in. From inside I could hear them arguing about how best to aim me, Wayne saying they should adjust my trajectory first and then just let go, be precise with it, and Con said it would be easier to keep the spool like it was and just shove one edge of the thing a little harder than the other since the hill'd taken it from us when we'd manhandled it up there, so there's no way we're finessing shit. I'm not entirely sure which method they decided on. Wayne tossed a crutch in with me and then I was rolling.

How was it?

So I think it was the crutch that broke my nose, but it's hard to be certain. It was definitely that or the impact with the tree. Either way, when everything stopped, I thought I'd died. I could still see, sort of, but my hands and my face were covered in blood and everything sounded like I was far away, underwater, and I felt there was—.

I don't know, something—.

Something like a sucking-empty of my head, like when you, throat closed, try to puff out your chest and the pressure fucks with you? But that feeling all over in my head.

How that felt, it was—.

Sort of it felt—.

[—.]

—Roy?

I don't know, sorry, just it's I'm finding it hard to think of something else for comparison aside from good heroin, but I'm coming up short. Maybe quaaludes, maybe. But it felt like Heaven. What I felt right then was what I thought Heaven was probly like, the nod of it all. Everything close but nowhere near. A thrumming hum in my head and a kinda, I don't know, a kinda *silver* feeling spreading itself all across my scalp, across my neck, drifting down and drifting in.

I could hear the basketballers applauding forever. My brothers' shoes, it seemed they slapped blacktop louder and louder for an hour before Wayne pulled me out by my armpits, before he held me off the ground and against his chest, before I threw up down the length of his back.

Jesus Jesus was all Con kept saying, but Wayne kept holding me, holding my hurt against him, and Wayne asked me if I could stand and I said I didn't think so, that I hurt, that my crutches were somewhere, I don't know. Wayne told Con to go back uphill and get my other crutch, but he said it with a sort of ventriloquism I'd never heard before from him, hypodermic-thin, and even in my state I tensed at the sound. How the words came out. How the words came out like how Dad said things, twisting with a braided kinda tension you'd only ever notice if you're one of the few of us who knew what Dad really was. Con ran back up the hill.

Wayne lowered me so my feet were touching the ground, and even though my nose was gushing red all over his shirt, he kept holding me. He said *I'm sorry*, Roy, *I'm sorry, I'm sorry*, and I told him It's okay, it's okay, and I'd buy him a new shirt when I could save up enough, but he shushed me and told me to pinch the bridge of my nose as tight as I could to stop the bleed. I grabbed at it, but the pain was impossible. Deafening. A deafening, dwarfing whistle of pain that lunged through my face. Wayne said I think you broke it, and I whimpered.

By then Con was huffing it back downhill with my crutch. He could only find the one from the top of the hill. The other one, it turned out, was crinkled up pretty good on the other side of the tree from the spool. But, like, right directly on the other side, sort of like the tree was the meat in a sandwich between spool-bread and crutch-bread, and to this day I have no idea how that worked out.

I was still spigoting blood, but as soon as Con saw that I was sort of standing and not really crying too bad he calmed down and started worrying about our story, what we were going to tell Dad about how my face happened and why, and how we'd managed to crumple one of my crutches.

What do we do? Con asked, once at first and then again and again and again, but Wayne said Don't worry about it, I'll take care of it. But Con wasn't having it. Honest, neither was I.

That he had it handled?

That it could *be* handled. That anyone could have run such a set of circumstances by Dad and come out the other side. Stressful, but at least I wasn't Con, him all mangled up with worry, no, at least I had something—a nose—to focus on.

So we hobbled back, every few minutes one of them offering to carry me, but I could walk by then on my one good crutch, just it was slow going. Halfway back I was still oozing, so Wayne tore off a piece of his sleeve and made me stuff it in my nose as best as I was able, considering the pain. I protested on account of the shirt, not the nose, but he said the shirt was already ruined, and he was right, and he had taken it off anyway. Hurt like a sonofabitch, but it made it easier for me to walk without having to tend as much to my busted-up face.

And Conrad?

Well not that he ever completely shut up about it, but it seemed like he reined himself in reasonably. At least until we got closer to home, anyway. Five, seven blocks left he started spreading that worry on thick again, but not that I entirely blamed him.

What are we gonna *tell* him, Wayne, what are we gonna *do*, Wayne, *what?*

Con's badgering can be relentless but I, too, was curious about Wayne's hypothetical Master Plan.

But still, your dad told him just to relax. Just relax, he said, and take Roy around the back when we get there and clean him up in the kitchen as best you can, I've got it dealt with.

Con said, we should use the bathroom, it's further from the living room. And what am I supposed to do about this? I remember Con asked, too, and he waggled my bad crutch in front of Wayne's face.

We'll use the kitchen, Wayne told him, bringing out that Dad Voice again, and it shut Con up something quick.

So after, I don't know, another hour of walking it was starting to get dark and we came around the side of the house to come in the back. Mom was at the store, thankfully. Dad, predictably, was watching the tube.

Where you been, we heard him boom before the screen door'd even swung itself shut.

I didn't know what to say or if I should say anything at all, even, even if I'd had the words. Con's squirming beside me told me he felt the same.

But Wayne didn't say anything either. Soon as Dad'd boomed at us, Wayne just left us in the kitchen to walk straight down the hall and into Dad's bedroom.

What the fuck are you doing I thought you—? Con whispered as loudly as he could, but then, from the living room:

You say something, Conrad?

And we heard him getting up.

They made it to us at the same time, Wayne and him, and I can still see Dad standing there, beer in hand, jaw slacked, just standing there in the doorway, saying nothing. Must've been quite a sight, me looking like I'd been hit by a coupla cars and Con, holding what was left of a ruined forearm crutch and doing that floaty little nervous dance he did whenever, brainlocked, his body'd decide that it must do something, anything, anything but stand still, and there, right there at Dad's side, is Wayne, looking right at the man, holding that goddamned belt all folded up neat in his hand, buckle out, dangling heavy. Felt like a week before Wayne started talking.

Wayne says: We went across town, way past the boundary, and over there we found a spool for telephone wire, and I thought it would be fun to put Roy in it and roll it down a hill. We did that, and Roy hit a tree, and we think it broke his nose, but he seems to be okay except for his nose and some bruises. In any case, it was my idea, not theirs, and I made them do it, so here. I thought I'd save you some time.

And right as he finishes speaking, Wayne tries to hand the belt to him.

Now that whole time, all while Wayne said all that, Dad'd just been looking at me, and when Wayne finished talking at him, when Wayne'd said his piece, I remember Dad sort of shifting his gaze over to Wayne for a second and then came right back to me, how like when you're watching a ballgame and it's close and someone touches you.

And then Dad did something I know none of us ever forgot. He walked right through Wayne's outstretched arm, bumping it aside and the buckle, all the filigree on it, I remember it made this sniffy, zippy little sound as one tooth or one barb on it whispered across his work shirt as he jostled past Wayne like even the buckle or the shirt or the both of them were just as startled, too, and I remember he slapped his beer down on the table, and the instant later, as he went past it, it tipped over and Con flinched, and I remember how it emptied and rolled across the placemat until it fell to the floor, and Con made a quick move in the direction of the dishrag with his arms but he didn't even move his feet, but then Dad came down on his knees in front of me, kneeling in the beer that was still leaking down from above, still pooling, baying itself about his knee and the denim, sopping it up. Then he was holding me. My crutch fell to the side of us as I put my arms around his neck.

Are you okay? Are you okay? Dad kept asking over and over, and I told him I'm fine, I'm fine, I'm okay, and his hands were like big paddles against my cheeks, but they were so careful. And soft. He touched every part of my face in sequence and then removed his fingers just as quickly, like my head was a hot handle he needed to grab but he was unsure of the temperature.

Does this hurt? Are you sure you're okay? How's your eyes?

I reassured him and all of his questions because really, aside from my nose and the rest of me feeling, generally, like I'd been thrown down a hill, I felt pretty fine. But I remember while he inspected me, the one thing I couldn't strip my focus from was these four splotches of my blood near his collar, where my nose had been when he first came down.

This whole time they just stood there, Wayne with his arm still out and that belt at the end of his wrist, and Con, like a sloth in a spotlight, them both totally out of their element.

And then?

And then Dad drove me to the emergency room.

And?

And some resident there checked me out and put plaster on the bridge of my nose after he numbed my whole head and set it, and I had to wear that little bit of awful for the end of the summer and part of the fall. Did me no favors with the ladyfolk of the fourth grade.

And that's it?

I guess.

You guess?

For that part, I mean, yeah. I guess.

But what happened for you?

Were you not listening?

But there must be more, here. What do you remember? What most?

So just ask that. Don't fuck around. Say what you mean—Christ, it's not that hard.

So?

So why are you so curious?

If there's nothing else, I guess that's fine.

I never said there was nothing else. I asked you a question.

Is it something bad?

Yes, sort of. But no. I dunno, whatever, I asked you a question. Why. Are you. So curi—

Why *sort of* yes? What happened?

Just—.

—Oh, what the fuck.

[—.]

—**Roy?**

What I remember most from the whole ordeal is how I was pouring sweat all the way home from the hospital thinking now that I was taken care of, Dad'd take care of Wayne.

And did he?

Well Wayne must have been thinking that too, because he was sitting on the couch in the living room when we got back, just sitting there quiet, in the dark, alone. We walked in the front door and I remember going wide-eyed seeing Wayne there and assessing the scene, flipping back through all the lessons Dad'd taught us all so well and trying to figure out which of them would now play out, right? Which would it be?

The belt?

The basement?

The iron?

Some silence. Then: Everything okay? Wayne asked him, not me.

More silence.

Then he told Wayne, Go get three bowls for ice cream. Strawberry.

I tell you, your pops—he sat for a full ten-count before going, expecting that there'd be something else, and we stood in the doorway, too, Dad's hand on my shoulder, his clip of keys fisted in the other and those keys, the half-scrape and half-jingle that pulsed soft from his hand as he clenched it up tight and then loosened, again and again while we stood, just standing, just each of us waiting together to see.

But then there wasn't something else.

Wayne went, and he paused again at the end of the couch when he came back with the bowls, but the T.V. was already on and Dad didn't seem to even notice he was there. So Wayne sat and passed two bowls down, two to Dad, which Dad took without looking, and Dad handed one down to me and said, Don't forget you're numb. We're not going back to the hospital tonight.

So we ate ice cream, the three of us, and said not a single word while we watched Koufax one-hit the Giants. The game ended and Dad turned off the T.V. and took the bowls, rinsed them in the kitchen, and went to bed without saying goodnight. It wasn't until after he'd shut the bedroom door that Wayne and I got up from the couch, but as he stood, Wayne said, I wonder—. But he never finished that sentence.

Do you th—

I don't know. I let it go. Figuring out what Wayne was thinking, I mean. I wondered, but then I wondered about a lot when it came to my brother, even then, so I did little but lump it in with the rest of the things about him that I'd just assumed I'd never know. And not to say that the missing half of that sentence was a puzzle that occupied much of my head in the ensuing years, but sometimes, when I'd be standing in line at the grocery store, or sitting in gridlock, or watching a three o'clock teakettle boil when sleep could not find me— sometimes I'd discover myself mulling about it. What knot Wayne'd been untying; what loop or end he might've, at that moment, gotten a fingerprint on. But it became just another of those *things*. Add it to the list. Something to maybe ask about directly, when, you know. Whenever we next spoke—.

But then one morning, without even trying, it just clicked. Just came to me like a face on the street you hadn't seen in years might walk right by you while you're rolling along and smile at you, swivel your head but it's already gone.

What did?

What Wayne'd discerned on that hot night forever ago— what, perhaps mercifully, he hadn't said. What had eluded me. What had eluded me and, with its elusion, had kept this trinket, this small souvenir I'd long prized safe, safe and away from the grime that Dad'd ground into so much of the rest of that life. Perhaps, even, it'd still be safe but for this nothing, bullshit, boring morning, waiting at the bus stop on my way to work some thirty years later, decades since I'd really spoken to Wayne and longer since Dad'd died when I was, for no special reason, replaying this little moment that the three of us had shared, when it clicked.

I mean I know Dad'd been talking about the ice cream and me freezing my tongue or something, or maybe biting it, right, since my head was still numb from the setting. But it wasn't until this moment, lifetimes later, that, for no reason I could ever quantify for you, that it clicked completely, that that night, what Dad'd said right after he'd handed me the ice cream? Yeah, well, those two clauses—.

Those two clauses hadn't been related at all.

CONRAD/BAKERSFIELD, CA/2008-07-24
16:21:23—16:38:58

Assume I'm not even here.
How's'at? You're right there.
Try.
But you're right there, though.
Humor me.
But you're right. There.
So humor me anyway.
[—.]
—Why?
Why what?
Humor you. Why should I humor you?
Talk about driving.
I—. Drivin'? Why?
Why not?
Like how to drive? But you drove up here tod—
Your work as a driver. Talk about that.
Oh—. Well why all that shit, though? I—
I thought you were humoring me.
But—
Conrad.

—But. Uh—.

Just talk, Conrad. Like I'm not even here.

Um. Well, like, okay, so drivin'? Fuckin'. Whatever. Fine.

Drivin' trucks came natural after my deployment on account of part of the time over there I was wheelin' convoys in the backfield, right? Ammo, food, troops sometimes. And I was good at it, too. M34s, M36 longbeds, rain, no rain, typhoon, didn't matter. Gimme your shittiest M109 and I'll show you a van that can climb a tree. I had an officer, Miller, who told me I was the best with a sprague-drive he'd ever seen, and he'd seen lots of the heavy.

But why driving? Over there, I mean.

Ah, I was smart, see. Draft Day—you know how it works, right? Where each county has a quota and then Washington ranks all three hundred sixty-six birthdays live on T.V. and then each county goes, okay, June twelfth is first, so all the June twelfth guys are in, and then they count how many guys that is and then they go to, I dunno, let's say August ninth is second, so they grab those guys, and then the next, and then on and on down the three-sixty-six until whatever birthday puts the county over its quota for bodies and they're done. If you're early, you're fucked, and if you're last, you're golden.

Well, my birthday was marginal when they pulled it, so I hedged bets and marched down to the Army office and signed up on the spot. Figgered if I volunteered before I got the mailgram, the least they could do's gimme some sorta preference where I go, what I do, so I got my ass down there and told them how my father was a long-haul and he'd taught all of us how to drive just as soon as our legs was long enough to reach the pedals, so I'm in if you'll let me wheel, I'm good. And it worked. They dumped me in the depots after basic and that, as they say, was that.

But past that? I dunno. Gun to my head I guess I'd say the M34 was my favor—

Talk about driving back home.

—Fave. Okay, what the fuck? Are you askin' questions or am I talkin'?

You drove tankers, right?

Just—. Yes. Fuckin' yes, I drove tankers.

Gasoline?

No, fuckin' chocolate milk. What'cha think?

Gasoline? Or diesel?

I—. Um. Gas, mostly, I guess. Why?

Details matter, is all.

Huh?

I'll get to that. Keep talking.

Well, like—. Okay, yeah, I drove gas tankers, mostly, through Cali, and I mean I dunno, I guess drivin' back here wasn't *that* much different from any other drivin'-type gig you might've heard about. It was lonely, but it was prolly the only place for me back home, at least right then. Similar enough to what I'd gotten good at over there, but without the brass nor the box-kickers breathin' down my neck or a clock to punch, and it gave me time to, like, decompress, you know? Figure out how to be a civvie again. Just get this trailer to Los Angeles, and get it there by 04:30 Thursday. Try not to wreck, but more, try not to get hijacked. Simple gig.

Not always easy, though.

Oh?

Mm. Fucked up that second part. A few times, actually, three times. Three in four years.

Is that number high?

For that time? Where I was? Eh. I mean, yeah, but it's not like that was a shitload, no, I know some people got jacked more than me.

Why so many hijackings?

Simple—gas prices. Hilarious when you fill up today and try to remind yourself that, yes, there was a time when sixty cents for a gallon of gasoline seemed like fascist, drag-'em-to-the-Hague type shit. But, even then, like now, most of your dollar wasn't Joe Gaspump wanting to squeeze you, because if he's selling at sixty, he's buying it from Exxon or Chevron or whoever-'On at fifty-two, maybe, or fifty-four, and he's payin' his lease mostly by poppin' dents and smoggin' cars, sellin' candybars and Vivarin.

But anyway, the unsavory types, they figgered out they could work in teams to jack trucks, sometimes two at a time, and daisy-chain the scores to the back of a third rig that they've got papers for, maybe, to take the edge off the heat if they get pulled over, and then they drive them out of state or down the street, find some Joe who's just gettin' by and empty the tanker on him for twenty, twenty-five cents on the gallon and then dump the empties on the side of the road.

Clever.

Mm, but that was then. Now? I dunno if they're still doin' that shit now, but I doubt it what with all the computers and satellites and every vendor running on credit, even, not just the buyers, and then most drivers're prolly packin' iron now anyways. It's just too risky out there anymore, but back then, yeah, before. Clever and common.

What was it like?

Gettin' jacked?

Yeah.

First time was terrifyin'. Second time, not so bad.

But so for the first one, it's February 9, 1976, and—

You're sure about that?

—And. Hm?

The date.

Oh. Yeah, the next night's when I started—.

[—.]

—Conrad?

Whatever. I'm sure. Don't interrupt me.

But then I'm stopped at a red light in Hollywood, right, and two guys just hop on up in the passenger door like I'm a Checker, and one of them has an M1911, black and pretty, and he tells me to take it up through the intersection and get out next to the fenced-off car wash at the end of the next block. So I do. When I'm out, Handgun gets out too, and he marches me over to the fence, and I'm puzzled, right? How I can't believe I'm about to get shot in the street, middle of the day in downtown Los Angeles. He tells me to turn around, and I'm like, well, shit, how's this supposed to go? *Mother Mary fulla shit*—but he doesn't. Shoot me, I mean. He pulls out a set of cuffs, and he cuffs me to the fence and then the two of them skip on back to my rig. Handgun rides shotgun and Other Guy drives 'em off. I guess Handgun was the guy with the idea and the guy who could drive the rig was, well, the guy who could drive the rig. Cops came after maybe half an hour of me hollerin' at traffic.

I can't stand L.A.

But cops unhook me and I rode with them to where my rig had already been reported sittin' peacefully at idle. Trailer's gone, but the cab's fine. Better than before, actually. They'd wiped down the dash.

And the other incidents?

So here's where it gets good. Few months after this I'm workin' for a whole different company, different rig, and I'm fuckin' up a cheesesteak at some diner in Gilroy after sittin' through two hours of Bay Area rush. I'm done, and I walk back to my cab, hop up in, and fuck, there's two guys lyin' down inside. I see one of them has an M1911, black and pretty, and he says, Holy shit, man, how you been?

I tell him I'm fine and I asked them how they were likin' San Francisco, and they said the cops were slower and the food was better and the heat was on down south besides. Handgun laughs about how it's a small world and so on, asks if I remember the drill, and I tell him, Yeah, which fence? and he directs us to a closed-down service station a quarter mile up, and then I'm cuffed again, but this time they apologize, though, for the inconvenience.

So they're off, but this time a sheriff happens by not thirty seconds after, and there I am, all flailin' and flailin' once I see their cruiser coming up around the bend, and they light up and slide to a stop, and one's out the door almost before the car's stopped movin', and he's shoutin' *What happened what happened*, and I tell them how I got jacked and they've got my rig not even a mile away, and they unhook me and yell to get in the back so I can point out my rig once we catch up.

Cops redline it, which is fun. If you ever get plunked in the back of a car, hope you get lucky enough they get called out on a chase before they can dump you back at the precinct, because that shit is F-U-N *fun*, the giddyup in those things and how good a badge can be at drivin' 'em. Prolly my best ride ever in the back of a prowler, that day. Top three for sure. But yeah, they redline it all lights and sirens and we catch up, and then, outta nowhere, boom, a dozen or so cars and a chopper, even, but the guys. The guys, they just won't pull over. Not for nothin'. We're halfway to L.A. before they're outta fuel.

Did you have to testify?

[—.]

—Conrad?

—Mm? Oh. No. No, nobody testified. Handgun and Other Guy blazed out of that cab like Cassidy and Sundance, and they bled out right there on the asphalt. Shame, really. They seemed like pretty okay dudes.

What about the third one?

Third what?

Hijacking.

It. You. Who told you there was a third one?

Three times in four years, you said.

Never said that.

I can rewind th—

Two. Two times, only two. Let's talk about somethin' else.

What happened after—

We're talkin' about somethin' else, I said. Or it's gettin' late, and you can go.

After the second time, I mean. What happened after the second hijacking? Those guys got shot, and then—?

Oh.

Yeah, I caught a lift back down south, and my office gave me the rest of the week off. I told them I didn't need it but they said it was protocol. Fine.

What did you do with your week?

Nothin'. I don't know.

[—.]

Y'know, Wayne called me that night, the night that it happened, but I don't know how he had my number. Never told nobody that before, that he called. I'd just moved into a new place, but he had my number, but I don't know how.

God, it'd been five, six years since I'd heard his voice on the phone, and there he was callin' me on the night I got jacked of all nights. What a coincidence, I remember thinkin', but he beat me to it, told me he'd heard I's famous now that I'd been on the news and asked how I's doin', if I'd been hurt, if I's okay.

Fine, I told him, I'm just fine, and then I was about to ask him, you know—ask him how he'd landed my number, how he was doin', what he'd been doin' and where in the world he was livin' these days, but he cut me off before I could get a word in, just started talkin' right after I said I's fine.

Good, he said, after I said I's fine, and then he started with the ear assault like he does, talk talk talk, on and on about all kinds of shit. Books he'd read, mythology, philosophy, and science shit like chemistry, physics, metallurgy, all this shit he'd been working on in school like I could understand a single goddamned thing about what he's talkin' about and I kept wantin' to tell him slow down, man. Slow down. You're in school? How are you? Where are you? But I couldn't even get a word in. I hadn't heard from him since right before I shipped and here he was, weirdin' up my already-weird day with his ramblin' on about all this shit I didn't even care about and all I wanted to know was what he'd been doin' for the last six years.

Six years is a long time.

Yeah but it's not like I never tried calling him, you know, because I did. Try. When I could. But if I'd try, his phone'd just ring and ring, or it'd be disconnected and it'd be months before Mom had a new number for him.

I remember him being difficult to reach.

Mm, well, finally I got a word in, asked him how he was. Fine, he said, fine. And then it was that chilly kinda quiet on the phone—you know the kind.

Hm?

You know. Neither one of you knows what to say. The longer it goes, the harder it gets to be that one who breaks it up. The kinda quiet gets bigger on silence, y'know? Like, eats it? I dunno. Eventually it's me who breaks.

What'd you say?

Asked him if he remembered how last time I saw him, how we drove way back up into the hills and he showed me constellations. Set a fire and laid out until I fell asleep to him talkin' and going on and on about all this cool stuff like the old stories that happened before there were books, and how people had to pass them stories down by mouth.

Or how'd he say it—? He said—.

That's right, he said they had to pass shit down by carvin', or by carvin' up the sky, star by star, to reason out shit about the world that they couldn't explain. To feel less alone, I 'member he said. I remember him sayin' that. That they did that to feel less alone beneath the vast and the cold. A sort of nightlight, sorta. I remember he said that. And I told him how I 'membered how we talked late—or rather, I guess how he talked and I listened because he was always the big talker between us and it was nice, that night, just to listen to him talk. Bet he's still a talker, isn't he?

Not so much these days.

No? Huh.

Well, when I still had him there on the phone I was rememberin' that night, tryna to tell him about it but I guess I was just excited to have him on the phone, so I just sort of blurted it out in one breath, all that, and then it was quiet again for a beat, and then I said, We should go again, I said, Maybe there's some good hills out here in California, I don't know. Are you in California? What cities show S.F. or L.A. news? I don't know which you saw me on, but a bunch, I bet, but how far from Burbank are you? Let's go eat, brother. Whatever you want. I'm buyin'.

He told me he wasn't in California.

Before I could ask him, you know, Huh?—about the news thing—he said he had to go, but I even shouted at him, told him, Wait hold the fuck on, what's your number at least, gimme your number. But then he was gone.

That's tough.

Hnh—.

—What happened next?

I dunno. I remember throwin' the phone, and then I remember pourin' a drink, and then I remember sittin' there in the dark for a while.

What'd you do?

—Mm? Oh. Nothin'. Just sat there. Sat there and thought for I don't know how long just sittin', thinkin'. Maybe I finished the bottle.

What'd you think about?

—Just how things used to be so different, y'know? How things used to be with him, I don't know if you know, but how he and me got along pretty decent back before all our shit, all those bad years. Different maybe than me and Roy or him and Roy, prolly, 'cause everyone's different with how they relate, right, but it's all special, you know? Do you have a sibling?

No.

Sucks. Guess you don't really know what I'm talkin' about, then. Not exactly. Maybe you're married or somethin', it's sorta like that, but it's not quite like that because it's just as close, but you don't get a say in whether you get a brother, so brothers's closer in a way. Not that I've ever got hitched, but I can imagine. But a brother, a sister—that's a closeness you can't really find somewhere else, and I'd missed that, my brother, all that whole time. Because I had Roy but it was never the same with all his—. Uh. Well, with all his shit.

Like what?

—I don't wanna talk about those things.

Was it the drugs?

Yeah, so——. I dunno. I don't wanna talk about it right now. Maybe later.

Why? Were you using, too? Were you pushing?

No. Never. Never in my life, not once.

But why wouldn't you—

His junk never came from me, never. Not for him. Not for anyone, ever. You hear me?

Conrad, we're just talking here.

Still. Just settin' you straight. Never did that shit.

Fine. So then back to what you were saying before.

Yeah, okay. Good. What was I sayin'?

You were sitting in the dark.

Oh yeah. Yeah I just kind of sat there and thought about shit, how we'd gotten where we were, what happened.

So what happened?

How much time you got?

I'm in no rush.

Hnh. Well——.

[——.]

Well maybe some other time.

—Conrad?

Just I wish we could've talked more over all those years, y'know? That's sort of what I thought about there in the dark, thinkin' how I missed him. That I missed him and that I'd *missed* him, if that makes any sense. That I'd missed out.

Why didn't you write?

—But I did. Don't know how many I wrote and sent him, hundreds, maybe a thousand, one at a time, half a dozen, sometimes a brick of letters unless—oh.

Oh you're clever, you. Is that what you wanna talk about? If that's what you wanna talk about you can just ask. You don't have to come at me all crossways.

It was just a question.

But he got them, then, right? He got my letters?

I don't check his mail.

But he told you, right. He told you about them so that's why you're askin', right, but why'd he send you? Chickenshit thing to do sendin' you to talk about me writin' him when he could just be comin' himself, why don't he just come?

He doesn't know I'm here.

Huh. Okay. So why're you here, then?

I'm just here to talk.

That's fine and all, you know, it's fine. It's good. Good to see you for once, I mean, you're taller than I thought you'd be, but why? Why are you here?

We're just talking.

But why the recorder if we're just talking, hm? Are you—? You're prolly gonna take these right back to him, then, right? For him to listen? To me? That's a chickenshit thing, that, and you know it, too, dontcha. You're aiding and abetting his chickenshittery. Why doesn't he just come?

Maybe the tapes are for me.

But why?

Do I need a reason?

Well. No. I guess no. But it's a little fuckin' weird. You know that, right?

I suppose. But humor me for a bit, hm? Later I'll explain, and this should make lots more sense.

—So you're not gonna turn it off, then?

Talking, Conrad. You're talking now.

Hey you don't have to be an ass, y'know. Fact I'd rather you weren't, actually, I was just askin' a question, I—

No, Conrad. That's exactly it. This is a conversation I'm making you have. Now make like I'm not ev—

I don'—. Wait. What?

Listen, we're off topic. Your letters.

No but—

Conrad I just explained it to you.

Explained what?

Why I'm here. I just said it. Just now I said it exactly.

But I don'—

Listen, don't worry about it. I bet it'll be clearer later.

Bu—

Now. Your letters.

But—. Oh whatever. My letters. Yes, I wrote him letters. And you didn't answer m—

About what?

My—. About his letters. You didn't say if he got them.

I told you I don't check his mail.

Fine, fine, whatever. But I decided to write him, yes.

You decided that night?

Sorta.

Why?

Hard to say. Why that night, I mean, because people write letters all the time.

But not like you've written. How many boxes do you think you have?

In this room?

Or total.

Well—one, four. Eight. Twelve, thirteen. Sixteen, looks like. Sixteen in this room.

And they're all letters?

Prolly. Haven't opened 'em in a while, but prolly. Mostly unsent but some that came back. But there's other stuff in there too, it's not all just paper.

Like what?

Oh, bits of things. Old stuff from way back that I kept just because. There's prolly half as many again in the other room and storage units downtown. Boxes, I mean. I've only got two units downtown.

Why so many?

Huh? It's just two units, and they're not even the bigg—

Boxes.

Oh. Well they're not all to him, you know. Believe it or not, there's other people I've written to before. Still write to.

That came back? Or that you never sent.

[—.]

—Conrad?

Actually they're mostly all to him. Just him, actually, not even mostly.

Can I see?

26

No, I'll show you some other time, don't open those.

Here, I won't take any of them I'll j—

Stop it. Sit down. Get away from there.

—Don't do that again.

So they're all to him, then? The letters? All of them?

Yes, just. Can we not talk about the boxes? Please?

Why?

I sometimes write letters to Wayne, okay? Mostly to Wayne. But I think there's a few letters in there to some others folks who're gone. Who aren't even—. Look I'd just rather not get into it, okay?

Another time, maybe.

But like I wouldn't go reading your diary, y'know? Know what I mean?

I know. It's okay.

So, Conrad—.

[—.]

—Conrad?

Just don't do that, okay? Touch my things without askin'. A man's things're private and I don't want just anyone touchin' everything, pokin' around in my shit. It's mine, okay? Never was meant for you so just don't, okay?

Fair enough.

Thank you.

Why do you write, Conrad?

—What?

Your letters to him. Why? Why did you fill up so many boxes?

Why?

That was the question, yes.

No, I mean why do you want to know?

It's just a question.

But—. Oh whatever. You're awful at answerin' questions but I don't know that I much care right now, I don't have the energy.

But why do I write? I dunno. Why does anyone write?

But to keep writing, I mean. So much and so long. It's extreme.

But it's like talkin' in a way. Even if there's nobody on other end, it's still like talkin'. And it's a sorta talkin' the other person can't do a goddamned thing about. They can hang up the phone or not pick it up at all, but they can't keep you from gettin' your head down and out of you, onto paper, whatever, and then maybe someday sendin' it or givin' it. Can't nobody stop that.

When did—

This idea come to me?

No, that's not—

Came to me that night, actually. Sittin' there in the dark and drunk. But funny thing about it is how it came to me, how I was gonna do it just to be a dick, right? To make him feel bad someday when I could hand him a bundle and say, Hey brother, fuck you, I love you, and hand it to him. Show him he's the one, right, that never tried.

But—

But yeah, I was just sittin' there, enjoyin' my drunk but wantin' more bourbon, but out, so I decided I deserved a trip to the liquors and as I was lookin' for my car keys I was still thinkin' about it, how I could reach him, make him feel bad, when it hit me.

That I could write.

That I could write and the idea hit me all at once, that I could—that I was gonna write. That, fuck it, I'm gonna write him every day if I can, and so what if I don't have his address. I'm gonna write him and keep all the letters until I can send them, and then I'm gonna send 'em or give 'em, because fuck him. Fuck. Him.

It's somethin' he can't stop, see, he can't stop me. Never could.

Nobody can.

SEVENTY-TWO

10 November or 12, I stopped keeping track. I find myself having a harder and harder time remembering things. Small things, yes, but still. I am beginning to get worried. They said this would happen, that this is the way it would start to happen, but still. I am worried. I am not sure what to do.

It was my car. I could not find it in the parking garage and I walked around for more than an hour. There were just too many floors, and at first it was just that I could not remember what floor it was on, but then after I had looked through all the floors I went to security. When I was there they asked me to describe the car, and.

And I—.

It was on the tip of my tongue, but the words would not come. The man there, how kind he was, he could see that I was having trouble so he tried to look at the tapes, the security tapes he could rewind to whenever I came in. I told him I was going to the mall for the holidays, and I had breakfast at home first, but I had misplaced my watch.

Your watch—.

I cannot find your watch, I have—. I have looked—.

I was not sure what time I arrived, but it must have been close to noon. The man, he went through the tapes, scrubbing

29

through while I watched in case any of the cars would trigger my memory, and we looked and looked and watched maybe a hundred cars come and go as the timestamp zipped by. On and on and on. Until I arrived. Until I saw myself on screen, right there, in black and white, but I was riding my bicycle, and the timestamp read 3:41.

He asked me if I was okay and I started to cry. He asked if he could drive me home and we could put my bike in the back of his truck, but I was so upset that I could not recall where I lived; I could just say that my first name was Wayne, and that I lived in a blue apartment by the railroad tracks. He had to read my address off of my driver's license. He did not want to leave me here, but I lied to him. I lied to him and told him that you lived with me and that you would be home soon. Home soon to take care of me. Home soon.

I have been sitting at this table for more than an hour. I managed to calm myself, and I have my head about me again, but I did not know what to do. I almost called you. I tried to, even. I tried to but I could not. The last three numbers, I—.

229-0.

229-0—.

I have them written down. I have them written down and as soon as I finish this I am going to find the paper with all of the numbers and I am going to call you and ask you to come, I am so ashamed. I am ashamed of myself, of my life, of the things I have done and the ways that I am. Of how these disappointments have disenchanted you. Have dissatisfied you.

I am going to call you and tell you about these tapes so you will know. That is what I will do. I will call you and tell you and you will come and I will show you the panel in the wall, and the tapes and tapes, the lifetime of tapes I made out of cowardice, I am so sorry. I am going to call you and ask you to come, and this will be the last tape. I promise it will. We will make a pact: listen to these or burn them, or both, but no more tapes—only talking from here. I will tell you everything I know, everything I remember, before it all leaves me. I swear.

This is the last tape. There will be no more.

Since—. Since this is the last tape, I am feeling compelled to end this disgrace upon some purer note, some small, lucent something so that this nonsense might end like the way that I wanted. Right. Good. Hold on.

[—.]

I have returned. I have returned from the box with a tape. With my favorite tape of the thousand I have wasted, and the label is smudged, but I remember its smudging. I was eating an orange, once, and pulled it out to listen, but the juice on my thumb, it—.

It—. It is still—. Even though I once—.

No matter. Perhaps it is fitting. I will play it now. I will play it into this microphone from my other recorder. I will leave it to run. I will leave it to run while I go search for the paper with your phone number.

Just listen. Please listen. Stay with me. Please stay.

[| |]

Today is 19 May 1986. This is tape seventy-two.

Good morning, Kidlet. As a break from my brothers, I mean to tell you about something interesting today. But first I want to spend a moment talking about something important to no one, save for me.

When most people remark on their favorite thing, their one, singular moment that happened to them that they would place above all others, their happiest time, they go with the things that most people fixate upon. Their marriage. The birth of their child. Becoming a grandparent or any other from the list of Important Things. But mine—mine happened on a mostly-unremarkable Saturday.

When you were four, maybe you remember, I had you on Mondays and Thursdays and every other weekend. I lived in a terrible little apartment with no furniture, because I gave everything to your mother even though she never asked me for any of it. My half of the house, half of whatever paychecks I got from whichever jobs I held down; it just seemed like the right thing to do.

So I plugged along in my tiny apartment, going to work, coming home, but always spending every waking moment looking forward to my next day with you. Even though I had no money, I always tried to plan things for us to do on the weekends you were over. The duck pond, if you remember— how we would go there with a loaf of bread and feed the ducks until the bag was empty. Or Tahoe, when I could afford the gas, where we would throw stones from its shore until our arms would not move.

But one weekend—one weekend in particular, I hope you remember, because I remember it well. It was a free admission weekend at the San Francisco Zoo, so I took you, and it was impossibly crowded—approximately everyone was there. How I held you on my shoulders at the gorilla exhibit. How you squealed with laughter at the hippos with their tiny, flippy ears.

We went from the zoo to the Big Surprise, which was a short helicopter tour of the bay. I had saved up enough money over the course of three months to take you up in a helicopter, and you were so excited. It was only half an hour or so, maybe less, but it was the best money I have ever spent.

We landed and you were hungry. I had some snacks in my bag, but you wanted spaghetti, but I had no money for spaghetti. But then. Just then. On the ground blowing by:

A twenty-dollar bill.

In all my life, that has been the only twenty I have ever found, and I found it, just then, as you asked for spaghetti and I was preparing to explain to you that it would have to wait for another day. I stomped on that bill, and I picked it up, and we went to the closest Italian place I could find.

And that is my moment. My favorite moment. My one thing I go back to whenever things are hard, is that one moment. Sitting with you in a highchair, your face and hands covered in marinara and the noodles are everywhere. You were so happy—.

Anyway—.

That already feels so long ago, now, and I was drifting again through that moment this morning when, for the first time in my life, I think, I felt old. While I was sitting in the kitchen, listening to the birds, and the sun was just about to come up, I felt it clear, and bright, and as *there* as the cup in my hand.

Old.

Even saying it feels odd, feels foreign. Like, when did this happen? Was it today? As I was reading the newspaper with my orange juice and my toast—did it just happen? That I became old? Does it happen like that? Or is it gradual and I noticed only now that the process actually *is*. Actually exists. Like a child growing, how a relative is able to remark, *Oh, look how you have grown*—but a parent. How a parent is too present, is too close to the thing growing and the incrementality of it, of the child, to see as the relative sees.

And of course I know that a child growing taller is a procession, is just a product of that child advancing toward adulthood and then later, beyond. I mean something different. That perhaps this has been happening to me, is what I am trying to say. The ascent into agedness. That shift. That maybe it was gradual and I am, merely, dense.

Or is it a *density*, perhaps? Does that make more sense—that I underwent some transmutation while I was not observing? A change of phase? Adult to old. Liquid to gas.

And then disregarding the nature of the mechanism, what if in the morning I feel young again—am I wrong today or am I wrong tomorrow? Or what if someday, much later, I feel young again after years of feeling old—what rule would that break? Would that change the corporeal fact of my age? Or could it be that age, as I struggle to describe it, is some other thing entirely?

And what if a meteorite flashes through this roof and sublimates me as I sit here, as I speak. If that, then was I old at some earlier time? Is there an equation for this sort of thing? And if there is, and if I had been recording this at the park or in another state when this room was fisted into the gut of the earth, would my newly-avoided, earlier agedness still apply to this formula and the balance of its outputs if, accidentally, I had lived on? Is every possible permutation considered in its calculation?

All of this wonders me. I mean, what of its nature, age? Is it a toggle that, once flipped, cannot be set back again? Or is it a toggle at all? Could it be more a ramp? Or a lever, perhaps, or some other, simpler machine. And if it is a ramp, is it a ramp that goes up or is it a ramp that goes down, and if it is a ramp, how far do you think it goes? How long is it, do you think, before the slope itself seems a separate sort of age? A sort of helplessness, perhaps. A resignation. A death.

Who knows. These are just things I am presently mulling, and maybe there are no answers. Maybe it is all of these and none at the same time and then, after all of that, maybe it is different person to person, life to life. Hm.

Sorry. I feel fine. I mean no worry and I mean no morbidity, merely, my old-feeling was something new and it got me considering. Considering that someday you, me, your friends, the people you will never meet and everyone else—we will all become some kind of old, even if only for a moment.

I hope, anyway. That you live to be old. And maybe you already are—how about that, Wayne-o? Hm? How old do you think that kid of yours will be when this tape gets its first listen? Fifteen? Thirty? Sixty? More?

Hey, happy birthday by the way.

But if—

[—.]

—*What was that, Kidlet?*

Hold on, you want something.

[| |]

Sorry. Back. I never like stopping and starting the tape, but you were calling me from the kitchen. I always hear you wake but it seems you grow stealthier by the day, and I need to remember to keep the cereal on a lower shelf. But you are presently situated and cartoons are on and Papa-has-some-work-to-finish, so. What was I saying?

It was—. Ah, okay.

So if it turns out you already are—old, I mean, if you are old as you are presently listening—well, welcome. Welcome to age. Welcome to age and I hope that the weather is nice whenever you are and I hope I turned you out okay. That was—is—my continual hope. That I screwed you up minimally, I mean, and that you hold no hard feelings in regard to all of my—peculiarities, I guess you could say.

But what peculiarities, Daddio—I thought you were the paragon of normalcy?

Well, child, I do sometimes speak into a tape recorder when I am alone, so. What else. Once, I decided to go a whole year writing only with my right hand, so I taught myself how and I did it and I never faltered. How many people do you know of that would endure such frustration? Or how about how people say I sound different when I speak, but nobody yet has been able to put their finger on exactly why. Or why I will not shake the hand of a working musician. Or why I tip thirty-three percent, to the cent, and how I will not open doors with my left hand, or why I kept things from you deliberately through your entire youth, inclusive of those childhood years that are yet ahead of you.

All I can say in my defense is that there is a reason for each of these things and for each other peculiarity that I have not said here or may never even say aloud. Reasons for each, well rationalized and purposeful, and maybe someday you will even understand some of them.

But wait, I can hear you wondering, *hold on a second old man.* All of that tipping nonsense and handshaking inanity is well and good, but what was that bit about keeping secrets, hm? *Just how big a jerk are you?*

Fret not, child, for I am no monster. What things I have withheld are not robbing you of anything. In fact, these tapes are a fine example of just such a secret—which is such an odd dichotomy, really, considering that I have not yet decided their fate and whether it includes a ribbon and a card, or a shallow pit and a pint of unleaded—but that there are, what, more than seventy of these things already and you have no idea. How many do you think there will someday be? And do you feel deprived? How could you, even?

But there are others things I have hidden, too.

Like what, jerk?

Well, like just how hard things were for me at times, and not just the suffering that hovered about your grandfather, no. I mean, what purpose would it serve you or anyone to rehash the many stretches of months where dinner was a bag of oranges because oranges were six cents cheaper than apples? Or about the times worse even than those, when dinner was a hammered-open can of beans because the beans were stacked furthest from the grocery employees? Or what other things? Too many things.

Things that I have done that I cannot bring myself to say even here. Not directly.

Anyway, the list of my peculiarities is already taller than you and will continue to grow long after you do, and all of that— well, perhaps all of that serves to keep me spry. Maybe keeps me balanced enough inside so I only screw you up just enough to become an interesting person, no more, no less. Just enough. Scoff if you must, but the spotless are a boring people.

And if you are wondering, I attribute some of my own spots—even most of them, maybe—to your grandfather. So. How about that for a bit of parity, hm? And not that I speak of him to you, and not to say that this is a theft, because my silence—my silence is maybe the only thing upon which we will ever agree, your grandfather and I. The hiding of him. His want to have transpired, to have had materialized sans history and to have existed with that story rubbed from the world. And I have deigned to be complicit in that want. Have chosen to be. And this is not a theft. The theft of his history will see you no worse because of it. I know this. Am certain of it. Certain beyond reason.

But then here—?

Here in these—*things*?

Here, who knows. Here I might bury my contingencies. Here is where I may say *in case* about a lot of my life, even though I cannot foresee any case in which, for example, what little is known of your grandfather's history should ever be at all needed.

Hm.

Well on with it, then, yes? Why not?

So, there was a time in my life, shortly before and after your grandfather's death, that I sought as much information as could be mustered about him, and this was because I hated him. I hated him and I wanted to know everything about him so that, perhaps, I might understand him. And whether this push for knowing about him was due to some want to diminish or to magnify this hate is something that I still do not know today. But still. He is the only thing I have ever hated completely, and I knew that even then.

I knew why. I knew why he was so deserving of my ire. And even in your present youth, when you ask about the other kids and their participatory grandparents and you wonder about yours, I tell you that your grandfather was very mean to me and you know. You understand because even you, today, can understand that there are mean people, and mean people do things that you should never do to an adult, let alone to a child. That a child can understand this concept only galvanizes my rage.

But there was so much more, I think, to my emotions about that man, and I think that is what I was trying to do during that stretch, to find out more about him, to search for a better understanding and, perhaps, some *something* else that might cast some different light upon him. Not that I was searching for some excuse for him—of course he was inexcusable—but that there must have been some reason, some other something that deprived any possible understanding of him. *Something.* That search was the engine that ran me.

That was my hate, I think, for him. Not just that he broke the four intermediate phalanges of my left hand with a ball-peen, one at a time, for touching his tools, or that he shaved off one of my eyebrows for thinking that he saw me raise it at him, or any of the other inflictions big or small, no, not just that. That those things were done to me would have been encumbrance enough, but that they were done by someone with no history, someone outside of time—*that* was my hate.

See, I knew my life, where I was from, that I had two siblings and who they were, and your grandmother would sometimes, while she was making pancakes, tell me stories of being a girl and of traveling base to base around the world with her father, haggling in hot bazaars, netting fish in brown rivers and learning games played with stones and sticks. But that your grandfather remained a mystery and strained to keep that shroud about him. That he could not even dignify me with the honesty of being tormented by a man who you could say you really knew—that I could never know just how he *became* so that, at the very least, I could know the littlest pity for his cowardice and could resolve myself to never make those same mistakes that he had had some choice in making. That I could not even be granted that minuscule consolation.

That was my hate.

So I began my asking on the day he died. It was a rough time for everyone and for me, too, but not for the same reasons. Your grandmother had lost the cold rope that had knotted itself about her life, but that rope had long since become the only thing that she had known, and that rope— that rope was also what Conrad lost, but it was the thing that he had most looked up to, the thing that he had wanted, most, to become, though I would wager that this fact would surprise him even today. And Roy? Roy was already going and your grandfather's death just cast him further away, and Harriet—. Well, Harriet had already escaped him, had already gone to where we could not follow.

But all of a sudden your grandfather was dead and nobody could or would talk about him. Not his family, not his friends.

Nothing. In fact, nothing substantive was ever again said of him, if you would believe that. And this was no wave of grief, no collective mourning, no. They put him in the ground, tamped him down, and it was like he had never even been. Just—*nothing*. Like maybe we had made the man up, or had just outgrown his company, or that maybe they still feared him— that perhaps they might speak ill of him and that he could still hear, could still come back to reckon them.

Or, what, did they worry that I could somehow sully his name? That I could spread such dreadful rumors about town to say that, shockingly, he was not a saint? I like to think that nobody wants to speak ill of the dead and that, simply, there were no kind words of him that anyone knew to say.

But so I went to the library. I went to City Hall. I went to the Army records office with his death certificate and got a clerk to lend me their copy of his file. I did all sorts of things like this until I could piece together his life, and I did it by myself because I asked the others for help but they each turned me down in their own way, so I kept going until I had put together a story that satisfied me, and some other day I will share it entirely. If it much matters to you, the bits I will next describe about his meeting your grandmother are things that she would confirm for me and expand upon during one of our brief conversations some many years after his death.

They met at the county fair, your grandmother and your grandfather, where she was working a booth and he was there with friends. Your grandfather was just out of basic and had been stationed at Fort Carson, and she told me that the uniform he wore that day made him glow. I surmise that she was attracted to him only because her father had also been Army and they had been close, and her father had been at Peleliu some four years prior, but they never found his body. But they met at that fair, started dating, and were married a few months after that.

Then Korea happened.

By the time he got Purple-Hearted back here, Harriet was there and two of us boys were slobbering around the house,

Conrad being born a few months before he shipped and me about eight months after his last day stateside, and then Roy arrived early, less than a year after me.

Your grandfather came back different, they say, but I can hardly be the judge in that regard. My first recollection of the man was not until I was seven, which is interesting when you consider that people say a child can first form muddy memories from about the time they learn to speak, give or take, and arguably-reliable ones by the time they reach three or four, certainly. Well, my first remembrance of him is from when I was seven, of me walking into the garage at night to find him sitting on a stool with his back to me, the bench light on, no radio, no sound, just him sitting, just him breathing at the wall, and he tells me to leave without turning his head. That was the first. And I wonder, often, about what from those early years I am not remembering.

From there we could easily continue into a much longer story about him, but as I said a moment ago, perhaps that is best saved for a different time—because there is plenty of it. Of him. Of time. And we will. We will talk about it, all of it, because you should not suffer as I have suffered, which is to say that you should have your history given readily and not be forced to claw it from the groun—

••
••

—ptember 2006, tape. Sevensomething. Seven hundred two. Or three.

A quick note before I forget from yesterday, I just grabbed one. A tape. Smudged label on this one, so probably this is fine. Probably a throwaway. But continuing from yesterday because the microphone cut off but I kept talking for quite a while before I noticed, and then I was too frustrated, so I went to bed, and this morning I took that tape out and redid the boxes, but I forgot to label it. That tape. So who knows which one it is now or where it cut off, exactly. Maybe you can find the first part when you look. If you look. In the box. The blue one, not the green one. Blue box number nine. Tape seven-something, low.

But continuing, no, I never know what to tell people when they ask if I have any family, because what am I to do with that question? Not that I have a problem with answering, just that the answers make people uncomfortable the way that I tell them and I am uncomfortable enough and the subject seems so tired to me, so——. Often, I tell them that I have a child and that I was married once, and then hope that they will let me leave it there.

But then what? What when someone insists—because of course you must ask these things of people? What when they ask about my parents? My mother and if we do holidays? Thanksgiving?

So if ever the question is raised, I respond by saying that she died long before they buried her, and that usually changes the subject on the quick.

But what of your father, then?

A viciousness.

Oh.

And if this continues, a typical asker's next question will mark a last, desperate effort to bail my scuttle:

But your brothers, then, if you had them. Sisters? All of that must have been hard on you. Or were you alone?

Yes. Yes, but.

And the *but* there—Yes, *but.*

Yes, I had brothers and I had something like a sister.

Yes, sort of, but the ones that are left are no family of mine.

Yes, but some of them are dead, and some of them are gone.

Yes, but how do you explain absence to someone who was never there? This is the question I have never been able to answer in a satisfying way, and that is the crux, really, the thing that feels so heavy. That truth.

But this gets to what I have been thinking and what I outlined on the other tape for when you find it—the question of whether that specific weight, the weight of truth, is illusory or if it is actual—and I have been vulturing about the answer for some time now. Long enough to stop hedging, at any rate.

So, simply, truth is weight. I hold this as fact. And I hold this fact as incontrovertible.

Since I have come to accept this, more and more I am noticing that everything I do anymore is ballast, is a particular heaviness to bear, so my truth? Your truth? Theirs? Immaterial, all, but they weigh something, each.

And from there, things get complicated. If we extrapolate, then the truth of the fact that each truth has a specific weight is itself a separate truth, a separate weight, and if we accept this, then logic dictates that nothing is weightless—not massless, weightless—and if nothing is weightless, then everything must accelerate downward at some relative speed. And what is down, then? Down, from a higher point to a lower. Down, the direction of gravity's pull. Down, until we someday strike the ground.

Is it that, do you think? That our truths rope themselves about us to drag us down together? Or is it the other way. That maybe just it is you that will pull, and, in your pulling, you find that even what were the lightest things, all of everything ends up subject to your gravity, gets guzzled up by the black of you.

Like Harriet and her headstone that I brandished too high above them. Why? For what? For them to acknowledge my truth? That mine was better? All my fuss and it gained what, exactly, aside from a weathered stone that nobody visits?

Harriet—.

Harriet and my brothers. Them and the childish fantasy of the pictures I yesterday described. How long have I been hefting such worthless burdens? And why?

Even just to consider the carnage about me in the aftermath of that slow tantrum, the cataclysm that I never dignified, the space. The depth of the fractures that your mother filled and refilled until I sipped the last of her light away. Even to place just that upon a scale, alone—.

Or you. That you were perhaps the lightest thing—you were—but that now the thought of you yokes itself about me like an X-ray smock because I squandered your reverence, and that our youths are spent, and that I spent ours wronger than I should, your youth.

My youths.

Mine and ours.

My millstone—.

[—.]

I miss you, and I love you, and I am so sorry.

Goodnight. Wherever you are.

SIFTING THROUGH STATIC
DRAMATIS PERSONÆ:
(OR, THE FLOTSAM SINCE THE SEACOCKS BLEW)

For the wrenching of reticent heads out from ramshackle hearts; for the futile assertion that a hand with four fingers, three and a thumb, remains as a hand:

Roy: You littlest digit—you're certain that some things can't be fixed. Like a never-oiled engine revved long in the red, you say, some things will just seize. To free such an engine from itself, someone must sledgehammer its pistons in firing sequence, you say, but you have the arms of a child and legs that were never really there. You're certain that you could hardly lift a sledgehammer.

And Conrad: At seventeen you were a sculpture hulked from battleship salvage, but today you're a figurine, waterlogged and listing. Today you're a rotary telephone. A rabbit-ear antenna. A vintage with no value. Today you're the loose leader of a highlight reel flipping and flipping, and today you're the longest finger left, still calloused, still grazing at the downy fringes of forever ago.

And you, Wayne: You father of mine. You tacit sentry. You empty sentinel. How your elisions yet muddle, and how your

47

dubieties still smolder small holes. How I've sickened of your silence and your closed-casket curios. Of how you were thin through your thirties, wound tight like radio wire. Of how your clothes were secondhand, stolen, or traded-for, and your boots, when you wore them, could be used to hammer nails. Of how you kept a beard that you kept pencils in and the mane I know from pictures, you, of how your hands were a mess of scabs and how your shoulders were broader than your shadow, you wasted light. You structured dust. How you're the teeth on my tongue, and how you're nothing but nothing. How whenever your brothers will speak on your provenance, I've little to add but:

He's——. Yeah. All that stuff's rather tangled.

Families, yeah—always some kinda sticky. But what about yours, though? What about your childhood?

No siblings, and we didn't——. They weren't——. I don't know. My mother divorced him when I was quite young.

That must've been hard.

No, because I never knew, because it was never an issue.

Oh. Either ever get remarried?

Neither ever really left since we were all they ever had.

So they——? But dincha say they divorced when you were young?

Sort of. I don't know.

ROY/LONGMONT, CO/2007-07-24
07:21:04—07:38:22

But am I happy? Sure. I guess. But things coulda been much different, y'know? Things coulda been better. And I don't just mean my legs. You grow up broken and that's just the way things are, so you make do and you get on with it. Not to say that that's easy.

Never assumed it was.

Mm. Took a while for me to come to terms, to be honest. Lots of anger. Lots of my problems, that's where they set roots.

What changed?

Guess I grew up. Decided to stop wasting energy on shit I can't do anything about and refocused. Got square with the world.

And how'd you do that?

It's mostly lotsa sobering conversations with yourself. Okay, so I never won a Heisman. Boo-fucking-hoo. Plenty of Heisman winners can't take apart a carburetor—shit, plenty of Heismans can't even point out a carb on a bench. And further, who needs that stress? Winning a Heisman, being scrutinized and constantly worried you're one blown knee away from starring in local car commercials. Get that into your head and, shit, those crutches? This chair? Downright liberating.

Basically the whole game's just that you make do with where you're at and what you've got and you get on with it.

And how's that sit with you?

Oh it sits fine most days. Sometimes, though—. I mean, I'm not perfect, right? Everyone's got some shit days. But I've got a lot, really. Of good. So don't think I'm complaining. It's just—well, you know. It can sometimes be tough. Thinking about what coulda been.

—But enough of me.

Your pops, then. Your pops was good with a wrench. Better than me, even, at lots of stuff.

Like what?

Well way I see it, there's two kinds of mechanics in the world. One can tell you, from the hip, the cam angle on a 1946 Ford Sportsman, or the compression ratio on a 1972 Chevy small block 350. Thirty-six degrees and eight-point-five to one, respectively, in case you were curious. That mechanic's generally a few steps removed from an assembly line servo how he knows exactly what to do, how to do it, and can bang out almost any typical fix just about as fast as it can be done by a set of hands.

And the other?

Other kind can turn a vacuum cleaner into a can opener with five minutes and a flathead. That second one, that's your old man. We were kids, he'd take things apart to see how they worked and he'd put them back together and sometimes he'd put them back together different, and sometimes they'd work better. And he'd build things, too. He'd build amazing things and then just take them all to pieces again, sometimes without even telling anyone. And that was frustrating for a guy like me to watch, because I always wanted that.

Why?

Well I mean anyone can memorize an engine manual, right? But you can't really memorize a sewing machine that runs on diesel with a three-speed manual, clutch from a riding mower, and even a respectable chrome job on the exhaust.

But, like—

Well but what do you mean?

Whatcha mean, *what do I mean?*

I mean what'd he do? What's something that he did?

He once made a sewing machine run on di—

You know what I meant.

Hmp.

Okay so, like, every Fourth of July, for example, our dad would go out and buy a crate of fireworks. And I don't mean a pack, I mean a crate. He'd bring them home but we weren't allowed to touch them because they were for him and his work buddies, but usually he'd pull all of us outside at least once to watch him set some off, though, and one year he even took a bunch of your uncle Conrad's army men, you know those little plastic ones? and he taped M80s and Black Cats to them and set them off. *Blam!* And then they were gone, just scorched concrete where they were. Me and Con'd cheer, and Harriet'd laugh and laugh and—ah. And ah.

And she'd what—?

—But like so this one year Dad was—

No, Roy. No. Harriet would laugh. She'd laugh and laugh and she'd—? Finish that sentence.

Dad was taking empty soup cans and he'd—

Roy.

What?

Why are you being evasive?

She's nothing I want.

Why?

—I'm tired.

We can—

No, I mean I'm tired. I'm tired of it. Of her. I'm tired of wanting, so I'd rather not, okay? At least for right now.

Maybe later, then?

[—.]

—Roy?

—But so Dad'd turn a can over and punch a hole in the bottom with a nail and then he'd suspend a firecracker or a Black Cat beneath by sticking its fuse up through the nail hole right up to the ass of that fuse, and he'd light it and hop back and then thing would go off and the can would jump up about one whole, entire, glorious foot in the air and he'd be standing prouder'n a honeymooner's cock and he'd even salute that pitifulness, and he'd make us salute it, too. Made us sit there and salute, actually, until he'd used up most of the crate. I didn't really mind but for my arms were getting pretty hurty by around halfway through. I guess the work boys were busy.

Well but so the next evening I was inside reading and I heard a huge *thwack!* out front and I figured some of his buddies had come over and they were out front drinking their way through the rest of the crate, but then I heard a big ruckus in the kitchen and heard the front door slam open and I heard him yelling, yelling loud:

The fuck you think you're doin'th my shit?

And then there was another huge *thwack!* but then there was no more yelling. A minute later, another *thwack!* and I was curious enough to get the ol' braces on and hobble out there to see.

But what I found out front was incredible. Dad was sitting cross-legged on the driveway and Wayne was out there and the concrete was all wet. Next to Wayne was a watering can and on the ground in front of him was a pie pan and a soup can. I got closer and Dad noticed me and he looked up from the driveway and he said, Roy, come check this out, and he picked me up and set me down next to him because it's hard for me and my braces to get down to the ground without help.

So we're sitting there and Wayne is setting up. He's got one of the rigged-up, nail-holed soup cans ready to go, but he's set it in the pie pan and he pours a bunch of water into the pan, around the soup can, until the pan's overflowing. He pulls out Dad's Zippo, lights it and hops back.

THWACK!

And when it goes off, the water goes everywhere, but it doesn't launch the can a foot or two, no—that can gets enough height it could clear our house. Shit, I bet it'd clear the big willow we had out front. Thirty feet? Fifty? I don't know.

But Wayne tosses the Zippo at Dad and Dad flinches but he catches it right in front of his face and Wayne just walks back inside. I figured he was gonna catch flack for that little toss, but he didn't. At least I don't think he did. Who knows. Anyway, Dad showed that trick to all his buddies later that night when they were over, and of course Wayne didn't get the credit.

I don't remember any other fireworks shenanigans until a few years later, maybe a coupla two, three months after Dad died. I guess Wayne ended up finding another stash Dad'd hidden, but he didn't launch soup cans with those.

Oh?

Hmp. Not even close—.

—And?

Hm?

Were you planning on sharing, or—?

Oh. Well, I mean—. I mean I guess if we're gonna go there I should start by saying my first real job, I guess you could call it, was working down at Jake's garage. Jake was one of Dad's old war buddies and he looked out for us when he could. I wasn't exactly the most efficient floor-mopper in the world on account of my legs, and flipping burgers is hazardous when you can't stand for more'n twenty minutes at a time and sitting puts the grill at eye-level, so it was tough for me to find your typical teenage gig. But like I said, I was good with my hands. You park me in front of a bench with half a manual and a crescent wrench and I can fix just about anything, so Jake put me to work on small engines for a buck-twenty an hour, but what did I care? Beat sitting in my room.

I started working there in the summer of '66 and by winter Jake was impressed enough he started letting me help with the smaller car jobs that came through. Popping dents, balancing wheels, wrench-handling for the mechanics that were doing rebuilds—that sorta stuff. And I liked the work a lot. Jake and his guys were good to me. Never once made an issue out of my legs or my arms or any of that, not really.

Not really?

Well I mean yeah, there'd be times they'd get merciless, maybe tickle me 'til I puked or put my lunch up on something high or disassemble my crutches or my chair, but they're good guys. *Decent* guys. Never an ounce of malicious in any of that, never. Most of the time they just gave me tasks like any other guy working there and they'd gave me hints when I'd get stuck, or a hand when something needed an extra set of fingers.

But anyway, that first December we had one job that came through from this gorilla who was home on winter break from CU Boulder or someplace. Wheel alignment. Simple job. Gorilla played football, I remember, because when he came back to get the car he threatened to strap me to a sled and cave my cripple chest for scratching the door of his T-Bird.

Good on you for hiring a freak, Jake, but keep this floppy piece of shit away from my 'Bird, yeah?

Yeah, he was classy. Jake assured him that he'd take the scratch out at no cost and walked him out.

Fuck right you will, Jake, or my dad'll hear about this and you won't like the story he writes in the paper.

When Jake came back he told me he knew the scratches were there when the car came in and the kid was fishing for free work, and that he was sorry I had to endure that. I asked him what else he needed done for the day and he told me to take the afternoon on him. He stuffed a fiver in my shirt pocket and told me he'd have me help him out with a tranny in the morning.

Fine.

Jake drove me home.

Wayne was cooking when I got back. He asked me if I was feeling okay, or if Jake had just run out of stuff for me to do and I gave him the whole story and Wayne kept stirring that pot of whatever he was making and said, *I see.*

Next day Wayne walked me to work. Said he wanted to catch up with Jake. They talked for a few minutes in the office and then Wayne flipped me a dime for a pop as he strolled past the garage door on his way back toward home.

Week and a half later, Wayne knocks on my bedroom door after dinner. Said we had a covert mission and told me to put on the darkest clothes I had. I wasn't doing well and I asked him why and he told me to meet him out front, and that the car was already running.

Fine. Okay.

It was dark, but I could tell his buddy Gordon was in there with him and they had ski masks all bunched up on the tops of their heads.

Ski masks?

Yeah. Like the kind that folks use when they're gonna stick up a liquor store or a bank, the kind with the holes cut for the eyes and mouth.

And this didn't concern you?

Not really. See, this is the thing to understand about your dad, and I don't know if he's different these days, but this sort of stuff wasn't so strange for him. He was always doing stuff like this, some mission, some something, so I heaved myself in and we drove across town while Wayne and Gordon planned a fishing trip for the next weekend and I thought nothing of it, really, just looked out the window and listened to them talk.

Where'd they fish?

Mm—fly fishing on the Colorado, I think it was. Yeah. Yeah, they were gonna knock off early on Friday after Gordon lifted some crickets from work because—that's right—because Gordon sold goldfish and lizards at that shitty little pet store off of Main, and I think the old lady that ran the shop looked the other way when he needed bait just so he'd stay working there. But the cricket plan led to a heated discussion over whether crickets made for better bait than grasshoppers, Wayne being of the mind that if you took the time to catch a grasshopper and glue a hook to its belly rather than skewer it you'd end up with a much more lifelike bait and the fish would throw themselves at you as fast as you could set up, and Gordon—Gordon argued that the time you wasted catching and outfitting grasshoppers was too high an opportunity cost. In retrospect, I suppose it was an odd conversation for the two of them to be having, but then, my brother is an odd man.

Anyway, they talked, and I listened, and Wayne drove, and eventually we parked. Wayne told me we were in Boulder and I believed him. And why wouldn't I? Nobody ever drove me to Boulder before but it looked sort of like how I'd heard it described. At least as much as I could tell in the dark.

The neighborhood we were in seemed quiet enough but for down the block from us was the largest house I'd ever seen and all the lights were on and whenever Wayne and Gordon would stop talking for a second you could hear music.

Wayne helped me out of the car and over to some bushes nearby and Gordon pulled a very familiar-looking crate out of the bonnet along with some blankets, another ski mask, and a small something or other bundled up beneath his arm. Gordon handed me the mask and wrapped a blanket around me. Wayne popped the crate open, unwrapped the bundle, and I began wondering how we were going to post bail.

What?

I didn't know what they were planning, but between the ski masks, the cherry bombs, the Wrist Rocket—a Wrist Rocket's a kind of hunting sling—

Slingshot, yeah, I know.

Yeah. But between all that stuff and the modeling clay, I couldn't see any way all three of us were going to make it through the night without getting arrested. Or worse.

I don't blame you. What—

Was the plan? Wayne explained the plan, but the explanation alleviated none of my anxiety.

See, he said, Roy, that's a frat house, and somewhere in that frat house is the guy who gave you flack at the garage a few weeks back, and tonight they're having a dance. Their building is shaped like a big square, and everyone's dancing in the courtyard in the middle, and I know this because I helped set up the lights, because I pledged there last week and they didn't bother to check to see if I was even enrolled. So, Gordon's packing these little guys in clay, and we're gonna park them in that party. It will be extremely loud, and the clay-splatter will be magnificent, and nobody's going to get hurt, it'll just scare them is all.

We all had a role, he said. Gordon would prepare the salvos, Wayne'd aim, and I'd pull. This goes south, your pops told me, and it's all on me. You were never here.

How the hell am I gonna get away from anything? I asked, and he told me, Don't worry, any cops come I'll take off and they'll chase me, and you and Gordon lay low until they're around the corner, then you split, and then Gordon bails me out in the morning.

We could get in real trouble for this, I told him.

It's foolproof, Roy, he said. What could possibly go wrong?

So we prepped. Gordon had a toothpick and he was drawing designs on the clay around the bombs after he'd packed them. First one was a smiley face. He passed it off to me and Wayne extended the slingshot up and out toward the castle down the street.

On your mark, Wayne said, and I loaded up and pulled back on the rubber tubing with both hands.

A little higher? Wayne asked.

You sure? Gordon said.

Wayne says, Hm, you're right, that's probly good, and then Wayne angled his arm down some. Gordon lit the fuse with Dad's Zippo, which Wayne'd somehow acquired, and Gordon began speaking, and we could barely hold ourselves together.

This is your slingshot. There are many like it, but this one is yours. It is your life. You must master it as you must master your life.

And then I let go. I couldn't hold it steady between trying not to laugh and trying to keep the laughs I couldn't keep in quiet. We watched it arc across the stars, the fuse sparkling like the world's saddest tracer round.

Gordon was wrong. A little higher would have been great. The first round punched through a window in what must have been the attic of the house because it was near the roof and one of the only rooms that wasn't lit up. A second or two later we saw a flash and an instant after that came the *THUMP*. And then—nothing. No screams, no wave of people pouring out the front door.

Music must be loud, Wayne said, and we were dying again.

Again again, Gordon said, and this time the design on the clay made it look like one of those pineapple grenades. I pulled back and Wayne said a little higher? and Gordon said Nah man, we nailed it last time. More laughing, and I pulled back a little more. Gordon lit the fuse.

You must fire your slingshot true. You must shoot straighter than the enemy who is trying to dance.

And I let go. Wayne stood up from the bushes and saluted the missile and Gordon followed suit. We saw it disappear over the roof of the house and a few seconds later: *THUMP*. Followed by shrieking and what-the-fucks we could make out clearly even from a block away.

Down down down, Wayne said, and we all got on our stomachs and peered at the house from our cover while probly a dozen guys, big guys, came pouring out the front door and started scouring the outside of the building.

Find 'em, we heard one yell, and we lied there breathless.

Probly ten minutes they searched and searched until one of them said, *Fuckin' Sigma Chi*, and they shuffled back in after tossing a few threats out into the darkness.

We waited until they were back in for a minute before we got up off our chests. Gordon was the one to break the silence.

Did you see those Sigma Chi assholes? Man those guys are assholes.

Sure are, Wayne said.

I feel like I need to send that party an apology on behalf of those Sigma Chi assholes, Gordon said. Hey, anyone seen my toothpick?

The next shot, marked up with a few choice sympathies, floated over the crest of the roof, and this time they came out with bats.

Time after that it was more bats.

Time after that we saw one of 'em had a rifle, and it was roundabout then we decided to hit the road.

I thanked Wayne after we'd snuck back to the car and he told me don't mention it.

Gordon said he wished he had thought of the idea but he was glad he could help, and said he had a present for me, too, but it was a surprise he'd hit me with on my birthday. I told him he didn't need to get me anything and he said he wasn't getting me anything.

Where'd you guys go next?

I dunno—.

[—.]

—Ride home was weird.

How so?

Weird how Gordon and Wayne, they're talking the whole time again about fishing, and then about hunting, how Gordon wanted to go hunting but Wayne wasn't so hot on it, and then a big discussion about how different were the two, really? and Wayne's making the argument that a fish wasn't much more than a potato with eyes—

Potatoes have eyes.

Har-har.

But I mean they're talking the whole time without ever mentioning, laughing about, or checking the rearview over the shit we'd just pulled and instead, Wayne's in this impassioned argument how a fish is just a vegetable, basically, and so in that way fishin's just like picking vegetables and further, it's a vegetable you can replant if you don't want to take it home and there's no harm, no foul, how, thirty seconds later, a fish's totally forgotten that it'd ever been yanked out the water.

Hard to replant a buck, Gordon.

Wrong you are, Waynus, I've seen plenty of bucks replanted onto walls. It's no different than picking flowers, really. Putting 'em in a vase.

But you don't shoot flowers into a vase.

Maybe *you* don't.

And it went on like that, back and forth, back and forth about fishing-vee-hunting, around in circles but never with any hostility, just exchanging opinions, and then at the end of the ride they decided that they were gonna go steal golf balls from the driving range instead and lift a club or two from the Salvation Army, maybe spend an afternoon replanting.

Did you chime in?

What, during the ride?

Yeah.

No. No, I just sat.

Why?

'Cause there's no room for me there. Not between them. Never was.

And how'd that make you feel?

—Left out? I guess left out, I guess. But not exactly. Wayne and Gordon—I dunno. Trying to join in between them's like trying to change the color of your eyes because you like your brother's better. Just as hard. So no, not left out exactly because yeah, you've still got your eyes and they work just fine, but also there's something right there in front of you that you'd much rather have, I guess is the best way of saying it. You don't need it, you don't think—or maybe you do, I don't know, but you don't, like, *need* it, but at the same time it's something you long for, right?

And you don't feel shame or whatever for—.

I guess I mean mostly it's just that there's that, right? There's *that*, right there, alive in the front, and you're in the back, and your brother's driving with someone else riding shotgun, and you're just kinda there, in the back, resigned to accept a hard fact for what it is. And for what you're not. But also, I dunno—. The other side's that you're also learning to be grateful to just *be*. To just even be sitting in a car with something so beautiful at all.

So—

But yeah, so then we were at wherever it was that Gordon was crashing, and they kept talking until Gordon was out of the car, and then again for another couple minutes while he leaned in to rest his forearms on the open window and they talked until Gordon said, after a pause: Alright.

He dug around his jacket and then popped a match with his thumbnail for his cigarette as we backed out of the driveway, and I remember the cherry on the end of that Camel glowing up his face as he took the first drag, his hair tied up from his face but chunks of it still hanging down out from the tie, falling curvy to frame his face, a red face, dim, and then dark again when he pulled the cig away to exhale.

And then I remember as Wayne was putting it into first, Gordon clicked his heels, saluted, and we all three of us had one last good laugh together even though Wayne'd already reached over to roll the window up. We saluted him back, and Wayne drove off, and I never saw Gordon again.

And there were no repercussions?

None that I was aware of. Unless——. Well.

Unless what?

I guess it depends on how you define repercussions. Like, which direction counts, or whether or not they can ever really end. Whether there's an upper bound on the time before it's just a fresh, unrelated grievance against the instigator, I mean.

What do you mean?

I mean Gordon and the gorilla and my birthday present, how I guess Gordon skipped town not too long after that night, but later that year I got an envelope in the mail.

From Gordon?

No return address, but it was postmarked Los Angeles, and it was sealed with a cheerful little sticker of a cake with candles. I open the envelope and there's no note, no card, no nothing. Nothing but just a picture of a Brandywine Red '59 T-Bird in mint condition, save a two big ol' greek letters—a sigma and a chi—keyed across the driver's door.

FEBRUARY 10, 1976

~~Qayn~~
~~Wanye~~
Wayne:

Hello from your not drunk Conrad brother. Remember me? I am not drunk right now I know you are wondering. Not really. I was pissed when you hung up yesterday and then I started drinking and then I spent some time thinking about the last time that we talked and it had been so long and then I remembered that a few years ago I wrote you a letter but I never mailed it how right after I wrote it found that nice old lady next door dead and I was torn up about it and I could not mail you because where do you live? but I did not even try hard to get your address but then I just now thought that that whole thing maybe was not such a terrible idea and that maybe I just got soured up on all of everything again after another dead friend died is all but then I remembered that I sold that typewriter a while back and my handwriting is still shit so I decided today is new typewriter day. So there. So fuck you.

Sorry. Not really. Kind of. I miss you.

Anyway I am drunk because of you because I am mad at you. Not that you care. Ha Ha! I got drunk and I went out and

I bought a typewriter and I had a fun. And now I will tell you about it. You cannot stop me Ha Ha! Brace yourself asshole. I found two whole sheets of paper I forgot to buy paper. Ha Ha!

First I went to the Sears but they only had typewriters that were way expensive and I only spend medium expensive on assholes so I said to the pawn shop I said I want a typewriter and I want a heavy one and he asked me what do I mean heavy and I told him you know heavy like none of those electric Jap shits with all the switches like NASA and he said there is an old Royal and he wanted $15 I said fuck you $10 and he said $12 and I said $7.50 and he said fine $10 take it just take it and go please leave just please go so here we are this iron motherfucker and me and that is how you haggle.

How are you? Great! Good to hear it! I miss how things used to be when everyone was around and we all hung out and we talked and shit fuck man those were good times remember? Remember when we got Roy drunk the first time and then we played Monopoly and we were ten? I remember you took a shiner but I took one too and it was a good time but Dad told Roy his hangover was plenty good punish and do not do it again and Roy never ever wanted to drink again after that how messed up he was the next day and even into the start of the one after that. Remember H. was taking care of him and made him soup but Dad told her not to but she made it anyway? He never could tell her what to do.

And then I went to sleep.

brother

ELEVEN

Today is 12 August 1985. This is tape eleven, side two. Story continues from side one.

I had not been expecting to see Conrad that day but he came in earlier than usual. Weekdays his shifts ended at seven in the evening and I always had to leave for work by six. As he came in, I had been chopping carrots for the stewpot, hoping that, before morning, Roy would revive long enough to feed himself from my stand-a-fork-in-it stew, beef, with red onions and purple potatoes—Harriet's recipe from the stock on up. If anything was going to coerce him to eat, I had my money on the contents of that simmering pot, comically oversized atop your grandmother's tiny stove.

I removed all but one clock from that house on the day that your grandfather died, and if you are listening to this, you know that I did not wear a watch until 1984—the staunchlooking one that you gave me by proxy, plated, too-big and too much. But even—.

Well, actually, as a brief aside if you would permit the indulgence, about the watch. It is a lovely watch, and I am, in fact, wearing it now. But though the gift was expressly stated to be from you-and-only-you, I must contest that claim and contend, rather, that your mother had some role in this watch's provenance. And how? Upon what grounds could I possibly base such a claim? What shred, what thin filament of deceit did I first pick at when unraveling your ruse? Well, child, it was obvious. The note on the box said *To Daddy*, but it was in your mother's handwriting, so. Come on now. But then, that there was a watch at all was telling enough that perhaps she had picked it out and paid. Unless—. Unless you found a watchmaker who would accept a barter in Cheerios? Hm.

But this is all to say that even without a clock, I knew that Conrad must have been early. We were standing in the same room, after all.

So he ambled into the kitchen looking ragged. Both of us had long hair then—mine longer than his if you would believe it—but his was uncharacteristically unkempt. Twelve-hour shifts at a warehouse can empty a person, but still, he always went out of his way to be presentable. I mean, he was the sort who would shower and arrange himself *before* going to the gym just on the chance that anyone he knew might be also there. And when we were kids he would stand in front of the bathroom mirror with the Brylcreem, combing thick globs of the stuff across his scalp, sculpting, shaping the hair until it was just right, until everyone else was waiting in the car and the horn-honkings began. But that day, on the steps between the garage and the kitchen, he had an eight o'clock shadow and a rumpled collar beneath his shoulder-length shock of unwashed blonde.

The dark spatter all across his jacket told me that it had started snowing again, but lightly, and only recently, and that maybe I should turn the heat down in the house. He trudged across the linoleum, poured into a chair at the kitchen table and swallowed his face into his hands with his elbows on the placemat, this last detail telling me that his news, whatever it was, was preoccupying enough to break the House Rules, moot then though they were. But I should have known that by the kitchen door, left open to the cold.

I asked him if he had been fired and he asked me if I had been watching the television.

No, I told him.

He said Jesus, man, we have to check your birthday.

Last I checked it was still in July.

No, idiot, he said, and then proceeded to tell me all about how Selective Service had held a lottery for induction order, how when he saw his position, how he ran from work to the bank, and then to the recruiters on West 5th. How he paid a sergeant there seven hundred dollars—everything he had—to forge the date on his enlistment application to show he had volunteered the previous week.

Only two hundred for the stamp, two hundred to find and properly file his forms, which, amidst the bustle of record recruitment, had slipped behind a desk, the sergeant told him. And for an extra three hundred on top Conrad could have a Journalism degree that might get him in the newsroom, though this, of course, could not be guaranteed.

What was I supposed to do? Conrad asked the wall behind me. What am I supposed to do now?

I told him to go to my car and I would be right behind him. He asked why, but we were short on time, so I told him just to go outside, that I could explain on the way.

What about Roy? he thumbed into the living room.

[—.]

That room—.

I can still see it.

The lack. The dim. The room, a scorch irradiated by the soft of a television tuned to no channel. The drapes, yellowed in smell and yellowed past possibility and the unwound grandfather showing an always-appropriate time. The mausoleumed knickknacks, beshelved and forgotten since purchase and the jaundiced carpet, peculiarly adherent, it seemed, to certain kinds of feet. The furniture as immovable as it was ineluctable, and Roy, swaddled up in its dinge. Roy, a smudge in the smear of its blurring fixtures and the valleying of its cushions, a ghost, a ghost fit for a ghostly topography of yawning valleys, their bottoms then dark, and down, and far from the soft of that room's strange, gray sun.

What about him? I replied as I turned off the burner. Conrad shrugged. I told him to grab the gas can from the garage on his way out.

We drove largely west. We had a mostly-full jerrycan of unleaded sloshing in the back seat, a few carrots, a bad radio, and hours of road ahead of us. With the sun almost down, there was no earthly way for us to make it to the clearing before dark, but that was better. Conrad asked for a carrot, since he had emptied his checking and payday had just come around. I passed him one and he turned it in his hand.

I can make it, he told me, Cigarettes work wonders and I can steal from Roy after Mom stocks him up. He barely eats anyway.

We talked a little over that first stretch. He asked me about work but I doubt he really heard a word I said, so I let him speak. He spoke about his tyrannical boss and that he probably did not have his job anymore, not after how he had left the warehouse that day.

Just as well, he said, I could not stand that job.

I asked him how Colleen was doing.

He was quiet long enough that I considered changing the subject, but just before I did, he said he was frustrated at her seeming so out of it all the time. I asked him why, but he told me it did not matter, that he was planning on ending it when he shipped out anyway, so who cares.

What little traffic there had been thinned once the last of Denver's already faraway lights had tucked themselves behind the horizon. A mile past that, maybe, and the asphalt gave way to gravel, and then gravel to dirt. Houses you could see from the road became infrequent as we traveled out until it was just undeveloped land around us, desolate for the most part, haphazardly punctuated with barns and tractors, old horses plodding toward wherever.

We drove for hours—so long I was sure I had missed our turnoff, and Conrad was getting antsy, and the weather was not helping matters, pleasant though it was. December had arrived during our drive and everything, everywhere, was snow. The headlights were thin but holding. There was no discernible horizon. The road was the color of the sky, which was the color of the road, and we drove down it for hours.

The space in a car, how it can stretch, how the breadth of a car can blossom if you let it. Sitting there, driving, but somewhere else inside, I drifted. At one point I remember catching myself thinking of Harriet, thinking she would have liked it in the car that day had she had the chance, how, when we were kids, how she had these beat-up black galoshes she would wear whenever the weather went bad and then for three or four days after the snow had melted. Who knows where she got them. Probably she borrowed them from your grandfather's closet and he melted just enough to let her keep them.

You know she bought me that old toboggan? The one in the garage if, when you listen to this, you remember. She saved up for it and gave it to me on my thirteenth birthday. In July. Toboggans, it turns out, are cheaper in the summer. But then that winter after, a friend and I spent almost every weekend bicycling that thing out to the far side of town where the hills are better, by the school. You had to strap one side of it across the handlebars, perpendicular to the frame, and then the other guy would have to do the same to the other side of the toboggan across his handlebars, and then you would ride side by side until you got there, reaching across the width of the wood to grasp at the other edge to keep you on the bike as you went. You turned the whole apparatus by having one guy pedal faster, and we even made snow tires by sticking thumbtacks through the inside of the tire tread, pointing out, and then inflating the tubes carefully. Fantastic fun. Complicated, the whole process, and I suppose we could have towed the sled behind one of the bicycles, but then, our method was an opportunity to experiment with coordination, with precision. And it was more interesting than towing the thing, anyway.

Sometimes getting the toboggan to the good hills would take hours and we would have to sneak out of our houses at two or three in the morning, but once we were there, believe me, we would blast that thing down streets, through intersections and sometimes in traffic, even, if the conditions were right. The hardest part was getting out there early enough after a good storm, before cars tore up the snow and ice, and once the plows started running we were usually done for the day. Those days were good.

But back with Conrad, my radio stopped getting reception—it was not a great radio—and Conrad clicked it off, but I clicked it back on because, well, white noise—. Leave it on low and things. Things seem to sort themselves out.

We stopped once on the side of the road because Conrad wanted a cigarette. I stretched my legs down the shoulder while he leaned on the fender and smoked, shivering. When I returned he was grinding his palms into one another and blowing into his fists. He never complained.

I turned off the main route once we were deep in the Front Range and, assuming nobody would mind, cut across what was probably private land, our maybe-trespass bringing us to the small, nameless path I was looking for that much faster then any honest road ever could.

Conrad asked me where we were going. I told him we were close and he did not ask me again. He fell asleep soon after, probably to escape his frustration with the whole day, but even as he drifted off I knew that my saying we were close was a bit of a stretch. He ended up sleeping for something like another hour before we arrived.

When I stopped the car, Conrad woke with his face all a twist of cheeks and eyes much as every person does when the car they are in stops moving, when the vibration from the engine ceases and its absence becomes tangible, becomes an essential resource, now exhausted, that sleep suddenly requires.

He stretched, and asked, as he did, if we were there. I told him I was fairly certain we were, and I got out and started walking into the night.

The ground had been powdered ankle-deep, but it seemed that the hills would only see a cough of a snowfall as the clouds had broken and some stars were already stinging through, and the night was a flavor of dark that you never find in a city. Comprehensive. An eye-level skin upon the world. The last quarter moon's glow upon the scrappy snow was just enough for us to find our feet a way through the brush, but the space between our knees and the stars was a cavity that no light felt disposed to fill.

I think Conrad was mad by then, but if he was, he kept it to himself, as he usually did. All I heard from him was heavy breathing and the slop of the gasoline he carried.

We came to the clearing about a mile later. It was as untouched as I had hoped, and quiet, and wrapped in pine trees shelved with white. There was no wind. I told Conrad to start collecting anything that would burn and he set off across the middle and into the trees beyond, searching. Another hour and we had emptied the woods of most of the dry-enough rot and scrub within a hundred yards of the center and then, having enough, we piled it all in the middle of the glade in silence.

Somewhere along the way, both Conrad and I had taken our shirts off while we went about our task, each then an embodiment of our own testaments to youth. Conrad, at nineteen, was a specimen of musculature. An atlas of flesh. And I, at eighteen, was a wire, drawn tight and twisted. A spring under strain. I noticed us, then. I took notice. I had thrown my shirt on the top of the pile and Conrad had done the same. We must have had a good reason to sacrifice them, but whatever it was evades me just now.

Grab me the lighter, I said, Front pocket of my shirt.

He bent to the pile and pulled his cigarettes from his shirt pocket and the Zippo from mine.

Smoke? he asked, and I ignored him.

Why do you have this, anyway? he asked, flipping and snapping shut the lid. I ignored him.

He sighed, lit his cigarette, and tossed the lighter to me after he took the first drag.

The fuel sent the pile up instantly and the forest came alive with light. Not just the middle of that clearing, see, but everything. The wind picked up. The sky cleared. We stood hushed and reverential through the blaze's birth, its adolescence, its middle and advancing ages, its senility.

The fire then in its hospice, I made to lie supine in its ring of newly-exposed grass, the grass's snowy shroud having been coaxed away by the radiance at its center, and that was something—the grass so mild, so damp after the melt with its warmth on my shoulders, on my arms, on my back against the chill across my chest, my stomach, my wrists. Opening upward, I welcomed the constellations, counted and recounted them.

Orion and Perseus.

Taurus—a favorite.

Canis Major.

Conrad seemed bored, so I told him to lie next to me and I would show him what I knew.

Cassiopeia, the vain queen, had boasted that her beauty surpassed even that of the Nereids, and the brother of Zeus had boasted back with Cetus. Cetus, I told him, rose from the deep and ravaged the coast until, in their desperation, Cephus and Cassiopeia offered up their Princess Andromeda to sate Cetus' anger. But Perseus, returning from the slaying of Medusa, happened upon Andromeda and, removing Medusa's head from Athena's wallet, cast the Gorgon's gaze at the abyssal horror and saved the virgin princess from its clutch.

Conrad listened. Maybe intently. Maybe it was one of the only times I ever had his full attention.

I recited everything I could remember. The crates of books stacked in the corner of the attic, the National Geographics piled high in the cellar. Eventually he began to get cold, so I stopped talking and stood. He asked me where I was going, and I said: Home.

Is that it? he asked, and I told him Yeah, and I started walking back to the car.

We made better time getting back, but not by much. Conrad bundled himself up in the army blanket I kept folded in the back and he slept again, and I ran the heater for a long time before that car felt warm.

My radio decided to start working once we were almost back, crackling into the first downbeat of *Come Together* like the cosmos had long been planning just such a gesture. Abbey Road had just come out and the song had been all over the radio for months, but still.

It was nearly dawn by the time I dropped Conrad back off at his miniature apartment, and he asked me if I had any cash he could borrow or have. I dug six singles from my pocket and scrounged a handful of change from the glove compartment, and he thanked me.

And then he said: I miss her.

I said I missed her too.

He said: I was hoping she might for the holidays, you know, but maybe she will call on my birthday, and if she does, maybe you or Roy could get her address so I could write her from wherever I end up, okay?

I dialed the radio's frequency up, just barely, until the then-wailing John Fogerty became the hiss of no station, and I backed out of the driveway.

SIFTING THROUGH STATIC
A PROLOGUE, A PURPOSE:
(OR, THE PRICKS OF MY PROBLEM)

So how I plot the places you've died. How I pore. How I survey your bygones and cordon your graves.

Bemusing, still, how each of you would check the calendar. How you'd flip it back and forth. How you'd run your wrinkles over the ink and squint.

I'm not sure, the two of you'd say, Maybe here. Or here. Or maybe between these two days, but who can tell, really. But then again I'm here, aren't I? I'm here, I'm here, and someone would have told me, surely.

But who? Who would speak to you now?

And you'd spurn me with an audible sigh and a loose-fingered flick of the wrist. An adjustment of the jaw and a turn of the head. A peer into middle distance.

A wait.

And then, toward the windowpane:

But wouldn't I have gone somewhere, though? Don't the dead go? Somewhere?

ROY/LONGMONT, CO/2007-07-24
08:08:12—08:44:49

So I had problems. Everyone has problems. You, me, Wayne, everyone. And your problems, mine, dude on the corner, they're all the same problems at the base, really. Just doesn't always seem that way when you look at how shit manifests and more, how people go about tryna solve themselves.

Meaning?

Meaning that guy gets slapped around so much as a kid something breaks inside and then he's a shelter dog, wary and jumping every time something gets close, or that girl hurts all the time and the pills go like popcorn, or this guy hates his job and drinks too much, that one gambles, that one puts the grocery money in his arm, etcetera and so on.

Everyone's got a poison, is what I'm saying, and yeah, some folks mix and match a little from this pile, a pinch of that. However you slice it, though, the fact remains: it's still poison. It's just that most folks don't let it get away from them.

But it's amazing. Pharms, powder, grass, booze. Theft. Porn. Sex. Fucking QVC. Almost anything you can imagine, really, someone's out there well and truly under its thumb while it eats them up a little more each day.

So what's your poison?

You already know about my many poisons I'm sure, so there's no need to be all cutesy and rhetorical, but.

But—.

But I've come a long way, though, so let's just say that at my worst I was doing a lot of mixing and not worrying so much about the matching, and I can say that because I've come to terms with what's hanging over me. All that reckless and selfish and stupid and scared, it'll always be my baby to run my fingers through its hair, y'know? Watch it sleep? But it doesn't scream so much as it used to.

Does it hurt to talk about?

It doesn't scare me so much anymore. It'll always be scary, sure, but I can't let it keep keeping me up nights if that makes sense so yeah, talking about it when anyone feels like lending an ear does help. Helps you, maybe, even. Helps me. Helps me stay connected to my past so I can keep focus on my future, and maybe it helps you for this—whatever it is you're doing.

It does.

Mm, well—. Well anyways, I ended up pretty deep, and as long as we're being honest, it's kinda impressive I'm even here talking to you at all.

I guess that's something to be proud of?

Proud's a funny word, but yeah, I'd go so far as patting myself on the back if I could move my arms that far.

But so you were in a bad way, then.

That's a dainty way to put it.

Well how would you put it?

I mean you could've killed a pony with a bag of my blood in 1972, so—. But then who cares, really, how it's put?

How did it start?

How I guess anybody starts, more or less. Everyone's road's gonna be different, sure, but nobody throws themselves into the far end of the pool from the get-go.

Explain.

Well first you put your toe in and then your ankle and you work your way down. Sort of a—what do they call those?—a structured plan.

But you, I mean. How did you start?

Oh I started on scrips. Lots of folks start with the bottle or the joint and get bored but for me it was the scrips.

For the palsy.

And for the other shit that they never quite figured out, yeah. They had me on near everything at one point or another, always trying to dial it in to that sweet spot where I wasn't hurting and also I wasn't an astronaut, and it's harder than you'd think, really, for docs to figure that shit out.

Sounds rough.

Again with the dainty.

What was that like?

What, the treatments?

Yeah.

Well that whole time coming up, all that struggle, all of it made me so I'm convinced those whitecoats don't know what they're doing most of the time. Sure, eight times outta ten there's Medicine B matches up with Condition A and everyone knows that and it's just a matter of figuring out what you weigh and how many refills and you're out the door. That's easy. That's memorization. I could do that. Had to do that, even.

Self-prescribe?

Well that came later if you mean what I think you mean, but even before then I was still sorta doing that whenever I was dealing with the green docs who're fresh from the study halls, whenever the fates would deliver me one of those poor, pink chaps. I've no idea how many of those I ended up manhandling:

No, they tried that.

No, if you mix those two I'll never shit again.

No, have you even read my chart?

No, I'll bin that scrip on my way through the lobby so write something else, and don't roll your fuckin' eyes at me.

See there's normal, right, A and B like I just said, but then there's the exotics and the chronics, the outliers like me who've got problems they're still figuring out, probly never will figure out entirely.

Seems that'd be frustrating.

It is. It's an endlessly frustrating cope with an endlessly frustrating existence. And then double that up when I look back at what happened to me and wonder if maybe if someone had ever been able to figure me out in the first place, if maybe I might not've lost so much as I did.

So, frustrating? Frustrating starts sounding like one of those kindergarten words you outgrew roundabout when you stopped pissing the bed.

But yeah, so every few trips it was a different cocktail, but sometimes they'd have me on so many different things they'd get scared they were gonna box my liver or something and they'd cut me off. Mostly the kid docs pulled that, but I guess that's something I can respect now that I'm in the neighborhood of sixty and my guts are still puttering along. I might not like it, but you have to respect that foresight when you consider I'm a hard case to treat and, generally, am also a pain in the ass. That some of the docs still listened—most, even—and tried hard, and didn't want me to die no matter how much I sometimes wanted to.

No, what I can't respect are the other doctors, the arrogant pricks who just liked playing god, who thought they could read minds and nerves and they'd strand me in a place where I'd have to bribe an intern at the emergency room to forge scrips for something I knew would work for a while when my legs kept hurting and the docs had told me it couldn't possibly still be hurting and had cut me off because of course they knew better than me, the fuckers.

And that actually happened?

Yeah they can cut you off for whatever reason.

No, I mean the intern thing.

Oh. Yeah.

But how?

Okay just today and then no more of this for at least a few weeks, at least a few. A few or maybe two. No less than two, though, no less. Not unless it's really bad.

Cut to a montage of bad days—really bad ones, man—that are first a couple of weeks, then ten days, then seven, five, three, three, and then two days apart and you've got a routine, now, a routine you can control for when these bad days come, how you can come home and you can have your five Percos and your sixer of silver bullets and sure, maybe you've gotta set a few extra alarms, but it's okay. Mornings at work are a little rough, but it's okay. Nothing a pot of coffee can't fix.

And it just sort of goes like that, on autopilot, and it's not so bad at all.

But oh fuck.

Oh fuck oh *fuck* you're dry when that audit comes.

Momentary sadness—or is it panic?—ensues. Momentary, but then, oh, chin up, trooper! Your wife's got her Valium in the medicine cabinet, right? Or hey, don't I still have a few Lorcet in my travel bag from Winnipeg last fall? That's gotta be close to the same.

Whichever. Whatever.

It won't go quite the same but it's like comparing flavors of chocolate ice cream how it gets the job done. Smash cut to tomorrow and you feeling more in control than ever because now there's a menu you can go to, now. So you do. You order, and often.

Now that menu, it works like a champ but goddamn does it work better than maybe you realize and things start to go watery, how Saturday morning you fix up and the weekend falls away and it's Monday already? Then Christmas and Thanksgiving feel like they're only a week apart. Then your birthday comes and goes, or maybe it was your brother's birthday? but it doesn't really matter because it's not like he called you anyway. A grain at a time is how it goes, little by little like an hourglass until everything's upside down.

But eventually you find that menu? Well that menu's too small now, man, you've—your problems—have outgrown it, so maybe you try some new stuff on for size because these *people*, man, you just need to take the edge off how stressful things've been with so many people wedged so far up your ass lately, so your buddy's got a guy who knows a guy who gives you a little bag of something or other and you decide, you know, that it's just only this once because these *people*, man. These *people*.

Once becomes just another item on the ever-expanding menu and, correlatively, this is where shit starts to rattle apart.

First you get fired, but fuck that guy, good as he was to you in the past, he's just showing he's not someone who can stick it out with you, you know, he doesn't get it how hard things are for a guy with your list of problems.

Then your people start evaporating, but fuck those fair-weather assholes, you were always there for them, weren't you? You're better off.

Then you start losing half-days at a time entirely in strange, low places. Or couples of days. Who gives a shit.

Then you blow back home one night or morning to find you can't get in the door because Mom's changed the locks to the basement and she won't answer the door or your call from a payphone even though you know she's in there, you bitch, I can see your car in the driveway I know you're in there how could you do this to me? but she's stronger than you maybe ever gave her credit for. That or she walked to a friend's, knowing that this would happen. Either way, you bust a window and heave yourself in to gather some things and you move yourself to the small town of Plymouth Rambler.

Then you decide you're done with Colorado when you hear about someone distant, someone through one of your strings that'll put you up for a week in Reno so long as you bring whatever to barter, so you float westward.

Reno is a colorful mud puddle.

You check out for a while.

You wake up bleary, cottonmouthed, head pounding in a shitty San Francisco motel room and you pick your head up off the pillow and, wobbly-necked, look at your toes, look at the wall past them, look out the window in the wall to see, somehow, it's winter. You turn your head to look around you for the first time in a long time.

Where are all of my things?

Who the fuck is this?

I don't like this place.

I want to go home.

But the last thing you can piece together is getting thrown off a bus in Oakland—bus because, apparently, you've sold your car. Or traded it. So now what?

Do you have anyone to stay with? No, you don't really know anyone in California. Your brother might be running tankers up and down the West Coast but maybe it was the Eastern Seaboard.

Your other brother, you don't even have his number.

Mom, it seems, has changed hers.

So, okay, how much money do you have? Empty those pockets, let's see—sixteen dollars, some change, three looks-to-be white crosses, maybe a gram of jet. Looks like sixteen bucks and a cerebral afternoon is you and all you're worth, but.

But then the hole.

Then the hole starts humming up soft, like a tube T.V. on with the volume off, like an amp that's hungry for a line-in, *mmmMmmmMmmmMmmm*, wavering, breathing, droning just loud enough so it knows you can hear, *mmmMmmMmm* until the humming starts sounding out words you know, words you've heard before in that selfsame, godforsaken tone that crumbles your best intentions, saying, *Hey now, hey now child, hey, it's not just sixteen bucks you're holding there, is it? It's also a way out, isn't it.*

See, something scary's moved in and maybe you notice or maybe you don't notice just then, but how even in your worst moments you're not thinking of money as just a means to any end anymore, no. Not ever again. See, even forever from now dollars'll still be dollars, sure, but forever they'll also mark a separate, ephemeral rate of exchange, how you'll be holding a note and see the numbers five, ten, twenty, a hundred—not as *values* but as *quantities*, see. Because anyone can turn sixteen bucks into a bunch of sandwiches or a pork shoulder and rice and beans and oranges enough to feed you for a week. Anyone can do that. That's easy. You find the right guy, though, and sixteen bucks'll land you five folds of brown and hey, there's two birds with the same stone. There's your weekend plans and you won't even be hungry. There's your way out—.

[—.]

So that's how it goes.

Or so I've been told.

But really though, the way out, that end, that's gonna be one of two things—or rather, it leads one of two places eventually, I guess that's the better way to put it, that it leads you either up or under.

And your way?

[—.]

Mm—.

—Roy?

[—.]

You smoke?

No.

Me neither. Mind reaching up top of the fridge there? Behind the—yeah. Thanks.

Got a light?

I do.

Don't smoke but you carry flame, hm?

Somebody's got to.

[—.]

—*Mmph.*

Thanks.

And hey, that Zippo. That Zippo's lookin' pretty familiar.

No it isn't.

Your pops give it to you?

No.

So it just looks like the one I know quite well, then?

I bet lots of Zippos do.

True. But mind if I see it?

I do.

Afraid that I'll, what, immolate myself?

That's exactly it.

Mm. Well—.

Hey don't go telling the wife if you run into her, yeah? About the cigs. I quit.

Sure.

So hey, tell me something.

I'll try.

Why don't you smoke?

My mother smoked.

Hey how is she, anyway?

She smoked. How's yours?

Dead.

Sorry.

Of?

Of an awfulness you've probly not even read about.

Try me.

Creutzfeldt-Jakob disease. Heard of it?

Remind me.

Well it's rare, and there's a few flavors, but hear me good when I say that you want none of them. It's—well, basically the way it fucks you is a prion apparates, and—well do you know what a prion is?

Remind me.

It's death. It's death itself come as an eensy particle of protein, practically invisible and nigh indestructible. Basically, there's a few kinds of prion and they each cause a different kinda obliteration, but with CJD, what happens is a prion pops up, says *Hey, brain proteins, you're folding wrong!* and whatever few brain proteins nearby are made to say *Fuck me, you're right!* and then those few little Brutuses go fire up the armageddon. Every fold they make—every copy from there until the end— is wrong. Two bad proteins turn into four. Four into eight. Sixteen. A snowball of bad fold after bad fold all while each and every protein, new or old, is also still causing its neighbors to go all fucky, and all of it all keeps on compounding and compounding up wronger and wronger until your whole head's a blender and you're poured, gingerly, into a coffin. It's like if M.S. and Alzheimer's decided to start a supergroup inside your skull and they cranked the knobs to eleven. It's horror.

What caused it in her?

A prion. Basically the way it fucks you is—

That's not what I mean.

Hmp—.

Worried, are you?

Call it a curiosity.

Well I hope you're not worried. Some shit in life deserves worry but CJD's certainly not one of those things, because there's nothing could be done even if you lost that lottery and could know. Not that you could, even. Know. There's no screening, really, just the death sentence once—if—they connect that ruinous constellation of symptoms early enough to run the gamut of specialized tests that they only break out for the presumably condemned.

But Mom? Nobody knows. Shit was first identified in 1920 or so, but that was just sort of, you know—naming it. Something for the toe tags. By today they've figured out that there's a kind you can catch if you're so nadirous to do so, and there's a hereditary kind, and there's another sort that only pops up in younger folks. But insofar as she was a military brat, well—. Who's to say, what with all her hopping place to place? Maybe she ate something as a kid and it slept until it sprung.

Or then again, maybe she didn't.

Point is, once the diagnosis is locked, the kindest course of treatment'd be just to prescribe a pistol.

That bad, huh?

Mm. At diagnosis, I hear they bring you a coupla dice and they have you roll 'em to see how many months you've got left.

I see.

Yeah, and what's further's you're rolling right after they tell you that probly the last two-thirds of whatever time you've got left's gonna be godless—gonna be you losing every faculty, every memory, every figment and fragment of soul that you've got until diapered, babbling, bedridden and vacant, you just sorta sputter out. No cure. No hope. Just sixty-to-zero. Adult to child to carrot to ground.

That's all to say that—.

[—.]

—Roy?

Wait, what were we talking about?

Funny.

Ha, no. I mean really. Mom. Your mom. Sm—

Ah, yes. Smoking. I asked you why you didn't smoke and you said your mom smoked. That's where I was going.

So a related question, then: what, if any, affect do you think your mom's smoking has had on your decision to not smoke?

None.

Liar. But I'll bite.

So none, then. No influence. Fine. Even if that were true— even if you could say that were true and mean it, mean it truly—don't you think that's more than a little bit of denial showing its face there?

Why?

Why? I mean influence, why. There's nothing's cut and dry out there in the world, nothing. You, me, everyone, we're all connected in how we affect each other, what with this small thing affecting that slightly-less-small thing or maybe just affecting several much smaller somethings. Butterflies and hurricanes, all that shit. There's some truth in there, is what I'm saying. That maybe you're just taking it too personal and're ignoring something that's neither good nor bad about you and who you are today, but something that's due to how things were and how someone else was. How someone's action can change your opinion for a long time, is what I'm getting at. For forever, even.

Can you elaborate?

[—.]

—Roy?

You wanna spark me again?

Sure.

No, hey. No you don't have to look for matches, I just want another. I don't really care about your precious little doodad, it's—

Found some.

—it's. Ah. Whatever.

Thanks.

[—.]

So. What were you saying?

Mm—.

You know your pops and me, we used to go for walks with me when we were younger. I don't know if he ever told you.

No.

Well not quite every day but most days we'd go for walks if it was nice, and if my legs were bad he'd push me around the block or down the street or wherever we were going. This was way before skateboards really took off, but it shouldn't surprise you how he took some roller skates—you know the ancient ones that were like wheeled struts and you clamped onto whatever shoes you had?—and he screwed them to a board for a rig that then hooked over the axle on my chair.

He'd stand on it and shove off with one leg and I'd be in charge of steering since he'd be holding the handles on the back of me, and we'd play chicken where I'd hold my arms out like an airplane as far as I could reach them and he'd keep shoving and shoving us down the street or toward a hill. First guy to grab the wheels or drag a foot loses. He won most of the time.

But so eventually I started telling him I didn't feel like going, that my back hurt, that the meds had me tired and I wanted rest, and he'd tell me Alright, man, tomorrow, I'm bugging you tomorrow and we're going, and I'd tell him Fine, that tomorrow I'd go, and usually I would.

Well eventually I'd tell him Fine and I'd lock my door. He'd still ask, though, through the door, with me sitting up against the door in the dark and him on the other side with his back blocking light coming underneath, asking, asking, and I'd sit there quiet until he was quiet and at some point I'd look down at all the light beneath the door and I'd wonder how long he'd been gone.

This slide, this—whatever you want to call it, where I'd stay inside a little more each day, when I'd stop thinking about much of anything but the pills—this started in late 1969. I don't remember the day because I don't know if there was one day, but 1969 was when I started bribing interns, when, for a while there at the start, I was still on top of it, still had it figured out, under control and feeling good. But then somewhere. I don't know. Somewhere that flipped a bitch and I think that was in 1969, maybe, or maybe early '70. Certainly by mid-'70 I was inside most of the time, so to speak, though if you caught me in a good mood you could convince me outside with you.

One day early '71, though, I hadn't seen the sun in probly weeks and I think only Wayne really noticed. Mom was working two or three jobs, I don't remember, and Conrad, I assume, was driving a van through a jungle, or exploding poor people, or running away screaming, depending on the day. Wayne, though—Wayne was working a few places but he still asked me, every day or almost, if I wanted around the block and this one day he asks me, and I go, mostly so he'll leave me alone for a while. We start down the street but he doesn't turn left at the end of the block like he always does, he keeps going.

Just up here, he says, I wanna show you something.

He pushed me what must've been a mile or two. Even tried playing our chicken with me once but I never even tried and he just stopped playing before it really got serious and he didn't say anything about it. One mile, two miles, who knows exactly how far, but eventually he stops us in front of a motorcycle dealership and turns my chair to face the showroom and makes noises like the tires are squealing when he turns me.

The fuck's this? I ask him.

He points to a '56 Indian Warrior I can see huddled all wretched behind the shiny bikes in the front window of the shop.

See that one back there? The green one?

Looks like shit, I remember saying.

Well now, maybe, he says, but give it a little polish and I bet it'd look great.

Mm.

Then he says: A little more enthusiasm would be nice, Roy, since I'm buying it in the morning and I need your pointers on fixing it up. When it's done we can ditch your chariot and go for rides.

Whatever. Take me home.

I didn't expect he was actually gonna buy it, but then he strangled it up to Mom's the next afternoon sounding like he'd tossed a handful of marbles in the manifold, Christ was it smokin' somethin' awful. I didn't even know he could ride a motorcycle.

Well, whatcha think, he says.

I could hear you for a mile.

I know, right? he says with one of those shit-eating grins.

That's not what I meant.

Hey everyone look at Roy, he says, Mayor of Frowntown.

I gave him the finger and rolled back inside.

But work on it went pretty quick—quicker than I thought it would. He did a bunch of it on his own in Mom's garage and I never once saw a manual. Artistry, really, to look at something foreign that needs fix and, without instruction or foreknowledge, just begin. It was only every now and then that he'd even need to call me out to the garage for some question, and maybe half the time I'd even make it there to see he'd have something or other stripped to pieces on the bench and he'd do most of the talking with his hands, picking up this piece and touching it to that one, holding these two parts together in this hand and gesturing at them with whatever was in the other. That's how he thinks.

Anyway, sometimes I was able to help him because he was stuck and the solution was pretty indirect. Like, turns out one snazzy thing about this bike was that whatever poor sap owned it before Wayne mounted a CV carburetor on the thing, and that style of carb was just then getting popular in England and almost nobody had even heard of it in the States. Stumped me at first but I was able to run it by Jake and get Wayne back on track.

And the rebuild went like that for a month or more, every night something else small.

Clean.

Replace.

Put it all back but better than before is how it went, a little each night, him doing most of the work himself and couple questions for me every now and then, and it just sort of progressed along nicely until. Until—.

—Until?

[—.]

Roy?

Until one night after I'd raided the last from the medicine cabinet and the runtiest connections I had left had ratcheted prices up past what money I had left, and I was actually contemplating the storage racks beneath the work bench and what bottles might do what beneath if only I breathed in a little bit, and I went out to the garage because I hadn't heard him, but he was there, ragging kerosene on a camshaft, and he said, Hey, and I blinked.

How you feeling, Roy?

I looked him in the mouth.

He turned his attention back to his hands. Looking good, right?

My eyes throbbed over to the bike. He'd put new tires on it and most of the engine was gleaming but for the few parts here and there he'd still had laid out on the bench.

Gonna repaint it? I asked.

Nah, he said, I kind of like it like this.

And I remember that making me sad.

[—.]

—Roy?

I can—.

Roy I can—

It made me sad because it was wasn't worth quite as much without the new paint.

—Oh.

Wayne was working long shifts the next few days, but I still remember hearing his car roll up that evening and somewhere, somewhere deep beneath the sea, hearing it watery and knowing that I'd rifted us, knowing even before it happened exactly how it'd go—how he'd come in screaming *Where's the Indian someone stole it where'd it go?* And he did. But I was barely there.

Gone the bike, was all I could manage once I'd found my lips. Gone.

And he looked at me there on the couch, just looked at me. He might've started crying a little I don't remember but he just. Stood there. For forever he stood there.

Inside that forever I had this, I don't know, this anesthetic vision where I rose from the couch without my crutches, rose and went to him standing there crying or not crying and frozen, and everything in the room frozen, and I wrapped my arms around him, put my cheek on his chest and stood there, holding him, wrapping my arms about his motionlessness. I remember I was there for a long time.

Then he moved all at once, just a great, colorful smear barreling toward me still on the couch and then I was up against the wall, my feet not touching the floor. Wayne grabbed me by the chin, my chin in his palm, and pulled my face toward him and into his face, nose to nose, and he just held me there, just held my face there. I remember I could smell the job on his hand. The bleach, the 409.

I closed my eyes—.

He smashed my head back into the wall and my skull caved the drywall where it hit. He let go and I crumpled and—.

—Roy?

Roy do you want me t—

And it only took him a few minutes to fill a duffel with whatever mattered, but you asked me once before and that's the answer.

The answer to what, Roy?

[—.]

—Roy?

His release, his letting go had dredged me from the depths to the shallows, and from that place I saw him in latencies, first here, still bent over a low shelf before smudging over to the cupboard while his low-shelfness faded like a polaroid but backward from color to sepia, sepia to spectral, and when he moved to the cupboard it was like watching a child paint with sponges how he moved through the room, his body streaking a memory of itself behind him that hung, and faded, and dissipated but never quite left the air, and the same to the dresser, and to the bookshelf and the pantry, to the basement and back while I gaped and pleaded and pawed toward the places he'd been until the snick.

—The what?

The snick. Of the door.

Snick.

And everything was gone.

CONRAD/YUMA, CA/2008-10-19
21:20:13—21:42:52

Don't know if I wanna talk about that. Don't know why it's relevant or what it's got to do with anythin', I don't like it.

But who does?

Talkin' about it, I mean. I mean I don't like it either, but I also don't like talkin' about it, I mean. People dyin', I mean.

It's nice out. It was a nice day outside and there're other things I think to talk about, nicer things.

Like what?

Anythin'. The dogs I owned or the fish I caught or the girls I fucked, any of that. Caught a bass once that was bigger'n my arm and I got some ladies in the archives let me tell you, some even foreign. French. You ever been to France? Some nice girls in France, smart. Don't you wanna hear about them? Nice day. I'd rather talk about that.

But that's easy, Conrad.

What's wrong with easy? Easy's nice. Life's hard.

You know—I'll just come back.

No no, just. I mean you don't have to be a pain in the ass about it, just some consideration for my dead, yeah? I don't often go digging is all.

So tell me a story, then.

But nah.

Nah, that's them, the liars, not me. I been lied to too much. I don't have the energy for it anymore and I don't think I even want that, even. Not here.

So just pretend I'm not here. Just talk.

Yeah, well—. My life's pretty well set in stone, but maybe I use this chance to set the record straight, maybe. Maybe that's what I do. With you, I mean. I don't know you hardly more than you know me by the pictures you've maybe seen so I reckon I owe you a clean slate because maybe you only know me by your old man's stories and that can't be good news for me. Maybe he told you some good ones but I know I'm—.

They're not all good stories.

Not all bad stories neither, though, there's still some good left. Or maybe the way I'd like it put, maybe you and me, we move on and you see there isn't much bad still in me. There was for a while, I know there was—it's not like your pops's stories about me are all made up or nothin'.

Oh?

Fact I wager they're mostly true or at least partly true, but they're not entirely true if he's made me out a monster. I'm not a monster. Some kinda toadish maybe, sure, perhaps. But mostly I just hurt myself and the people I love, nobody else. I'm not a monster.

Don't y—

But anyway. I guess let's get on with it if we're gonna do this record-set-straightin' shit. Don't want to, but I guess—I guess there's no harm in talkin'. Not like it matters much in the end. Colleen, then. That's who you're prolly after, yeah? Fine. Whatever.

She's n—

My dollar says that's the speck of dust in the middle of the snowflake, Colleen, but she wasn't the first. Wasn't even the second.

But Colleen and me, we met behind. Behind the. The ah—.

Actually.

Actually no.

No what?

No I don't feel like talkin' about her.

Okay.

How's *that* feel?

Fine?

I don't feel like talkin' about that so I'm not gonna talk about that so how about you just sit with that. Prolly not what you were lookin' for and I know I just said all that shit about us bein' all buddy-buddy but then what are you lookin' for, exactly? If you're lookin' to get to know me, I'm a lotta things and I can talk. I can talk for days. But that story, if you're looking for the endin' I can just jump to that if that gets your rocks off, get right to the point, I could do that and blow how it ends so maybe we can move onto somethin' else, yeah? Maybe some other shit I color in myself because I don't feel like colorin' their fucked up drawings anymore, my brothers, so yeah, let's do that. Spoil it and roll.

Conr—

I told her I was shippin' out and I was a waste of her time so she ate a shotgun shell. There. Scene.

So what do you wanna talk about now?

[—.]

—Oh? Silence? Just gonna sit there and I'm supposed to keep talkin'?

We don't have to t—

Talk about others? Why not, though? I mean, we're already here, right?

Conr—

Miller—I lost Miller.

Fisher and Fields, too.

Sklar. Hamada. Ruiz. All door gunners.

Hancock, McNabb, Harris, Lombardo and Lovell went down in a Huey.

Jacobs. I can go on. There are more.

Schaffer put one through his own forehead fifth week in-country, and the guitar—*man* could he play the guitar. Better'n Wayne, even.

Knopinski took a punji through the foot and whatever shit Charlie slathered on it ravaged him dead inside a week and the docs couldn't do much but hold his hand.

Veerkamp, Padua, Traverso and Harbuck—all dropped before we fragged the shooter.

Montroy got separated on a sunny day and the jungle ate him up.

I can go on. There are more.

Conr—

I got more names, too, if you wanna talk stateside: Edwin. Dean. Paula. Garth. Ivan. Elizabeth. It's just names that don't mean anythin', right? They're not even people anymore.

Conrad I d—

Everett. Everett was a guy at work, my last good job. He covered for me and I covered for him, real standup guy. He tripped crossin' the street and his head poked out just far enough past a parked car, and. Welp.

And Cheryl, she managed the grocers when I worked there in Stockton and she was a rare kinda kind. Nice, I mean, how some days I'd be feelin' dark and she'd catch it, ask me what's wrong and then sometimes she'd send me home and handle the baggin' for the rest of my shift and still pay my full hours because she knew I was never late, not a minute, and you could set your watch by my breaks and my lunch, and she's fit, too, real fit—marathoner, one of those types of fit—and happy, always happy. But one day she has a headache and goes home. Two days later it's still there so she goes to the brain doctor and he says to her, he says: You've got a tumor's the size of a clementine, so get your shit straight. Nine weeks.

I—

And oh, Jimbo. Jimbo walked in on his wife steppin' out and he scuffled with the guy right there in the kitchen and Jimbo, he got throatshot with a steak knife from the set he won from work. Bled out on the linoleum he'd picked out for her special, installed himself.

Then, oh yeah, there's Edith and all her strawberry daiquiris got her drowned at her own birthday barbecue when nobody's looking, and the coroner wrote how I broke more'n half her ribs tryna breathe her back after haulin' her off the bottom of the deep end.

Stephen and Bernice, my neighbors when I was rentin' a room in Winnemucca—their mail piled up for a week and her sister found them still in bed. What's that monoxide shit?

—Carbon.

Whatever. At least they were sleepin'.

I can keep goin'. There's more. There's lots more if you w—

Stop it, Conrad. Just stop. If you want to talk about everyone who's ever died because that's what you want to talk about, then fine. Talk. But I didn't come out here just to bathe in your rage.

[—.]

It's not like I'm some guinea pig you know. Don't know you that well and sure that's partly my fault but this ain't the way to get the ball rollin', you ask me. Could be doing tons of shit gettin' to know each other better than this, this—this whatever it is that you're doing but no. No, you just sit there. Y'just sit there and I'm supposed to keep talkin' and talkin' and then you disappear with that tape and I go back to bein' a picture on the fridge? Well fuck that. Fuck that and fuck you, you. I—.

Whatever.

I—.

[—.]

I'm sorry, I'm just—. I'm frustrated. With all of this.

All of what?

My life, I mean.

Why?

All this that it's come to. Wonderin' how'd we get here, you know? When did this become the world? Buddies at work, they tell me all about their nieces and sisters and moms and all that shit and I'm just Mr. Smile'n'nod who's got nothin' to add.

Something can always be added.

Right. Well I'm sorry. Let's start over.

Let's.

Start over—.

Jesus. Where?

Wherever.

But you're gonna think I'm crazy.

Even if that was the case, why would it matter?

—Just hear me out, okay? Crazy's not me.

So stop dawdling.

Right.

—So people around me just have a way of, I don't know, going away—if that wasn't already clear. And my brothers are the kindest example.

Elaborate.

I mean like they're gone, yeah, but—. They're both gone but at least they're still out there. He's still out there and I hope he's doing good, your pops. I mean I know we don't talk but I know inside that he's doing good he's gonna outlive us all, I know that—that's not what I mean. I mean I hope he's happy, y'know?

Is he?

Is he what?

Happy. Is he happy?

I thought we were talking about you.

Right, but—

So talk about you.

Okay but—. Okay.

So Wayne and me, we both went away from one another, repulsed-like, and maybe that was my fault but maybe it was his, I don't think you can assign all the blame complete to one column or the other, but alls I know's that somehow my life ended up here at this table with a cup of shitty discount coffee and a glass of good scotch and a mic in my face at, what, nine at night. So that's me. That's maybe not what I woulda picked how this sits now, but that's me.

Roy—Roy's okay. Not doing so well as he used to but that's partly the hand he was dealt and partly all the mileage he racked up through the middle years because he's been through a lot and I don't say that lightly and sure, he brought a lot of that down on his own noggin but he's been through a lot and whether you bring it on yourself or it gets shoveled down on you or it's some combination it doesn't matter so long as you make it through, and he made it through. Don't know how much longer he'll still be around, but he—he's had his share of experiences. Went some places I couldn't follow. We don't talk much, Roy and me. Don't know if we even know how, anymore. The calls, they never go good. We're too heavied down by what shit we can't drop.

Wayne, I feel like Wayne was there with him from a distance though, sometimes I feel that. I mean neither of us were *there*-there for Roy but I feel we were always both there for Roy in our own separate ways, maybe, and maybe Wayne more than me but I don't know. It's hard for me to explain. But Wayne went away, and Roy went away, and I went away too, each in our own directions, and as much as that sads me up, that—all of that's better than the rest of the people I've loved. People, how they—. People just—.

Y'see it all started with our father but you didn't ask about him. After that our family—.

Actually, no, it was before that. What's a good way to put it. Okay maybe, maybe our family is like magnets all flipped around wronglike, fine on their own but the closer you bring 'em the harder they push off each other, maybe that's how to figger it. Maybe that's the best way to start.

With magnets?

I dunno. There's lotsa of wedges between my family, I know. I know you know too. Lotta distance these days, lotta space.

And what do you think about that?

Early days, I thought it's all room to grow, right? Everyone's got their lot, I thought, and maybe it's all for the best us splittin' up—that us, we needed to air ourselves out. At first I thought hey, maybe a year, two tops, and we'll all be straight again, movin' past this. Thought Roy'd square himself up with a little nudge here and there from me, maybe Wayne, Mom.

Harriet'd fuck him up quick and get him back on track with one phone call if she'd give him a call ever but she split first and nobody really expected her coming back so that never happened. She was always the good around the house growing up, had her finger on the pulse of the place and knew just what to say to any of us when the chips were down, but she had to leave. If I'd've known how to get a hold of her I'd've told her how her brother needed help and she woulda called, I know she would. Retrospect, I think a call might've been the only thing that'd've snapped Roy out, brought him back, but—. But I dunno. That's not how things shook out, and for better or worse, here we are.

Here we are indeed.

Y'know—.

Y'know, what do even you want anyway, *you*, huh?

I—

You want the dead?

Conr—

You want the fuckin' dead you go talk to my brothers. They'll tell you things and you'll eat it up, you, they'll tell you this and that 'bout how they cried and cried when we put Dad in the ground but they're lyin'. They didn't even go. I was there, motherfuckers. Motherfuckers didn't even go.

They'll even tell you our sister's dead, how's'at, hm? You believe that shit? You know I bet you do, you, I bet you ask them about her and watch them froth at the chance to tell you she's a saint, she's the martyr swooped in an' saved us all, how she died and took our father with her, well *fuck*. *Them*. We didn't need savin' and she wasn't a saint. She's our sister and she needed to leave but she's comin' back and I know that for a fact.

Is she?

You know how I know? I'll tell you how I know, motherfucker. I know because it has to be true I can feel it, I can feel her out there and that's not all, I say that knowin' there isn't much I really even feel at all anymore and it's not like you'd believe me anyway if I tried to lie but I'm no liar. Too many years in the bottle maybe, sure, and I don't got much but she's maybe the one thing I've got, that feelin', and they can't take that from me, so laugh. Laugh at me. Go on. Keep suckin' up the bullshit they're servin', my brothers, how they cry and cry over a grave Wayne faked 'cause she never got buried, so fall in, go on, go do exactly that if that's what makes you happy, just don't tell me I'm wrong when I know that I'm right, I know it. She's out there and I know it.

Conrad—

She's out there I still feel her out there and she's the ultimate *fuck-you* to my brothers and the rest of them sayin' me, Oh Conrad oh you fuckup, you're it. All those girlfriends, all those people, all them and you in between, so how 'bout that, hm? What'd those dead all have in common? Hm? *Hm Conrad?* Well fuck them, they're gone, and it doesn't even matter. Noise, they're all just noise.

Harriet, I *feel* her but she's not just a *feeling* see? See I've got somethin'. I've got somethin' I've never told them about, my brothers, somethin'd fuckin' fuck up their world they ever found out but I'm savin' it, see, for a token of the faith and she and me'll be there when I drop it on the table sayin' how I never gave up, no. It's there on the mantle, look, left of the baseball right of Dad's flask, see?

See what?

The bundle, you see it? The postcards.

They're from her?

There's more'n eighty of 'em, stamped, mailed and fuckin' delivered. Eight-tee.

And she wrote you? They're not blank on the b—

Y'know this project—I'm liking this project of yours more each time we meet, you. Roy, Wayne. Hah! Hi there, liars. Fuck you from sunny Arizona, you can't see me wavin' but you'd better believe I'm wavin' at the tape. You'll wave at them for me when you play this back, won't you? That's what you're doin' with this shit, right? Please wave at them I'll even pay you to, here. Here, have a fiver.

[—.]

And give 'em a big sloppy kiss, too, while you're at it.

Conrad that's not wh—

Kisses, hey. Hey, now that I think about it, lemme take a moment to say that this beats anything from when we were kids me looking over at that mantle, motherfuckers. Neener fuckin' neener. Just like when we're kids I'm right and we're playin' my game like it or not except this time you can't just quit on me. We're gonna sit in the sandbox until it's over whenever over ends up bein' and yeah, maybe we'll all win when she comes back and the dust settles but I'd be lyin' if I said I wasn't gonna enjoy watching your faces the moment you know, how it'll be like losin' her all over again but different, yeah, hollow. Be a hollow you won't ever fill and I'll fucking bury you in it, because I kept the faith.

Conrad they're nev—

She's alive, brothers. She's alive and when she comes back you'll know I was right and it'll crush you how wrong you were but we'll dig you up, she and me, because that's family. We'll pull you up by the ears from your pieces and we'll rebuild us all together because. That's. Family. Because we all got some good left and because we're not monsters because it's still there, the good. It might've been hidin' but it's still there. It's still there and we're not monsters.

NINETY-SEVEN

Today is 29 February 1996. This is tape ninety-seven, side B, regarding the seventeenth in the series of Days I Almost Died. Continuing from side A.

An instrument for writing or drawing with ink, she said, Typically having a metal nib or ball on the business end and fitted into a cylindrical holder, metal or plastic, sometimes wood. A pen. And your name, actually. I have to put your name on here.

I floated inside to borrow a pen, but none of the other movers on shift wanted to give me one when I told them why.

Five bucks tell her I can give her five.

After a brief and increasingly frantic search, I found a Bic squirreled deep in a drawer, and back in the garage, she stuffed my two dollars into her shirt pocket and scrawled across the back of the form and told me, Here, write your own name in, whatever it is.

Wayne.

Well, Wayne, do it yourself anyway. Two bucks for a car, you should be filling this thing out as it is.

She stood and pulled a set of keys from a pegboard on the wall above the bench that was full of keys and lobbed them to me. She sat back down, stubbed out, and reached back for the pack, and I remember looking at all those little hooks and thinking that she had a lot of dead husband left to shed.

I was staring down at my keys in my hand before I had even pulled the cover off the car. Strange, I thought, that I was the owner of a car I had not even seen, and that was the only emotion about that exact moment that I can remember, the thought that anything could be under there.

Or nothing. Nothing could be under there. This could—would probably be—some sort of sick joke with me at the butt, and Conrad was probably hiding just outside the side door and would burst in at any moment with a camera. Or maybe it has no engine, something like that. Maybe I own two thousand pounds of iron and four flat tires, maybe, and now she extorts me for storage fees or some such.

A chill went through me and I almost tried handing the keys back to her and telling her this was all some great mistake, but she was already somewhere else there on the stool, just breathing, staring trancelike toward the wall with her cigarette already burning down. She was somewhere else entirely.

Stuck with it now, Wayne, I heard myself think, so you might as well get it over with. Take a peek to see what sort of heap hides beneath.

I braced.

I peeled the corner of the cover back and felt my pupils blow.

A Porsche. Nobody had ever given me anything and here was a Porsche. I ripped the cover the rest of the way off.

Does it work?

Mm?

Scrap job, right? No starter or something?

I think the transmission needs fix, she said, Reggie said it was on his list, but—. But aside from that and a headlight out, I think he kept it tip-top.

Looking at it, maybe the paint had been green in a previous life, but now it was much closer to white. It was missing a hubcap and the passenger window had a thin, wispy crack that split it into halves. The back right fender was starting to rust. The driver's door stuck a little. It was beautiful.

I parked in the driveway that evening and pulled Roy out to look at the car. He asked me how much I bought it for and just shook his head when I told him.

I need your help with some stuff on it, I said, and he said Sure. First order of business, I said, was I needed new headlights because I had already been pulled over once on the way home but the cop let me off when I explained that it had been my car for less than an hour.

Headlight troubles? Roy perked up.

I have no budget for tickets.

Got you covered, he said, but he refused to elaborate.

So the next day Roy brings home a new bulb from Jake's along with a plainlooking box so big he struggled to keep it under his arm, and when I tried to take it from him he snapped at me, *Careful careful, fragile.*

How did you even get home like that?

Master of Crutches, Wayne. I am the Master of Crutches.

Box and bulb out at the car, he pulled a flathead from his back pocket and started on the headlight assembly to swap out the dud.

What is this? I poked at the box.

I told you I had you covered, he said.

A few minutes later the headlight was working and situated and he pulled a box cutter from his other pocket.

These Carellos, he says, will bubble paint at a hundred yards.

Carel-*whats*?

High beams. Carellos. Technically, anyway. Carello housings but some illegal Eastern European guts in there that should make regular Carellos look like flashlights. No idea what the real numbers on these are, but I do know that regular-old Carellos, like, recoil the car when you turn them on.

And Jake sells these things?

Sort of. I bought them a while back from one of those foreign catalogs he has stacked up by the oil drums, and I was flipping through one, and I saw these and beneath whatever their real name was in whatever language, in quotes, was *Fingers of God*. So, I mean, how could I not?

But you should use them, then.

On what? My cripplesticks? No, a ride like this needs some wattage up front and I bought them mostly just to buy them, anyway.

Okay Roy. Whatever. Slap them on there or whatever you need to do.

I thought he was being dramatic about all of this until he said, Might need to pick you up a new alternator tomorrow, depends on what this one can handle, and you need special mounting brackets, too, but Jake is still checking on those for me.

He brought a new alternator home a few days later, dragging it behind him on a creeper he had tied through his belt loops, and he worked through the night. I offered to help him but he shooed me off whenever he said I was hovering, saying, Go away, go away, this will be good, just trust me.

But why, Roy?

Because go away.

Fine.

I slept and woke up early, still dark, and found Roy sprawled out across the couch. I put a blanket on him and went to see his handiwork.

Two silver domes, flattish in the front and smaller than I had expected, were mounted to the bumper, and the cabling was braided neatly to where each set disappeared through identical, brassy grommets he had installed in the fenders. Roy must have heard me open the door to the garage or something because he appeared next to me, but I had not heard him.

Since when can you sneak?

He said nothing.

This looks neat, what did you do up here anyway?

Roy told me to pop the back, because the engine on that car was in the back, and I did.

Then he said Okay, I still have to run switches into the dash but I can probably take care of that tonight after work, but in the meantime go stand in front. He gestured, as he often did, with his crutch. Start the engine for me first, though, and I can fire them up.

So I started the engine and then stood in front of the car, and prepared myself to be underwhelmed. Roy, now in the back, reached clunkily into the bay, his arms thin and unwieldy as ever.

I was about to ask him if he needed my help, but then everything went a white you could not possibly comprehend. A kind of bright to crush eyelids and snatch the air from lungs. I felt an uncomfortable warmth spread and increase across my shins and knees, and the loose denim of my jeans, I imagine, was flapping softly behind each leg as a flag in a field.

No headlight tickets for you anymore, eh? Roy was squinting and turning his head away even behind the car and kind of laughing at the same time. I still remember that, him laughing.

He undid whatever it was that he did to turn them on and everything went mineshaft-black, my vision reeling and furious from the violence of those lights in the predawn's cold dark.

Thanks, I told him, blinking, but I wonder when these would even approach practicality.

Mountains on a new moon, maybe. Who cares.

Or some sort of makeshift cooking apparatus, I said, for the smaller, roadside mammalian fare.

Or that, sure.

I walked over to give him a healthy slap on the back and I took him to breakfast, and life doddered on, and I think it was months before I even turned those highs on but for once or twice, just to chuckle. It was much longer before they would serve their true purpose.

Now, a while after the installation, one of Conrad's friends set me up on a blind date with someone or other, I cannot remember her name. From what Conrad told me, her interest was tepid at best until someone said I drove a Porsche and then her attitude changed.

Perfect, I remember thinking. Just the kind of person I want to know.

Conrad's response was that I needed to get out more, and he would sell some of my comics if I backed out. So I went. And he sold them anyway.

The day of the date came and I figured if she was going to be more interested in my car, we were going to do whatever I felt interested in doing, so I had set the time for noonish on a Saturday. I picked her up and she was wearing a nice skirt and one of those sweaters—what are they called, cardigans? One of those and a hairband that matched her shoes that matched her earrings that matched her handbag and she asked what we were going to do as she walked, beaming, to my car.

Hiking.

Hiking?

Hiking.

Oh.

So we drove. And drove. And drove and drove and I could tell she was having a terrible time but not me—it was a fabulous spring day. Fabulous, until somewhere way, way back up nowhere, when the transmission dropped a synchro with a splendid clunk and the car became a singlespeed.

What was that? she snarled.

I started laughing.

What was that, Wayne?

I think the transmission just imploded, dear.

What? What does that mean?

Looks like first gear still works, at least.

What. Does that mean. Wayne.

Car no go fast.

Are you serious?

No.

Really?

No.

She scoffed, and I said Hey, look on the bright side, we have to turn around if we want to get back before nightfall, and I figure with just first we can do almost fourteen or fifteen, maybe, even.

Fourteen or fifteen what?

Speed. Miles per hour.

Are you kidding me?

Yes.

Really?

No.

I figured it had been around three o'clock when the transmission went out and we had driven something like a hundred miles, so we were looking at about a seven, maybe a six hour drive and maybe I could even get her back in less if I could raise Gordon at a service station somewhere in between.

Fasten your seat belt here we go! I revved the engine to redline and dropped the clutch, and the tires roared, and the rear drifted to the left until the rubber caught, and then we were off, topping out at about twelve miles per hour with the engine screaming. She called me some names and affirmed that this would be our last date, and I made racecar noises while we lazed along, Num-num-num-num-num-num here comes a corner *skreeeeeeeeee!* and she ignored me and seethed for more than an hour.

Just before I hit the deer we were coasting through a corner at the robust speed of thirty, thanks to gravity, and she gasped.

I looked to her and said: What?

And then a buck—a majestic specimen, truly—soared roadward from the brush and I creamed it midair. He almost cleared me but he should have known better than to test mettle against the 1956 Porsche 356A 1300, famed apex predator of the Colorado State Highway System. The front left bumper-fender-area crushed his left hip and he spun as a *danseur* before landing on his right side, head still pointing off to the left shoulder like it was before his—well, I guess you could call it a *tour en l'aire*.

116

She was shrieking and in my shock all I could say was, Did you see that? Did you. See that.

See what, Wayne? Did I see what?

The deer did you see it.

Which deer, Wayne, huh? Which one?

That deer. Right over there.

She made a weird growly noise, got out of the car and started pacing and grunting and grabbing at her fancy hair and muttering while the buck was making this soggy, gargling sound and pawing at the air with its forelegs. An odd, yet somehow harmonious duet, I remember. Like peanuts and pickles. Chocolate and parmesan.

So I idled Reggie to the shoulder and got out to assess-slash-admire the situation I had created, and I say admire because every so often in life the stars misalign with a perfection that demands attention, and it occurred to me that this was one of those moments, how there, out of the car, I could see the animal was maimed and flopping, and my miserable date was boiling over, and my car would not shift out of first, and we were something like eighty miles from civilization, and the left of the Carellos my brother had installed looked bent and spritzed with fur and blood, and I was hungry, and it was too hot, and I had no water, and somewhere I needed find a stone large enough to kill a deer. It had to be a heavy. I needed a both-hands kind of rock because his flailing and his rack meant I would be ripped apart if I tried to get close enough bash him with a one-hander or use the knife I maybe had in the toolbox in the trunk.

I laughed. She was not laughing.

I marched toward the hill off the side of the road and she started yelling, Where do you think you are going? But that is not what she said, exactly.

I came back hefting a fifty-pounder, hoping without optimism that, in my absence, another car might have come around the same blind corner and obliterated the dying deer.

No joy.

I found my date huddled behind the car and plugging her ears to deaden the deer's rattle. It was trying to get up on its front legs, but its pulverized back half lay limp and still behind its struggle, and the noise—the noise it made—a dissonant concoction of wet strain and unholy howl that has never really left me.

She saw me with the rock, a big rock the size of a basketball and heavy and she said, Oh no, no no no, and I told her it was either this or leave it there to bleed out into its gut, and that might be in five minutes or it might be in the morning, assuming that a bear did not find it in the night.

She whimpered.

Feel like helping? This is just like hunting but easier.

She did not feel like helping.

After the first throw I ran to look for the knife, but there was no knife, but I checked twice in the trunk while it quivered, but no knife, so a second throw of the rock was the way it would have to happen and a rock is—.

A rock is no way to go.

Dreams. I still have dreams.

When it was over I tried to drag him off the road but he was too heavy. I gave up and left him there. I footed the rock over the precipice and watched it tumble down until I could not see it, and then I listened until it made no sound. I wanted water for my hands.

Walking back around the front of the car I saw with some relief that the Carello, the left of the ones that Roy installed, was not bent but rather the whole bumper was twisted up a little. And then I remember feeling sad. Not so sad for the bent bumper, no, because bumpers are there for bumps and who cares, no, I was sad because until I had money, that bumper would stay that way and the misalignment would render that impractical headlight even less useful. Aimed up like that, it would liquify the eyes of every other driver on the road.

I thought about fixing it. I tried later, even, with a mallet and a block of wood, but that got me nowhere, and then I contemplated a pry bar, but I worried about damaging something else, so I gave up. Or the bracket, I suppose I could have tried to bend that, but the brackets he got were special, and I had no desire to mess with that since I would have to bend it back if I ever fixed the bumper.

When I turned the car on, I marveled that, first, both sets still turned on, and second, that even in full daylight, I could see that the pines up ahead of the car were brightened by those Carellos. You had to look to see it, but that they were functioning and that they were brighter than daylight was undeniable.

At least the headlights work, I said more to myself than to her.

Headlights, what do you care about headlights I thought you said we had hours until sunset just drive me home.

These babies could cook a deer, you know.

She cared little for my joke.

I num-num-nummed us the rest of the way out of the hills.

Four hours later, I called Gordon from the first gas station we passed and he came in a car I had never seen before.

New ride?

Something like that, he said. Date not going so well?

Something like that.

She said, you know I can hear you. And I said, I know.

Can you give her a lift home? Couple beers on me.

Sure thing, Wayne.

And then they hopped into Gordon's vehicle—or rather, I should qualify that as the vehicle that Gordon was driving—and I never saw her again.

—So that all sets up the next part of this story, but before we get into that I think I should frame something, namely, that I doubt there is such a thing as luck, and that there is no luck is something I set out to prove to you with this story today.

Basically, this thinking comes from looking back at my life and assessing and concluding that luck could not exist in this world. Whenever there was some chance to catch a break, whenever I needed to roll a hard eight—.

How many times have I heard, *Sorry, Wayne, we liked you a lot but the other guy got the offer, it was so close.* How many times have I been the only speeder in a pack that gets pulled over. Every car accident, the other person has not had insurance—every single one of them. Every pet I have loved has been killed or was stolen or wandered off into the night. I, my life—. I argue that my life disproves any notion of luck existing.

But fate, though. Fate is a different story, I think, because some things just worked out sort of organically, matured into goodness on an observable vector. Like, I planted the peach tree behind your mother's house when we first moved in, and it grew tall, up and up before growing out, like a capital T, and it grew for years before producing any fruit, and when it flowered, it only made flowers at the ends of its tallest branches and by then, most of those were overhanging your mother's roof, and for the ones over the lawn, ten bucks at the hardware got me a few yards of netting, and by the time I was done, that tree was producing fruit that would plop onto your mother's roof or the netting and roll into the gutters. Every few days during the late summer, while other folks had faces full of leaves and ladders pitched precariously, all I had to do was climb the shed, pick peaches from the gutter and rinse the roof down.

How? Why? Peaches are supposed to grow low and wide and I have never seen another peach tree grow like that one.

Another example. My family, between all of my family and my brothers, what happened to Harriet and—.

And all of that.

All of that pushed me away, in a way. Pushed me away or maybe I just left in selfishness, my opinion changes daily. But either way when I left, I knew my next stop had to be college, anywhere, doing anything, and while I know that it was not fate that brought your mother and I together, fate certainly put me in Golden.

And this story, my car, my Porsche. Fate. Fate exists and my proof is still mounted on the bumper of that car, in whichever junkyard that bumper presently sits.

So getting back to the story—we had one road trip, Gordon and I, where I wanted to get Gordon away from everything, so we took a week around the Midwest to see as many of those Largest-Mudball-In-The-World type things as possible. Rubber band balls, mud, twine. Lots of balls, thinking about it now. Not much else out there worth calling Guinness about, I suppose. Probably we saw a dozen of these things over a week or ten days or something and there were endless stretches of driving in between.

Nebraska, Kansas, Wyoming, Iowa. All of that space is something that everyone should stand in the middle of, the fields and fields, the towering sky sphering down until the two touch at the edge of what you can see, and how on the roads through them, how you can listen to an album you know all the words on or the zealots that doomsay from the corners of the AM band, how you can lose yourself to one of those or both or to your head's own ephemera, and you drift until you return, amnesially, to look down to see that somehow you are doing a hundred through all that space with the windows down and a gale going through your hair.

I am not sure where we were or even what time it was. It was late, and we pulled into some mom-and-pop diner on the side of the interstate, one of those hopeless-looking places, bleached of all optimism. Its tattered candy-stripe awnings. Its weedy gravel parking lot. Its once-cheerful signage. Like some small, quiet war had long since been lost, and yet this solitary, losing battle forever crept on.

We walked up as the waitress was locking the door, but she was kind. She let us in once we told her we were fast eaters. Gordon ordered for us before we even sat down.

Two burgers, bloody, just walk them by the grill, fries or whatever comes with is fine, and two—chocolate—yeah, chocolate shakes.

Hey Merle you get that? and a large line-cook stereotype grunted and the waitress shuffled off toward the broom in the corner.

We sat in a booth by the door. I rubbed my face and Gordon put his legs up on his side of the booth and stretched out with one elbow on the table and the other arm draped over the back of the booth's cracked vinyl.

Gordon said he was tired.

So sleep in the car, I told him, I feel pretty awake.

No, he said. I feel tired.

I remember us talking about Lou Brock and Hank Aaron at length, and I remember him keeping his eyes closed until the food came.

He used to pitch, Gordon did. I cannot remember if he ever told you that or if I did, but up in Canada he used to pitch before he came to the States, but not officially, of course.

Well, okay.

Like so much about Gordon, it was complicated.

Is complicated. Is.

See, he never went to college, but you know that, and Gordon is a big guy, too, six-five and muscular, you remember, and fast—faster than me, even—and he said he had been that size since he was sixteen and he could buy booze from the time he was fourteen, he said, and for the last year or two before he left Canada he told me that he could just mill around college campuses whenever he had the inclination and he could get into parties and sit in on classes without much or any notice at all.

So one day, ambling around, he happened across some college's baseball practice, and after watching from the bleachers for a while, one of the coaches sized him up and asked him if he had ever considered trying out for the team.

Rather than explain his non-enrollment, Gordon just told him no.

You look good to play, the coach said, I can get you a glove.

Gordon—never one to turn down the chance for a good story—borrowed some guy's glove and whipped up some tale about how he used to pitch in leagues as a kid before his parents uprooted everything. The coach snagged a catcher and

Gordon made the team a few pitches later. Gordon was—. Is—a quick study.

I can only assume Gordon expected not to make the team, or at worst for the situation to implode shortly thereafter, but he said he actually started two games before he ran out of excuses for forgetting to bring his transcripts to practice, and when the coach eventually sent him off the field in uniform and told him to come back with the papers, Gordon just left town. Poof. Gone. Over the border and into our lives not too long after that day.

He had that way about him, doing that, and he was good at it, too, was equipped with all of the necessary skills. He had a Teflon tongue, was goodlooking, far smarter than he ever let on, strong enough and deft enough to hold his own at any labor, and fiercely dependable, at least until the next gig came along.

Best part of that story, he said, was that there, my name was not even Gordon. Always a new name for a new place, he said, always. A fun game for whenever he landed somewhere new.

And no, if you wonder, I never asked Gordon about it, about whether he—. If he. When he got here, if Gordon was really even—. If Gordon was even his actual name.

See I knew him. I knew him and he never lied to me, not once, so it never mattered.

But so we talked baseball while we ate, and when we were done, Gordon peeled a ten out of his thick roll of bills, dropped it on the table, and we were out the door. He hopped in the passenger seat and nodded away about five minutes later to leave me alone again with the radio and so much meandering black road, and not much happened for the next hundred or two hundred miles, who knows exactly how far.

When it happened—the point of all of this—there were other cars on the road, going my way or the other way, but not frequent, and by that point we were probably into Iowa. Had to be. I remember stopping for gas outside of Council Bluffs and we were eastbound on 6 because both of us driven eastbound 80 before, and this story ends before Des Moines.

Anyway, it came on slow. First the wink of those headlights small in my rear view, miles back and minuscule but ever-present because the Iowa interstate is eerie-straight and too flat, and I noticed them because there was nothing else on the road to notice, no cars, no stars, no moon. But then how slowly they grew, how those headlights grew in my mirror like watermelon vines, how the headlights grew like that, like how the vines grew when I used to watch them from a hammock beneath an oak, and the jays, and the summer's zephyr, and the shade of an oak on a hilltop outside of Parker while the distance ripples silent in its bleachy broil and the vines just crawling, growing, stretching to strangle whatever beneath.

Before long I could make out the array of headlights and it was a big rig, and it had its full set on high, running lights, auxiliaries, even a line of those little ones on top of the cab, whatever those are called, all on.

Whatever, I thought. The road is flat and straight and black and this is what high beams are for, and he probably just forgot he had them on. My radio had deigned to actually work for a little while, and Lightfoot was on. I whistled along.

But then he kept coming. He crept up and up and before long he was ten car lengths back. Then eight. Then four. I eased off the gas, hoping he would pass, but when I eased off, he eased off too. Then he was three lengths back. Then two.

I kept slowing down, slowing down, but he inched up until I had to adjust my side and rear view mirrors because the bright from his lights was more than I could take, and I had to hold up my hand—like this—to shield myself from the passenger side mirror that I could not reach, and—.

[—.]

Why did I do that? Just now, with my hand. Why do people do that, do you think? Gesture when speaking alone or on the phone?

[—.]

But anyway I slowed down to forty, maybe, and waved him to pass, but he would not pass. And those lights. Those lights, I can still see them. Everything was white and white and white, and he was still riding me, and I started to get scared. What do I do?

I tapped Gordon on the shoulder but he was too gone, and he did not wake up even after I called his name.

Then I thought, okay, I can just wait it out. We had made good miles that day and we were in no real rush, anyway. Des Moines was only a hundred miles out and if I drop it down to thirty and keep it there, he can sit behind me all night while I squint and either we get to Des Moines or the sun comes up, and at thirty, either or both of those were about three hours out. Good a plan as any, I figured. I let up on the gas.

But no joy.

Twenty minutes, maybe, he sat a car length or less behind me, both of us rolling down the interstate at around half the speed limit and I started swerving back and forth thinking if I got to the side of him he would just go around, but of course this did nothing. He would follow me on to the shoulder, into the other lane, everywhere, matching every move.

What if he ran me off the road? What if he ran me over? I was a tenth his weight and I could never outrun him with my bitty little engine—again, that Porsche was built to corner, not burn up the straightaways. So what do I do? What *could* I do? I spent a few miles thinking and weaving, getting desperate. Then the answer came.

I started veering back and forth, back and forth, faster and faster and shifting into third and then into fourth and he was doing a good job of keeping pace.

Did you ever see that movie with the fighter jets, what was it called? Where they pull the air-brakes and the plane chasing them flies right by? That. I did that. I pulled the brake and the car nosed forward into a halt because by that time, through the veering, I had sped it back up to seventy or so and I knew his mass would work against him. He tried, though. He tried to brake and swerve to stay behind me but I snuck by, just barely, and then his truck came to a stop maybe fifty yards ahead of my car, both of us stopped momentarily, and then I saw his cab chug-chug-chug and start rolling again. And it was over.

It was over, but now I was mad. My fear had given way to anger and I wanted for vengeance, for recompense, but how? I started the car moving again and I clenched my jaw so hard that my teeth hurt.

And then: fate. There, grinding my teeth and shaking my head, I happened to look over to the left of the wheel on the dash where there were two toggle switches that had been installed and mostly forgotten.

I have not even checked them, I thought. I have not checked them since right after the deer. But maybe. Just maybe. This would never work, right? Right?

Wrong.

I flipped the left switch and the air caught fire in the shape of a weapon, in the shape of an inferno aimed up, just enough. I corrected to the left a little and then sped up to close on the cab and bring the beam down a foot or three. Just back barely to the right. Now back a little.

And *there*. There it was. A white-hot lance of fanatical light striking squarely upon his driver's side mirrors.

His whole rig jerked like when your leg will sometimes kick just before sleep and he began to swerve like I had been swerving but my Porsche was infinitely more agile and drawing a bead with its holy fire was a simple calibration.

Faster, now left.

Slower, now right.

Aim. Aim. Aim.

And I was Yessing and flaring my nostrils and it was such a satisfaction to watch his doughy arm reach out to adjust the panels, but he had too many of them to account for the blind spots—the curvy jobs that keep everything in view—it was hopeless. His mirrors belonged to the Finger of God, and the Finger of God belonged to me.

Never had I felt as vindicated as I felt there in that moment, there on the highway somewhere in Iowa, punishing a man I had never met.

And how? How was I able to reify this retribution?

Fate. Fate for a cannon of a headlamp I had adjusted against the hip of a deer on a date with a girl whose name I cannot remember, a lamp mounted on the front of a car I had practically been given, a car I was driving in Iowa when I had no business in Iowa but to seek out Americana's most celebrated debris, and if not for this trip or for any other of the variables, like had we not stopped for food, or had we eaten a few minutes slower, or I had I told Conrad to sell my comics or had I just sold them before and sapped that leverage, or had the car come with two working headlights, then that lamp, that car, would have never realized their destinies. It was perfect. It was perfect and I felt righteous.

At first, anyway. It was when I noticed that I was squinting in silence, calibrating and recalibrating, while Gordon snored softly and the road rolled by, that the guilt began its wisping in.

Surely, this man had learned his lesson, yes? For twelve miles or more I had kept him pinned, and by now he had learned, right? So what was I doing? Who was I? Sitting there, softening the metal of that mirror array and redding his skin, whiting his eyes? That was not me. That was not who I was.

I flipped the switch. I dropped back to let him pull away. However fast we were going when I ended it, maybe sixty, whatever, he kept up that speed and I took it back down to thirty again and rolled the window down to enjoy the smell of the night and the satisfaction that justice brings, the justice that I had meted out but fairly, and that it had been more compensatory than punitive. Perhaps a touch too punitive, but then only barely, and I ended it before I could have. I could have torched him into Des Moines but I had relented, given him a stay. And that made me feel better.

I floated along the road and there were no other cars. It made no sense that there were no other cars out on the interstate, but we were close to the 80 interchange and whatever small highway we were on that connected 6 and 80 was probably just small and there would be more cars out on 80. Still, it was weird to go so long without seeing another car, I thought, but whatever, it was just me and the stars, and some clouds and my car, and Gordon, still unconscious, and everything was right.

But fate, it seemed, was not entirely done with me. An interchange or two and then some miles later, with the light from Des Moines glowing on the horizon, I came around a shallow bend in the road to find the truck idling and jackknifed across one of the eastbound lanes.

All of his lights were on and as I drew closer I saw a silhouette by the wheel-well, beside an open driver's door.

What was he doing? What do I do?

I closed at a cautious speed, maybe forty, until I could make him out clearly. He was a large man, wearing overalls and a cowboy hat and he had a thick, wide, white beard that came halfway down his chest.

And he was holding a rifle.

I slammed it from third down into second, mashed on the brights and fired up both of the Carellos and stomped my foot halfway through the firewall and he shielded his eyes. I whipped to the left, squeezing by the front of his cab and then back into the lane and I rammed it into third, and into fourth, and then I was doing a hundred with the engine wailing.

Faster I have to go faster, I thought, because even though I had gained some distance I saw his headlights orient themselves behind me again, and soon they stopped getting smaller, and then, slowly, slowly, they became bigger again. But I could go no faster than a hundred, and with enough time, I knew he could get a rig like that up through a hundred and five or ten.

Panic. I was panicking. Could I make it to Des Moines before he caught up? I had to. It was not far now, but he was gaining and it would be close. I had managed to put probably a mile between us before he started gaining ground, and he was closing at something like five miles per hour—so ten minutes or so—and I was starting to think that I was not going to make it to Des Moines in ten minutes since the outskirts had to be at least another twenty miles out. It would be close.

And where was the traffic? There were zero cars out on the road why were there no cars on the road? why had there been no cars this entire time, where had they been this hour or more no cars in so long why why why? and then I saw my exit.

I call it my exit because it was a billboard for a steak house near Des Moines and it read *Almost there, partner, not this exit but five down the road! Take the first left!* except the whole phrase was written in the wavy rope of a swinging lasso, and the man attached to the other end was a faded John Wayne, and immediately past that billboard was an exit for a rest stop.

I clawed off all of the lights and whipped in at full speed and came to a sliding stop near one of the parking spaces. Not good enough. I popped it into first and inched into a spot and squared, flipped the key, and the only sound was my quickened breathing and the clicking of the cooling engine. Less than a minute later the rig blows by doing better than a hundred.

Gordon returned. Why are we stopped?

This looked like a good rest stop. You feeling any better?

Sort of—no, not really. The matter with you?

Nothing just the headlights are kind of intense.

Gordon craned his head to look toward the interstate. Like, what, the other headlights? I see no other headlights, Wayne.

No these ones. Whatever I could go for a steak, I said, I just saw a billboard for a place do you want to check it out?

Not really, no.

Okay, I said, Just let me go throw up real quick and then we can keep going.

Gordon told me I needed to sleep and that he could drive for a bit, but he said he needed a smoke and a stretch first. I said Okay, and he puttered around that parking lot for a while, at times miming a tightrope on the curbs and at times lying on his back or sitting to stretch his legs as every sprinter does. The whole time, he hummed little nothings and smoked his Camel down to the filter without the cigarette ever leaving his lips.

I watched Gordon for a while before curling up in the backseat and trying to sleep, but sleep could not find me. I remember a soft rain awaking across the roof of the car: one drop, one drop, two, three, and then I remember hearing other cars start passing by again in synchrony, it seemed, with the rain: one car, one car, two, three.

And then it was Illinois.

I awoke with our army blanket tossed across me and sunshine blobbed up on my face. Gordon was shirtless and singing with the radio, and he was doing eighty or ninety and the window was down.

His arm out the window. His elbow bent forward. His hand up and down and the sun, the summer, the motley of tattoos thrown across his shoulders and arms and back and his hair licked into waves and his hand up and down like this, oscillating into the sun and into the driver's side shadow and into the sun again, up and down, up and down, up and then down again, and again, and again and again up and down inside that balmy gale.

SIFTING THROUGH STATIC
ACT ONE, SCENE ZERO:
(OR, THE INEXPLICABILITY OF ABSENCE)

The dead don't go anywhere, my father says, because I had two brothers but I know that they're gone.

Where they went, Papa?

Roy spent—.

Conrad is—.

[—.]

They went different places, Kidlet.

Is different places far from California?

They went far, far away.

—Papa?

Yes, Kidlet?

Why they go, Papa?

Dissatisfaction, he says. Dissatisfaction was their butcher, was the death beneath their hearts. It grew unnoticed in the pulsing dark and it wound itself about their organs like ivy. It slept them slow.

—They go to sleep?

Sort of. I don't know.

ROY/LONGMONT, CO/2007-07-24
09:29:59—10:12:12

It's hard to quantify my fucked up, you know? To work out how much havoc's on my head? It's hard.

What?

You know. The quantifying of it. It's a difficult thing to quantify.

But what do you mean, quantifying? Quantifying what?

To put it on a scale I mean, the damage I've done. If that's at all possible.

To put that to numbers?

Yeah with numbers or something, whatever. If it even matters. Do you think it matters?

The damage itself? Or trying to p—

Trying to put it all together on a page is what I'm saying. Saying I could have a page or some pages or a manual or whatever and I'd be able to look at it or read it and say, yeah, this is how much. This is what I did and how much it hurt.

But don't you already know that, though?

No I mean like for other people, how much it hurt. Not just my experience of their experience, is what I'm saying—

I'm saying objective-like. I'm talking about a thing I could look at to see entirely how much I hurt them. How much it trickled down. How far.

—**So but like a graph, though.**

Or a chart or something, yeah. You know. With numbers? I don't know.

A graph. A graph, for this, and not something like a book. A memoir or something. A novel.

I mean I've thought about it as a book, sure, and maybe a book—maybe a book'd work better. But I don't know. I guess I just always pictured it as a graph or something. Something with numbers.

But how would you—? How could such a thing even be organized into one graph? Or fifty, even?

Yeah, okay, so that's the rub I'm talking about. Like, should I be trying to measure just those worst years or do I go for all of them? And does that mean it's a column-type graph? Higher equals worser? Or all the times I picked up the phone but couldn't dial—are each of those a point on some line? Or maybe is it both of those things but somehow offset by the times I could dial but it didn't ring through, or the times I tried to go somewhere for them, be there for them even when there was no reciprocity nor welcome—should I maybe put all of that into one of those heat maps or one of those radar charts or something? I don't know.

Or maybe it *is* fifty graphs. Or a hundred. Or a thousand. I don't know.

But doesn't that all sound like something'd be valuable? Might matter for something?

Does it matter to you?

That's not what I asked, but thanks.

But I mean it must, yeah? I mean isn't everything supposed to matter? Be relevant? Not necessarily to me, I suppose, or to you, but to someone or something it must, right? It has to.

Why?

Well otherwise what's the point, right? What's the point of all of this if there isn't some score, some scale?

The point of, what—living?

Yeah.

You don't think that's a bit reductive?

I dunno, maybe. But maybe not, though. Maybe it only sounds stupid because nobody wants to admit that that's really what's going on, right? That it really is that simple and just nobody wants to say so?

I don't know—. I guess I'm more wondering why you're wondering, is all.

It just feels like—.

I don't know. I feel like if there isn't a scale then everything's a waste of time or something.

And?

And what?

And so what if it is?

A waste of time?

Yeah.

I don't know, Nietzsche, what if it isn't?

No I mean what's so troubling, really, about how things are? Right now? Who gives a shit about purpose, is what I'm saying. You're alive. You have your health. It's a nice day.

—That some sort of joke?

Did it sound like one?

My health? Really?

But am I wrong, though? Are you dead?

Have you looked at me lately?

I'm looking at you right now.

Well—.

Well if I'm not, then maybe I should be. And even if not now, then I should've been dead I don't know how many times, so—. So maybe I was, sort of. Maybe people don't ever really come back from shit like mine.

But you're not, though, is what I'm trying to say.

Not what?

Dead.

You so sure?

I mean—.

Okay fine. Fine so you're dead, fine. So why is this so hard, then, how you see your life? Why do you give a shit? How *could* you give a shit, even, about how things are, hm? If you're dead?

—Roy?

—There's different kinds of living.

You think I don't know that?

[—.]

—Roy?

It's just senseless, I guess. Just makes it all feel senseless or something.

What does?

That's why the scale, I guess—I don't know. I guess it's just something I can wrap my head around if that makes sense, that scheming up some map, some something I could hold in my hands that'd show precisely how bad I bombed my life back then, that maybe that'd be some comfort? I don't know.

But why that, though? What's that getting you over something less painful?

Like?

Fuck, Roy—like how about going for a walk, maybe? How about you go to the library and read the first bright green book you see for a whole hour, whatever it is. Or go brownbag a decent red and spend that hour feeding pigeons if you don't feel like reading, or if birds aren't your thing, then go down to a shelter and get a licky little puppy instead. How about go do that and then tell me it's still worth your time worrying about some goddamn chart or some wallowing, self-flagellating account of whatever shit's already behind you.

Hm?

—Roy?

It's the masochist in me maybe, I don't know. I mean I know people say you shouldn't dwell because it's bad for the soul or whatever, I've heard that. But then I don't have much else to go on, now, do I? I mean, like, any of those things or whatever else—that shit'll only fill up so much of a day anyway, right? So, whatever. Here I am.

Plus I'd find a way to kill a puppy. And that'd be the saddest graph of all.

If that's what you think.

I'd forget to feed it or I'd leave the door open, something.

Mm.

But yeah, but—.

But—?

But.

But actually let's go back for a second, yeah?

If you want. Why?

I'm starting to put it together, now, I think. I think it just hit me.

Put what together?

Why you're here. It's not all there yet but I'm just now thinking—. Yeah. Yeah I think my wallow's probly a corner of it, yes? Because I'm thinking now, and it seems we've really talked about is me and my brothers, more or less, right? Where all the pain's been sleeping? Am I wrong?

Hm?

Roy I'm just—

—here to talk. Yeah, I've heard that too. But maybe remove thyself from thine high horse, hm? If I'm wrong, tell me—please tell me. But if I'm not—?

If I'm not, then what's the harm in how I've been, how I've chosen to be? I mean don't we both get what we want if I stay how I am?

I mean—

I mean am I wrong? Is it not helping you, how I am?

I'm just here to talk, Roy.

Here. To. Talk.

Right.

So fuck it, then.

Whatever you want to say, Roy—I'll listen.

Right, well—.

Well?

So what's it you want to talk about?

Roy if you don't want—

Hmp.

Y'know—.

Y'know, I just figured something out.

What?

Maybe we'll—. Maybe we'll talk about it later.

Huh? What'd you—

Do you still want to talk about your dad? Is that what you want? You can just say if you do.

Could y—

Well so your dad left and I was less than okay, but you knew that already—already knew how I was fucked up something fierce, both on the inside and the outside, and I was bitter and I was angry when he left, before and after.

What were you angry at?

What *wasn't* I angry at? I was angry at Mom, angry at Con. Angry that Harriet was gone and angry at Dad's part in that. Angry at my legs. I was even angry at your dad for making me sell that bike, if you'd believe that—do you believe that shit? Sounds almost as ridiculous saying that out loud now as I suppose it must have back then, but that's where my head was, thinking that he made me do it because he wouldn't fix me and that anger—it only grew. It became a rage that stayed with me, consumed and became me, then and for years after.

But then he left. He fucking left, Wayne did, left me as a fucked-up sack of fury there in that house for the few days before I also left. And, surprise surprise, I was raging about that, too.

What got you off the couch, so to speak?

Oh I didn't leave by choice if that's what you were thinking, no. If I had my druthers back then I would've been there forever, I think, there on that couch.

Was it Conrad threw you out?

Conrad was already gone. It was Mom, actually.

Really?

Mm. Surprising when it happened, when Mom actually stood up and tossed me out on my ass. Really surprising. I didn't think she had it in her, really, and that's what I'd been banking on, that passivity. But I guess even the most predictable people can shock you once in a while.

So what'd she do? Change the locks?

Nope. Well I mean, yeah, she did that, but actually what she did was she called the cops, and they sat there and sipped coffee while I pouted and bitched and cried on the porch while the locksmith swapped everything out.

They were worried you'd, what—hurt her? Not leave?

No I think they were just there for her, the cops. And being honest I don't think she even had grounds for tossing me beings as I was, I think, still seventeen. But the cops in town always seemed to go out of their way to do things for her, so—.

Why?

The cops?

Yeah.

Oh, people wonder. I have my theories.

Like?

Like maybe we'll trade later.

Trade what?

Theories. You've got some, no? About her and why?

Zero theories over here.

Mm. Well—.

Well where'd you go from there?

Well—.

You ever lived on the streets?

Is that what happened?

Well I told you before—or maybe alluded is the better way to put it—but that I ended up in Reno.

I remember.

Yeah, well, Reno's where I woke up one day, on the street, and I'd been with some friends but they were gone. And I don't think they stole my car, but I can't be certain. Likeliest story is that I sold it to one of them for a few grams or a burger or I lost it on a gamble and they just forgot about me in the morning. Or maybe they stole it. I don't really care. It doesn't matter and I don't care.

Really?

About the car?

That didn't bother you?

Well I was angry, remember?

Still, though? Still angry?

Oh yes, I'm still angry.

That's not—.

Okay.

But so I met some new people in Reno, same as Denver, but I wasn't lying when I told you that Reno is, like, infinity kinds of awful. I don't remember much from Reno but I do remember not liking it, remember thinking that if I never saw Reno again it'd still be too soon.

What about it was so terrible?

—Have you been to Reno?

But what bothers *you* about it, I'm asking?

The garishness? The second-rate grandeur? The inescapable feeling that you're surrounded by people who're only in Reno because a flight to Vegas was thirty more dollars, and what the hell, they've both got slots so how different could they be? It's the armpit of the bourgeoisie world, Reno. And Reno's where I started sleeping on the street, too, so there's also that bit of bias.

Why?

Mostly because the good folks that run the shelters tend to be serious when it comes to their zero-tolerance policies, and I often underestimated the sway of my crooked little leggies.

So it was the streets for me, mostly—the cloying, neon, tiny streets of Reno.

Sounds lovely.

Mm.

So what came after Reno?

Vegas came after Reno.

And how was Vegas?

I remember nothing of Vegas.

So what came after Vegas?

I don't know. Some stuff.

Like what stuff?

I don't know.

Roy, we don't have to t—

No that's just it, I mean. I mean I don't know. No idea. Not really. Not but for some flashes and some smudgy bits.

You—

I mean after what little of Vegas, my next cogent *anything* is waking up in a hospital bed in Los Angeles, detoxing, and that just might be the worst thing that I've ever gone through with the shakes, the sweats. And the nausea—Christ, the nausea. The unbearable endlessness of it and the twisting headaches that I can't even figure out how to describe. Like slivers of white metal pushed through your pupils and wiggled. Like wringing the juice out of your brain like you twist a dishtowel.

How'd they find you? The hospital. Get you in there, I mean.

Someone dropped me off at Cedars-Sinai, they said. Dumped me out of a car in the ambulance bay like an abandoned baby.

But so you made it, though.

In there, you mean?

Yeah.

Well yeah, but only because I didn't have the means to kill myself. That's what was keeping me alive, to be honest—to stay alive and quasi-cognizant long enough to find a way to hang myself or to open a vein, but they thought of that.

But you made it.

But yes, I made it. The detox ended and I started counseling, took classes, all that stuff and they found me some cripple grant for some public housing thing and I started to get myself sorted out.

What sort of classes?

Oh all sorts. Algebra and classics, geography, I think some history. Even they had one of those classes that's just about ironing shirts and balancing checkbooks, cleaning a bathroom.

Did you do well?

Set the curve in most of them.

So they were a good distraction, then.

Well more they challenged me in a way that I hadn't really been challenged before, I think. I think that's why they went so well while I was in them.

How so?

Well I mean before this all happened, engines had always been an interesting diversion, but they'd gotten so easy for me before I went downhill that I wasn't getting much out of them anymore, right? No challenge. But then there was a psych class, and for the first time in a long time it felt like a bolt in a socket, how there's all these books, all these studies, all these folks thinking and writing about people and how they work, yeah? And then I read some other textbooks about kinesiology and physiology, but that was all just sort of—stuff. It was interesting enough but it wasn't really jiving because I think it was too much like mechanics, right? Like engines. And I was already good at engines. There was no mystery, no magic. But psych, though. Psych, everything's behind the veil. Everything's somewhere in that gray mush, grinding in the dark.

And did you find it helpful?

What, like did it keep me out of trouble?

I mean more like was it applicable. Did it help you figure anything out, or was it just a distraction?

Well I think it gave me a lot of answers, if that's what you're wondering. Or at least attempts at answers, because I don't think there are ever any definite answers when it comes to how people work and why, but I think there's a lot of good guessing you can do even though it's never going to be an exact science. So yeah, it helped me grapple with my anger— or I guess at least have some more understanding about why I was angry and why all of us were the way we were, and are the way we are.

Could you elaborate?

I mean it's simple, though, isn't it? Couldn't you figure it out?

I'm interested in your opinion, though.

Well there's how Con's always been so fucked up since Dad died because Dad was only vocal about being proud of *him*, right? Whether or not Dad was more or less proud of Con than any of us, Conrad's the only one ever heard anything on the matter. And Con got the new stuff, new clothes, new mitt, new whatever whenever there was money and there's only hand-me-downing going on for the rest of us, and then he's on his own with that, too, once Dad was gone.

And me? Well I'm jaded from how I was always treated, right? With kid gloves? *Best not to touch yon Noodle-legs, lest we break him!* Let's not even let him try to do anything for himself. In fact, let's punish him for trying, for being so inconsiderate as to risk his own health for some silly want for independence. Tell me that won't fuck you up.

And then Wayne—. I guess Wayne's never really been treated much like family, if we're being honest. Middle child, not sick, independent and a little fucking weird. He was always just sort of biding time, I felt, until then one day he was gone, and Dad knew that inside somewhere, too, I think. And he was less than thrilled.

And Dad himself, on the subject—I did enough reading, I can go back and make more sense out of the man now than I was able to before. I can sort of sort through the backlog and figure out that yeah, probly he did love us. He was a mean sonofabitch, but he loved us. Just, he didn't know what to do with that love. Does any of that make sense?

What do you mean, exactly?

About Dad?

Yeah.

Well it's endemic, right? For people like him?

Assholes?

Well yeah, but no—I mean you've probly heard how his life was terrible when he was younger, how poor he was, how nobody took care of him, yeah?

Something like that.

Well so did you know that his sister raised him practically on her own? They worked hard on the farm and it was a big family, and there were too much work to do for enough attention to be paid to each kid, and our dad was always last in line for whatever attention on account of him being the smallest and capable of the least amount of work.

That doesn't surprise me, from what I've heard about your grandfather.

Right? I honestly think that by the time he came around, his folks were over the whole idea of having kids, so he was never much more than a liability to them, and—take it from me—being seen as nothing but a liability'll certainly get you off on a bad foot with a begrudging set of parents.

Them? I thought his mother died in childbirth.

Mm? Oh, that. That's what he always said, yes, but that's not what actually happened.

What happened, then?

Well Gramps, I guess, maintained that she ran away when Dad was real young—that she got tired of feeling pinned down by her life and took off one night with no note and never came back. But then Gramps was also a meaner drunk than Dad, apparently, so it's plausible he might've gotten loaded a few times and lied to Dad, told Dad that Dad'd killed her by his coming out into the world.

So which is it?

Either. Both. Something else. Point is she might as well've died so far as the impact on Dad's concerned, because he was young enough when she dropped out of the picture that the guilt he carried with him's the same, I figure.

Point is, shit's so tangled up when you're trying to figure out anything about him, there's no saying for sure what really happened with her but for the fact that she was gone for the most of him.

And there's nobody to ask.

Who could you, even? Everyone's dead before Con comes around, and Dad was never much of a talker. They weren't hospital-going folk, either, so if she did die—if that's what happened—probly they just stood around a hole in the backyard, cried a bit, and then went back to tending after the hay.

But anyway, he was effectively orphaned by fifteen or sixteen what with most of his siblings already dead, the ones left being mostly useless, and Gramps having maintained a solid level of drunken loathing for Dad for every day of his life since the matron'd been gone.

So what'd he do?

Well Dad never finished high school, we know that. We know he went out and did odd jobs until he lied his way into the Army, and we know he couldn't even do that right and got sent back after a grenade on the range took off a hunk of his finger, once, when he wasn't where he was supposed to be. Or at least that's what he told us. He says he fought real hard to stay in, but a finger's a finger, they said. Whatever.

How'd he meet your mom?

County fair, I think.

And what'd they do until they started their family?

Well they were married less than a year before Harriet came around, so, not much.

That fast, eh?

Ten months, plus or minus.

Ten, you say?

Mm. Why—?

Just I've heard some wild things, is all.

Oh? Like what?

Like maybe we can trade later.

Cute.

Well, my proffer on the matter's that I found some papers once that had that math way off. Like, way, way, shit-doesn't-make-sense off, but then Mom said she got that cleared up. Clerical error, she said.

What'd they say? The papers.

Her birthday and birthplace didn't match up. Not even close. I asked Mom and she said there was a mix-up at the hospital and that they mailed them the ones with right date and place on them later.

How could a hospital fuck up its location?

Right? I asked if I could see them and she said she'd try to find them, but then she never came out with them and I never quite followed up. So who knows.

And you're sure it was her certificate? Not someone else's?

Reasonably.

How?

Doesn't really matter.

Bu—

Point I was making's that all four of us were around before long and our family embarked upon the shit-slog that mutated us into the people we are today.

But—.

But what?

[—.]

Hm?

—Nothing. There's such whimsy in your voice, Roy. Really.

Hmp.

—What was the problem, do you think?

With what, me? Or the family?

Either. Both.

There were lotsa problems.

But was there a main one, though?

I mean Dad, probly. Dad was probly the problem if I may be so bold as to blame the bulk on him. I mean we all had our flaws, sure, and we all contributed to make things worse in our own little ways, but he was the lynchpin, I think. And God was he ever a rotten lynchpin.

I've gathered.

But it wasn't just the drinking, you know, because even drunks aren't without their merits and their saintly types, no.

No?

No, it was the volatility of him, I think. His mercuriality, if that's a word.

How do you mean?

I mean how he could be so kind in the afternoon and thrash the life out of you for leaving the lid off the peanut butter after dinner. Or for any reason, really, you could get your face pummeled straight through the back of your skull even when you'd spent that morning hanging out with him in the garage, shooting the shit or watching baseball. And that kept us away, in a way. The constant wariness pushed us all apart and kept us from ever knowing him, and then he'd beat us for not knowing him, for being wary. It was so completely fucked up, but I do believe he loved us, I do. Just I don't think he really knew how, is all.

What makes you think that?

Hard to articulate, honestly. He was troubled by a lot of shit I'll probly never understand—things that occupied the most of his head for the most of his life, I think, and those things, they consumed him. Ate him up and we got what got spit out. And when he'd come up for air he'd just be so, I don't know—so goddamned *dissatisfied* with things, with us, and he'd spend that energy he'd found for us with his fists or on some genuine attempt at being present for us, but then still probly later with his fists because something didn't go exactly how he envisioned.

Like what's an example?

Of him trying?

Yeah.

Well take my birthday. Eight, I think. Or seven. But I was turning seven or eight and the whole run up to this party I was supposed to have on a Saturday, Mom'd been hyping it up all week.

Your father's going to have a great surprise for you just you wait, she'd been saying a few times a day.

And I spent that whole week trying to get her to tell me what he was doing but she wouldn't budge, and in retrospect I think it's likely he'd just told her he was going to do something but didn't fill her in on any of the specifics because he didn't have any specifics himself, due to lack of an idea, or money, or both. And also because it was never like him to tell her much of anything, anyway. Either way, she played it well.

But so Saturday rolls around and I've got my friends over. Or rather, I've got my friend over.

Actually that's a lie. I didn't have many friends.

How many, more or less?

Any friends. I meant any. Mom invited the kid from down the block for posterity's sake—Dennis—and I didn't like him. He was pale and too small, and he reminded me too much of me. But he came, and he was there when Dad got back.

Best as I can remember, Dad was angry before he came in.

How could you tell?

You could just tell. He had this way about him—this stomping, slamming way that you could hear down the block, how squirrels would scamper into their hidey-holes and birds would flock off ahead of him, and that'd be your first suggestion from the world that you should fasten your seatbelt for whatever's in the hopper, and by the time he'd slam that front door just that little bit harder than usual, well, it'd be confirmed.

You could distinguish that?

Yeah. It's difficult to articulate, the difference in his door-slammings and how he carried himself, but yeah. But the slamming—it was like how an alarm clock can wake you with the *snip* of its mechanism, before the buzz or before the music, how you hear that sound and you react reflexively and you're awake before the alarm or whatever song's started sounding.

Dennis didn't know this, though, and, for some unfathomable reason, he galloped up to the door to say hi to our dad.

Hi Mr. Roy! and Dad just sneered at poor Dennis, said: The fuck is this kid? And then the tears started.

Mom was there pretty instantly and was trying to console the crying Dennis, but this just made Dad madder.

Party's over, Dad said, and Mom attempted at this juggling act between the crying child and the angry husband and her baffled, party-hatted children sitting around the kitchen table. She tried to shush Dennis while protesting to Dad, but then Wayne started laughing because—I don't know. Because he's an asshole I guess. And that's all it took for all the balls to fall.

Dad marched straight over to that table, cocked back, and smashed Wayne square in the eye. A robust, mature punch, too, nothing corporal about it. Full step, pivot at the hips, smooth follow-through. Wayne's chair went over backward and he lied there stunned for a second, still in the chair, and he let out one or two little sobs and sniffs, and then he started laughing again but louder than before. And that's how my birthday party ended. Party hats and sucker punches.

Mom was the one to come to me later, before bed, to say there'd been a problem at work and Dad couldn't get me anything for my birthday, and that she or he'd make it up to me, but I didn't say anything to her.

But that's what life was like for us, though. Living with him. Dealing with that instability until we didn't have to anymore, until everything took a hard left when he died and we all shoved off in our own little boats—.

[—.]

So what happened to him?

To Dad?

Yeah.

A whole host of things like I said, the growing up—

No. I mean what happened to him?

You mean, what, him dying?

Yeah.

—Really you don't know?

It doesn't get talked about.

Huh. I mean I guess I shouldn't find that surprising, but still.

Well what do you know about it? About his death.

But so then you know how there's more than one story floating about, right? And that there are still some questions we'll probly never have answered? Right?

Why not? Why no answers, I mean.

Well there's a buncha weird still buried, basically. Like the CB dialed to nine, which is the restricted channel reserved only for emergencies. Like his belt buckle, flask, his lighter and his clip of keys missing. Like the zero investigation and the fact they crushed that car the next morning, I heard.

I'm not sure I follow.

You know—.

[—.]

You know actually I'm not sure it matters.

He was a drunk, and he was a bear trap, and he took the tumbler with him to wherever it is that the vicious go after marrying headlights to telephone poles and we were better for it, and maybe that's all that really matters, really.

Maybe he wrecked it on his own, and maybe he didn't.

Maybe he was sleeping with some cop's wife, or maybe some cop was a first responder and saw some stuff he could pawn, or maybe there's another story, entirely different than anything anyone could ever even dream up.

R—

Point is, even if there is another story, I don't think that's a story that I need or want to hear, and I'd rather not talk about him any further.

DECEMBER 25, 1979

Wayne I remember Dad was that guy who lived in our house and I remember he was that kid who grew up hungrier than any kid should because farms have a way of bringing that out in families the hunger especially when there is no money and you are the littlest. They all told him we all got to sacrifice Junior but some more than others. Soon as you are stronger and can work harder you can get more food but your brothers got to eat a little more so they can work a little harder so we can be not so poor Junior so sorry Junior. So he picked berries and carrots and tried to sell them in town but who is going to buy berries from a messy kid? So he would end up eating half and selling even less and get beat fierce for that even though it should have been the other way around the whole time because that is not how you should treat kids. Ended up fucking his soul up inside I think. I think maybe that is why he was always so savage.

I mean I will be the first to admit he could be hard on us. Too hard probably even. I mean I remember that one time when you probably should have gone to hospital after what happened he did. How he would just back off long enough to where you would start whimpering again and then he would lay back into it and it went on for hours it seemed until he in the end he actually picked you up as a ragdoll and took you into the backyard and I thought you were dead and there was blood on the floor and there was blood on the wall and that was not right. That was not right at all actually.

It is 3:19 A.M. and I had the dream again but the ending was different this time. This time I get close enough see there is not much left of the face from where it hit the windshield and there is not much left of the chest from where the fencepost shot through and the end of the post is like a hundred painted pencils reaching out the back window driver side drip drip dripping and there is a neat round of red beneath and you come up to the driver door while the other fighters on scene drag hoses lazy and you reach into the window with your right hand and you brush the hair off to the side of where the forehead used to be. The left eye is still there and when you brush the hair back I can see that it's closed. You reach down around the feet with your left hand and pull out the flask that's a little dented and you stuff it into your back left pocket. You reach back in and straighten the collar a little. The top button is unbuttoned and then there is one button done up and then there is a post punching through. You button the button. You hold the left hand hanging out the window with your left hand and you run your right thumb over the crown of the head front to back front to back front to back and shush shh shh shh shh.

Then you turn around and you walk over to me and say here and you hand me the flask and tell me he always meant for you to have this and I cock back and punched you in the face and that feels good even though the other guys are on us before you are even two steps back and they are all shouting whoa whoa whoa and they are holding us back and I am screaming fuck you fuck you and then I remember things calm down and the guys let us go and you spit a bunch of blood and walk back to the truck and you tying your hair back in the front seat and then you look out the window away from the road and away from me and I walk around the truck to look at you but no matter where I go your head does not move but your face does not turn. I am not sure how to describe it.

I always wake up bad from this dream all sweaty and upset. I sit up and I think about it and try to calm down but I am alone and there is nobody to help calm me down so I sit up and breathe or take a shower in the dark until the hot water runs out or sometimes I write to you when nothing else works because that sometimes still calms me down.

Wayne do you remember him? I mean really remember him? I wonder if you do. I wonder what you remember.

Do you ever talk to him Wayne? I doubt you do but I wonder that sometimes whether or not you and Roy still talk to him like I still talk to people. Or maybe you just think you see them some places like when you are in a bar and you hear someone order a drink and it sounds like them and it is their drink too but you look and it is not them. Or if you are at a comedy show or something and someone laughs at a joke and you know it is their laugh that you hear because it is one of those sounds that sounds like a fingerprint. Like the jingle of your own set of keys how it sounds only like your keys and nobody else can have keys that can sound like yours.

Does that ever happen to you? That you think you hear them? That you think you hear something that can only but belong but to one person but then you hear that one thing out in the world but it cannot possibly be it could not be because that person is gone been gone a long time but then also that sound cannot be without that person? I mean you know his keys right? You know the sound of his keys? What they sound like? We all did. Do. We all do.

Do you think that is normal? To keep hearing those things? Do you think it is normal?

Actually hey Wayne so I need to go Merry Xmas miss you love you. Hope you are doing good.

C

ONE HUNDRED SIX

Today is 12 June 1999. This is tape one hundred six, side two. Story begins on side one.

So she says, Hello?—and then she says What? What? What? Over and over, again and again.

She falls to her knees and the phone hits the floor at the same time. She slumps and sits, legs folded sidesaddle with her right shoulder against the cupboards, palms up on her thighs, and she will stay that way until Conrad collects her.

I was somewhere else, but Conrad says she had been mixing batter for pancakes, that the big yellow mixing bowl had been upset and the batter was gooped across the linoleum, already congealed by the time he sprinted home. He says the griddle was smoking when he leapt the hedges, when he flung the door almost from its hinges, shouting, and, in his haste, he blistered his hand trying to move it from the flame. He found her in that position, between batter and phone, the phone's urgent, off-hook beep-beep throbbing as fast as his heart. He flipped the burner off and blistered his hand on the griddle. He bunched a wet towel in his blistered fist and sat with her, with his arms around her on the floor until, however long after, Roy roused and advised them to clean the batter before your grandfather got home, but Conrad could not even tell him directly, could only insist that no, there was no rush to clean the floor. Roy stood and then sat in the hallway, and Conrad sat wrapped around her on the linoleum until the afternoon, until Conrad collected and carried her to the bed where she would stay for three days, and then he went to the morgue alone. She never, to my knowledge, made pancakes again.

For Conrad, this all was an albatross. This was early release from a different sort of prison and, strong and straight as he was, he was ill-equipped for the life that this death thrust him into, and Roy—.

For Roy it was like a small slosh of water on someone lying prostrate and dying of heatstroke. Not enough, and long past when it might have mattered.

But the thing of it is that when I think of them now, I see that yes, these decades later they have shown some genuine growth, but I remain unconvinced that they would have come this far had your grandfather lived to be old. The imposition of him was too great, too stifling—and not to tout bravado, but I just doubt that they had it in them, that same commitment that I had, to do whatever it would take to be free of him. And this is frustrating, looking to them, thinking of them and seeing where they are, thinking about what they could have been if they had wanted what I had wanted in the same way that I did.

Mark me, though, that this is not to say that I ever hold anything against them. If ever I do weigh them down with that responsibility, inadvertently or otherwise, I remind myself that despite everything that he was, a death—his, or Harriet's, or anyone else's—is something that a person never really gets over, no, just only gets used to. And with that settled once again, I am able to lid them back up in peace. I can return them to the shelf and return to myself.

But for me—?

For me it was different than it was for them, I think. For me it was as though a giant thumb had been lifted from the top of my head and it let me learn how to change. Not that I became great at it, no, but that I learned that change was possible. The framework for it. That there, on that day, began my misguided attempt at building something according to its guide, I mean, because I was only just realizing that I was capable of getting myself beyond him in the year or so before he died, and his death, I think, was the shove over that precipice.

But.

But you know, before I much continue, I suppose it best if I provide more context for him, some better landscape upon which to see his smudge. Because that was partly the point, yes? To assuage your biases? Because I know you have surely heard stories enough to write a book about the monster that he was and about the childhoods we spent cowered and pressed against walls, but that bias—sometimes I guess it feels unfair to make him seem so monotone. I mean, I know you have preconceptions of him as a tyrant, as a coldness that broke me, broke us in places that never quite healed. I know that. But is that fair? That you should think so of him when you will never know him yourself? While my two cents might say yes to both counts—excepting, of course, the truth that tyrants are simple creatures of want, of take, of hold—he was no simple creature. Yes, he was simple in many of those ways, but he was also more complex than I ever did, or will, understand. But I guess this is to say that despite my experiences, despite my sometimes salivating at the chance to paint him however I like, to lie about him would be doing him a service, I think, and would be impossible besides. To lie would be me still gnashing up at him from beneath the shadow he so enjoyed, and I left that shadow long ago.

So is it fair? Maybe. Maybe not. But either way, stripping him naked beneath the light is also the cruelest thing I am still able to do to him, and as such, will forever be my preference.

[—.]

—But so then, your grandfather was born in Oklahoma in 1930 and he was the youngest of nine if you count full-blooded siblings and the second youngest of the thirteen or fifteen total if you include the unofficials, though nobody is sure quite exactly how many of those there were. We think his oldest sibling, half or full, was a sister born in 1907, and the truth of his youngest half-sister is a story perhaps too distracting and problematic to discuss here today. For now, just know that that person was born in 1946.

And I suppose maybe you already know some of this information, but I see no reason not to tell it again here. Completion's sake and all. Just feel free to fast-forward if anything sounds familiar, I guess.

And also I guess before I go much further I should remark upon the hedging that often happens when speaking of him and note that this is not the result of lazy research or of disinterest or an attempt at marginalizing him, no, just that it is almost impossible to be certain of some of these facts, particularly with the rest of his family, because he never spoke about himself or his life but for the moments when something would slip through his fingers, and further, there is next to no paper on him before his enlistment, and there is even less on the rest of his kin—your grandfather and the two siblings born before him were born in hospitals but every child previous was born on the homestead or in someone else's home, and your grandfather and his next-oldest brother were the only two of the rightful brood that were dappled into school. The State did not know, even, about some of them until the first time they needed hospital or got arrested or tried to vote, I suppose.

But on the subject of those relations, I suppose it is also worth mention that, just like your grandfather, every of those legitimate family—and even each of the illegitimates that I know of—they each died of some kind of violence. What I pieced together from years of thin implication from him and also from my own excavations was that, as far as his full-blooded family goes, at least one of his sisters and probably a second, too, succumbed to the same, berserking pneumonia of 1918 that sledgehammered more than three percent of the world's population directly into the dirt, and some years after that, one of his brothers died in a threshing accident gruesome enough to earn mention during Lowell Thomas's nightly national news broadcast. Later, another brother would die at

Anzio and another at Falaise and then another at Okinawa, but before those brothers, his oldest sister was thrown down from the back of a motorcycle on a bright day, and there she smeared her sandy-redblonde locks across the interstate's asphalt. After those brothers—after he met your grandmother but before Conrad came, even—his youngest full-sister was found beneath a mound of leaves, having been unzipped, throat to pelvis, by the butterfly knife of an unsatisfied john.

Your great-grandmother, as you know, died giving birth to your grandfather, and your great-grandfather, *maybe* you know, was twelve-gauged on the lawn of someone's wife in late 1949.

And I know that this all sounds grim, I know, and also true is that those happenings tweaked him inside. I know that too. That that amount of death could envelope him is a lucklessness I have seen only one other time, but lucklessness has no bearing on truth and this is the lesson of it, I think, to look at such a person and not see the circumstance as some definition for them but rather as an impartial, elegant fact. Just that life could happen—that life could come to pass as it did and that that happening could shape him into *something*—and perhaps this is the leap, but to see that circumstance and its result as maybe the most beautiful thing about the man. That the adult he became was a laceration upon five other lives is just a correlative datum, I think, honestly. Nothing more.

But that being a first bit of context, the point here was to discuss the particulars of him, and as interesting or uninteresting as the rest of those people may be, those other lives will always be just footnotes and should be treated as such. There are so many other things about him that are less remembered.

Like how baseball, Roy could tell you, was religion to him. How the Dodgers were the flesh of his God.

Conrad might talk at length about your grandfather's pastel pencils of songbirds, of how one of them was mistakenly sold as a photograph.

Or like, unless I told you, how might you ever know that just about the only thing that ever really held his attention, aside from us, was engines? Model airplanes to Mack trucks and everything in between—he loved those things. I know he did. He hit them, too.

How when he was home from the road, how he had a fickle relationship with cars, driving who knows how many over the years until, inevitably, he would wreck this one or sell that one, or would want a new one and trade whatever in and he never told us when he was going to be bringing home something different, it would just be there one morning or he would leave in one car and drive home in another. We actually had a sort of betting pool, my brothers and I, even before we knew what a betting pool was.

Bet you three comics he has a new one before my birthday.

Oh yeah? Well I bet four comics and two Cokes he does it between your birthday and Thanksgiving.

That sort of stuff. Usually I won, and it was not always just because I made a hobby out of going through his things.

But he shuffled cars as often as he got bored, I suppose, but there was never a question as to which of them had been his favorite: a 1958 Edsel two-door hardtop, royal blue with white back through the wings and he called it Edsel, sans article—just Edsel. Edsel was blinding beneath its polish and polish. Chromed and heavy, low and mean. It was an artwork.

They are rare, Edsels. They were rare back then and they are even rarer today. The make only ran for three years and last I heard there were something like five or six thousand of them left, and most of those only come out for car shows and go back into their garages to sleep beneath their covers. They nearly never saw the road, then, today, or anytime in between, but.

But—.

But I am getting ahead of myself and I think before I go on, actually—.

I think actually there was more to say about him, about his life. Before Edsel consumes me again, I mean.

But so he led a hard life, your grandfather. He finished grammar school, we think, and if he went to high school, then the records did not survive. He certainly never mentioned a mascot to me and he never went to a reunion or any such thing or ever mentioned friends from his early life. He grew up poorer than poor and I know that he resorted to panhandling to feed himself at least once during childhood, though, if he were alive today, he would never admit to this. He left home before his father died and he painted houses and fences, sidewalks and roads, and he drove cattle and he drove delivery until he joined the military. He fought briefly in Korea until a blown-off finger sent him home in frustration. He met your grandmother at the Denver County Fair and made a family. He fixed cars and drove big rigs across the heartland. He cheated on your grandmother—not often, but there is evidence that he did. He drank. He beat. He died.

His was a simple, frustrating life, and we complicated it for him. His words, those, that we complicated things, and I suppose this is one of the few things upon which we agreed. We were not an easy family to have, rambunctious and under-stimulated and neglected and blamed. But that was us, our lives, our incidental nature, and my version is not the only one out there. They have stories too, my brothers. They know things I have no knowledge of, just as there are parts of my life that are still dark to them, and while I am not sure if any of us loved your grandfather, I will admit that we each of us knew him in ways that the others did not.

One thing I am sure they would touch on, my brothers, is how your grandfather was a smart man, how he had potential that went unrealized until the end and that he was a shopworn soul that rarely caught a break and was exorcizing upon us his justifiable frustration though, of course, through means that were altogether abhorrent. But understandable, they would say. I mean look at that life, right? How easy to pity a creature such as him, yes?

Well, I disagree with that notion. Fundamentally. That his potential went unrealized, I mean, because he was smart. A genius by some profane metric, even. Misguided, cruel, mercurial. A genius who rarely caught a break, maybe, but a genius, him, all the same.

Affirmation of this brilliance lay in his creativity, I think—how he was as creative as he was cruel, and if you consider creativity to be the mask worn by intelligence, well—. Because anyone can place a lash so as to conceal it from a teacher, and anyone can make a child kneel in the garage for an afternoon or stand at attention all night. Anyone could do that. But the delegation—?

Oh, his delegation. A treasure he kept close. How he divvied our punishments between us, how he made us into his hands. Not all of the time, no, of course there were beatings and of course there were weekends when we would not eat. Some Saturdays, even, he spent sloshed and slouched in a deck chair to watch us dig pits as round as a manhole and six feet down, him waiting for the depth enough when he could say his piece, when he could toe the edge and look down at his children, muddied and raw, and he could remind us how easy it is to vanish a person—how indifferent, the dirt, and forgetful.

But life was less flashy than this for the most part.

Hair pulling was a big thing, getting back to the system. Not tugging like how I would tug on Harriet's hair when I was young, no, I mean strand by strand by strand, out.

Pinch.

Pinch.

Thin as a needle. Ten for leaving the lid off the jar of peanut butter and five for speaking out of turn. Twenty for saying no when you should have said yes or the other way around. Two for making eyes—I mean I could still write out the entire, extensive chart if I needed to, because there was a chart written on the back of the map above the workbench and he often referenced it with a flourish. As if he needed the reminder.

The chart, yes, that was half of it. But again, the delegation was the sun at the center of that system, always that delegation.

See he never did the pulling, see. No, if my hair needed plucking, how Conrad would be the plucker. Or Roy. Or vice versa. How there was the punisher and the punished, yes, and there was the judge, him. And then there was the witness, the brother left over.

See, he never laid a hand during the usual, structured punishments. Not unless there was dissension. If there was, then his blows would fall upon the odd-man-out. Because why? Because solidarity, boys.

Because you need to stick together.

Because you are still smaller than me.

Because I feel like it.

Because my life was harder than I would have liked and I have drenched so long beneath the dribble of ire, boys, because beneath the missing finger that I still feel and the jobs I must work, and the plain picket fence, and the two boys and a half, Roy, lies my profoundly-limited sky.

Dogs. They, more than me, but we were like dogs that did not understand how to navigate an owner who beat with one hand and fed with the other. And even now. Even now, the question of how those moments of feeding or of just not beating, how do those moments, those small, ephemeral moments interface with the rest of my construction of your grandfather? Does it make me loathe him more? Or do I just especially appreciate those reprieves? Be thankful for them, even?

And then how do you reconcile the versions of him? He drank, as I have said, your grandfather, and of course this factored into his demeanor. Of course. But he was not always a mean drunk, and what does that mean? Because there were some days when he would swim into the backyard eight beers gone and start up the little barbecue—one of those squatty ones you bring to a tailgate or to camping—and he would sit there, cross-legged, and poke at a burger or some hot dogs, soak in the late sun and smile slow smiles and call us out to sit with him, to sit with him so he could tell us the lowbrow jokes from Jake's garage, or careful, sterile stories from his childhood on the farm. How he rode a horse once that got spooked and ran him under a low hanging branch that ripped his back open from shoulder to beltline. How he drove cattle through Wyoming one summer and went days without speaking.

That was a side of him that hid, mostly, so what does that mean? Or he kept hid, maybe. But my point is that when or if ever that version came out, it was an odd object, foreign and placeless in our understanding of him and of our family, and it has always stayed that way, and I have no answers. In many ways he remains a puzzle with no picture on the box.

Thinking of him now—.

You know, as much as I have tried, thinking of him still reminds me of nothing good. Or, rather, of nothing productive I guess is the better way to put it. Mostly when I think of him I am reminded of what he drove me to do and of how poorly I left that earlier life, that I made decisions and did things that have repercussions even to this day, and as much as I might like to blame him for that—?

He cannot stay the problem, is the thing. He died. He died too long ago for him to continue to matter, so the blame must become mine, I think.

But how I left, I mean, to take my last day there as an example and how from there I left Roy to twenty-some years, now, without speaking and your grandmother and I never really picked up the pieces either after how I left, how I left him and her that day when I left, and how full of rage I was, and how I had nowhere I knew to go but just to go. What of that?

Just drive, I remember thinking, just go. Just go, go. So I drove. I drove, and I dismissed them and planned a new life, until thoughts of them raged me and I bargained them away. I cried for miles with the radio off, and then I bottomed the AM band and listened to the sky with the volume turned low, and I drove. For two days, I drove, with no direction but for east.

Until I decided I had to go back. It came to me like a predawn glow, the light growing in logarithm, that I had to go back. I had to go back and do something difficult for myself in spite of the rest of my life. In the *face* of the rest of my life. I had to finish some Herculean task, and I had to do it in

Colorado. What exactly that task was, though, I had yet no idea when I started the car. By that time I was in Indiana, and twenty-some hours of driving back would give me plenty of time to think, I figured.

Somewhere around the Missouri-Kansas line, I remembered hearing some folks saying once that the Colorado School of Mines was the hardest school west of MIT and I decided that that was what I needed to do. That was a challenge that could consume me, could overwhelm me and crush me. That could be my ocean to fill.

I had no idea how admission worked or even where it was, the school, but I had an inclination that it was in Golden, and if it was in Golden, then it was close enough to Denver that I could rent a walk-in-closet to sleep in for ten dollars a month if it really came down to it. This seemed as good a plan as any.

But I got to Golden and, yes, the school was there, and the following December they let me in. I quit half of my jobs and began what would be my life for the next seven years, accruing debt and doing well while, simultaneously, feeling I was falling perpetually further and further behind.

The schedule—.

That schedule is part of why I still struggle to sleep. Classes always started at seven and ran until five and an hour for lunch, five days a week, and the jobs, and later the experiments I had to run with readings that needed logging every twelve minutes, plus or minus about twenty seconds, for four hours, and the only hours I could run the stupid thing were between about one and about five in the morning, so I learned to sleep as much as an egg timer would allow.

You remember as a kid with your stopwatch? when I could tell you to start it and then we could go about our day and I could tell you, Check now, five times every hour and it would always be on the twelfth minute, plus or minus some seconds? and how you always wondered how? told me I was cheating? that I had a watch I was hiding? Well, now you know.

Twelve minutes.

Dozens upon dozens, maybe hundreds of nights over those few years were splintered into twelve minute sleeps, and even on the good days there was just never enough time, and all these years later I still cannot get my nights to fit together as they should.

But the schedule and the brutality of the coursework aside, the third side of my Triangle of Misery was the many terrible jobs I held, and amongst those forgettable jobs, maybe the worst was the one I started a few years later as a lab tech. I enjoyed it, but it was as hazardous as the hours were long, and it was quiet, and it was lonely, and I had too much else to do besides, but I did it because I got paid in credit hours in addition to a token amount of dollars, and it was not dangerous all of the time, though, just some of the time. Actually, it was not that dangerous. It was only above-average-dangerous when one specific lab tech was also around.

One night I came in, late, and found that this other lab tech—this sniveling, sycophantic little creature—had reorganized the lab. Why? Well, because it made so much more sense to organize it the way he wanted to organize it. Everything should be alphabetical, not parsed by hazard—and the labels? The labels we used in the labs made no sense, clearly, even though they were only the federal standard. So he had decided to redo all of them. He even left me a note, ordering me to continue to implement his newfangled, awful system. Great. Thanks, but no thanks. I set out to undo all of his work.

About an hour into my un-reorganizing efforts, I noticed a few unlabeled glass jars open under the fume hood in the corner, the fume hood being one of those ones with the retractable glass panel in front and a workbench beneath a behemoth fan that can suck a thousand cubic feet of air in a few seconds and blast it through a vent in the roof like the sort you see in restaurant kitchens, and protocol—there, like everywhere—prohibited open containers being left out, so I went over, perturbed that, there I was, too busy with my own problems and still having to clean up after other purported adults, and I pushed the button to void the air behind the glass and, some seconds later, still distracted, I lifted the door and stuck my head and arms in to start cleaning while I was thinking about classes and projects, thinking about how much I disliked this other tech, thinking about the walk-in closet I had been renting as a room and about navigating that reality come the blind date I had lined up for Saturday, thinking about almonds—

—almonds.

Almonds.

I had taken a full breath and most of a second one before the panic wrecked through me.

See, in the lab we kept chemicals of all kinds, varying mixtures, elementals, a full palette of components for any of a variety of possible experiments, and amongst that varied inventory were several containers of potassium cyanide that the lab used when teaching the principles behind gold extraction.

Basically the way such a process works is you can take any throwaway rocks, typically throwawayable because they were the ugly sister rocks from an otherwise fruitful vein and were perhaps still full of ore but the ore might be microscopically unreapable. But this is the thing, though, the magic of chemistry how this gold-flecked junk can still be rendered, ground down to dust, lifted from dust and dissolved in one of a few, careful cyanide solutions—usually with $NaCN$ or KCN, but calcium cyanide works too—but you can do that and the gold remains in the aqueous solution that you can run again and again through finer and finer sieves to separate the dross and, a little evaporation of the final liquid later and, *ta-da*, pure gold dust from junk rocks. Sorcery, I tell you.

The problem with this process, of course, is dealing with the cyanides, the nastinesses that they are in how they demand a meticulousness of handling, a fatal fussiness how, for example, potassium cyanide loves to react with the moisture in the regular-old air and will emit small amounts of hydrogen cyanide through a process called hydrolysis. This is why KCN is kept in sealed containers, themselves kept in cool, dry cabinets lined with packets of silica gel—same as comes in shipping boxes—to suck out any moisture. Reason for this cautiousness is, where potassium cyanide stays solid up through around the melting point of aluminum, HCN boils at eight degrees Fahrenheit and becomes gaseous. Breathable. Quiet and quick.

Another interesting tidbit—whether or not you can even smell hydrogen cyanide depends on a genetic marker that about half of people have, but if you have it, then hydrogen cyanide smells just like bitter almonds.

Did you know that?

I did. I had no idea that I had the marker, but I had read that before somewhere, maybe some textbook, but in my distraction I had not noticed that the fan had never fired up after pressing the button and as my vision tunneled down to pinpoint I thought: Oh.

Oh almonds.

Oh no.

And I collapsed in the direction of the door, sucking for air, at air, grasping at it with my hands and thrashing for the door and there, on my final floor, came a ringing in my ears, crystalline, high and pure that swaddled the sounds of my flailing and as I scythed the tile my vision, my arms, my legs and head seemed to slow, seemed to stretch in time and as the world slowed, the tone dropped in synchrony, and as it dropped, it became more a buzz, and as the buzz dove further and my arms slowed to the speed of construction cranes, the buzz became bursts, small bursts, bursts of something, and then as I watched my arms slow to the speed of sundials, it became distinguishable. The bursts. The bursts of words.

Oh no no no. Oh no. Oh no.

My own voice.

Oh no no. Oh no. Oh no.

And then it slowed to stopping. It stopped and my arms stopped, and my head stopped, and everything stopped, and the pinpoint pinned down to a smallness beneath all measure and there, in the almost-black—almost-black but for the fleck of light left in the center of my sight—in that silence, in that nothing, we spoke, myself and I, and myself asked me how long I thought it would be before the body was found.

When, Wayne? Tomorrow? Monday? Will it be Monday when someone finds our blank body?

That will be hard, we thought. *To be found. For someone to find us and to have to carry that with them.*

And all sound ended.

And the only bit left was the fleck.

And slowly, slowly, the fleck began to expand, began to wake and open as a new kitten will open its eyes, later, slowly, later, until it spread enough to reveal an undergraduate kneeling by me in the night, his tallboy spilt across the concrete where it had fallen from his hand or had tipped where he had tried to place it, but him shaking me, yelling for his friend to call an ambulance and then his friend busting a softball-sized rock through a laboratory window and then making to knock out the remaining shards of the pane with his jacketed fist, and then Tallboy yelled at Friend, No the *door*, idiot, the door is open why did you do that just hurry.

I tried to stand but my legs gave out. My shirt was covered in vomit. I took it off and threw it toward the bushes and I remember the cool of the concrete on my back and the cool of the air in my lungs and the stars squinting cold above me.

At the hospital they ran tests and told me I was about one quarter of one lungful away from dead and, frankly, they were impressed that I was alive and that they wanted to Polaroid me for the break room if that was okay.

Fine. Whatever.

They released me the next morning against advice. They wanted me to stay and I told them I had no insurance and I had no money and I felt fine, and all the standard doctor stuff ensued: call us if you feel funny, or if you have a prolonged headache, or if anything seems at all off-kilter, please call this number or just call an ambulance, please, blah blah.

I asked if I could see the bill and they said it would still be a few hours to compile, so I asked if I could just settle it up tomorrow and they said, Okay, since they had my information anyway. I walked the four miles back to my closet and slept.

I had no idea what the bill would run, but I assumed that it would be large. An ambulance, who knows how many medications, two specialists, an overnight stay——. The following day I returned to try to work out my bill, dreading the visit for the entire walk. I walked, rather than drove, for the sake of having some sort of condemned-man's last mile, to savor some last stretch of medical-debt-free life before they fastened that fetter to my ankle.

But they had to have some way to finance an ambulance trip and a hospital stay, right? It would only take me about a decade at minimum wage, I figured, and I was trying to be okay with that, that it was better to be alive—that, worst case, it was better to be alive, and if it was between living with debt and just living, I could always expatriate.

Still I remember that, walking to the hospital, thinking about how I could expatriate. Could do it anyway, even, even if the debt ended up being manageable.

I could find new life in some humid, low place unpronounceable, in slipping through its reefs of Vespa, bicycle, old asphalt. I could come to know its beriddled bars that cough neon out into sultry dark and inside, beneath their head-high atmospheres of threadlooking smoke and the grime and billiard tables' crack, between the effacing susurrus of unknown language and the incandescence of the place and of its haggard barkeep polishing chipped glasses and of jukebox prattle and of the smut, of the smutty, almost-damp film, questionable, encasing everything and every split mended by crushed peanut shell I could sit, could surround myself with the denouement of hoary men. There I could sleep myself up in their tumblers and their dust. There I could rest between a barstool graffito's proclamation of presence—of galvanic, yawping presence—across a barstool that seems itself a bit of Hell and a forest of barstools. There I could age inside a strange ecology of little Hells, beneath and between them and the imposition of a thin, head-high nimbus that would never rain—.

So imagine my surprise when my bill had already been settled. Turns out, one of my professors had heard about what had happened and had written a check for the whole hospital bill early that morning. Done. Taken care of.

I hurried back to campus and to his office to protest, to find a way to pay him back, to—*anything*. He wanted nothing of the subject and only asked how I was doing, what happened exactly, all that stuff.

I know you are not the type to do anything so stupid, Wayne, he said.

I told him what happened with the fan, that it must have fallen to disrepair or something and broken and we need to get it fixed before we can do anything in the lab, or, who knows.

He told me he would investigate the matter personally.

And he did. He ended up looking into it and finding that that other lab technician, the awful one, had actually disabled the fan in order to save on electricity, as hard as that might be to believe. At his hearing, he claimed that that beastly fan had been—still was—leeching power and should be unplugged overnight and he was in the right for saving the department something like a half a dollar on the monthly utility bill.

They asked him to step into the hall while they deliberated, and they called him back in as soon as he shut the door.

I know he deserved it, but sometimes I still feel sad for him. Somewhere inside that misguided man there was something trying to do the right thing, trying to look out for all of our livelihoods. His myopia almost killed me, is all.

Anyway, after that debacle, the benevolent professor told me he was sending me to an electrical engineering conference in New Orleans in order to make it up to me.

Electrical engineering? Really?

Sounds fun, New Orleans. Go pick up a nametag from the conference and knock off for the rest of the weekend. Just, this time the hospital is on you, is all.

So I flew to New Orleans on his dime.

He put me up in this prehistoric hotel replete with peeling paint, screechy plumbing, wallpaper older than I am, the whole nine. No idea now what it was called, but it was sort of on the left side of downtown and it was a rundown building from the outside. Yellow, I think. Yellow with white. My room had a balcony and the night I got there I stayed out on it and ate apples and watched the drunks flow riverlike below as the fog swept in and it was perfect.

That fog—.

Thinking now, maybe what happened in that fog was the point. Of a lot of things. Of everything, maybe, or almost.

It was a peculiar kind, its features being still difficult for me to describe. Thicker. It hung. Walking in it was like walking through sheer curtains—a fog to make you think of Dickens, maybe. The gas-lamped streets, the yellow-gray quiet of it all. I finished my bag of apples and I had to go out, to be in it.

I picked a direction and decided to walk until walking tired me enough to turn around, because how better to get to know New Orleans than to know that fog, yes? To dive into it, to duck into some seedy club casting double-bass and saxophone out into a thick night, stay for a drink, and then leave without speaking. To lose myself. Maybe get mugged. Why not.

[—.]

But here. Here in this story. Here is where—.

I mean really. The chances. What could the actual chances be? Appalling. Astronomical. Impossible. Indiana and what sent me there. The years of school. The cyanide. The fog. The fog and the—.

And also, do you see what has happened? How I have ended up again at this place? Do you see? Do you see how inescapable?

But so I walked through that fog, street by street, feeling out the city barefoot because you get to know a street much better if you leave your shoes behind, and I let my mind wander. I brought the fog into my lungs and I listened to the city and I walked, and everything was right.

And then things started to drift away. Not me, I mean, no. I mean the rest of the things. My mind was off somewhere else and it would check in every now and then when I needed to cross the street or when something caught my eye, or when whatever—it would come back for a minute and then it would go away again.

It had to have been miles before I stopped on the sidewalk and I realized that everything was gone. No dogs barked, no tree branch swayed, no cars, no people, and there I thought back to those last few times I had checked in with the world and I realized that, successively, less and less of the rest of the stuff that had populated my immediate vicinity had been there each time I had checked in. Little by little it had left and I had not noticed its leaving until it was all gone, until its absence was present there with me, there, at the intersection of Who-knows and Nowhere, New Orleans. Just me. Just the city. Just the fog.

And just as I noticed this absence, it came. Around the corner, slow, slow. Headlights torching up the fog brighter than the musty yellow-gray glow of the gas-lamped streets. Blue and blinding. Chromed and heavy. It rolled up an empty street and everything left me. My knees felt like nothing. My palms went river. My feet wanted so badly to turn and to run but they would do neither.

Slow, it rolled, slow, cleaving out vertigo ahead of those headlights and into and through me, and I looked in, and the thing on the inside, it wore his clothes and it wore his skin. The thin eyes—his thin, brownblack eyes were there on its face and its lips were chapped like his lips were chapped and it wore his hair short, his short sandy-redblonde hair, and it was parted on the left like always, and the little ears, and the cruel, button nose, and the left hand, obfuscated by shadow—was it?

Was it the shadow or was the finger gone at the first knuckle?

And as it advanced I fixated upon this and spun down into a dark dampness I had thought long shuttered, and the thing on the inside, it just—*looked*. Just looked straight ahead as it floated past, never turning its head toward me or tapping a finger on the wheel in time with some unheard radio, nothing. Never so much as a flinch enough to be certain that it even saw me.

I mean, it had to. It had to have seen me, right? I was the only thing out there, the only living thing and it had to have seen me but the car, the Edsel.

Edsel purred down the block and just before it turned the corner I saw the license plate, dark green on light green with Colorado stamped beneath.

It rounded the corner and it was gone. My legs gave and I fell and they folded beneath me and I slumped, legs to the side and I propped myself up with my hand and who knows how long it was before I returned to find myself moaning and sobbing and shaking there on the curb in the fog in the middle of the New Orleans night.

[—.]

A dog barked.

A dog barked and that was what brought me back, what made me realize where I was and what I was doing and that my throat was sore and my eyes were bleatied from the crying. With some trouble I stood and I leaned against a lamppost. Other cars started passing by: one, one, two, three. Some suit and his date happened upon me and asked if I was okay and I think I just left. Without saying anything, I mean, then. I think I just left.

The next thing I remember was the hotel, being back at the hotel in my room with all the lights off but the lamp on and I sat for a long time waiting, wanting, yearning for the sun but the sun seemed never to come. I had no watch and my room had no clock.

I needed a distraction. I tried calling your mother but she did not pick up. I tried calling Gordon but the number was no longer in service. I tried calling some of the guys from the lab, from class, everyone I could think of but no one would answer and I called and called until there was nobody left but for the people I wanted least.

Anyone but Conrad, I thought. Anyone but Roy.

I almost hung up the phone as I dialed. I did, actually. I hung it up and I left the room and I tried to walk around the block but I made it as far as two doors down before my legs began to shake and I hurried inside for fear of what might still be cruising the fog. Inside, I returned to my room and told myself I was strong, I was strong, I was strong and I never needed them, then or now.

But I was not strong enough.

I finished dialing Conrad this time and he picked up on the second ring.

—*Hello?*

And I just started talking at him because I owed him no formalities.

It had to have seen me, right? I asked, but he did not know what to do with that question.

He said Wayne? over and over, just kept saying my name. Wayne? Wayne?

Do you think it saw me? I interrupted.

What? Did what see you? Are you okay Wayne where are you?

And things were going nowhere, which is exactly where I had predicted they would go.

I hung up.

I sat awake and left the room again only after the sun was pouring in, only after I tiptoed to the window and peeked to see that the morning was burning off the fog.

I gathered my things and ran to the Greyhound where I caught a bus back to Colorado. I never got the tag from the conference.

[—.]

Never have I told anyone about New Orleans. Never have I spoken of how it has kept me up many nights, that night. Kept me up thinking. Kept me up bargaining and rationalizing, passing off and reassuring, but still it is there. Hard as I try it to blot it away, its spot yet remains.

So many nights I am still there in my dreams, and everything is still thick, and still, and silent as Edsel passes slow, slow, just its passenger and me and the fog, alone, and I am looking through the lamp-lit haze and seeing something driving a car I know, wearing clothes I know, wearing a face I know exactly.

Some nights it all plays back but I shout as it passes and it turns its head and its neck but its face never turns.

Some nights it stops and it opens the door and it steps out without turning but it looks different through the legs and I am able to tell myself that it is okay, that it was just some impossible coincidence, that some doppelgänger—some lost, illegitimate brother bought and resurrected Edsel's mangled body, and the two of them then moved to Louisiana.

But then there are the other nights.

There are the nights where it stops next to the curb and it pops the trunk without looking at me, and I stagger toward the back even though I am struggling, pleading, screaming at my legs to take me anywhere but the trunk but they will not listen, and at the back of Edsel the trunk raises open and I try to look away but my head is pulled forward and my eyes are pinned wide and I am screaming as I look in the trunk and the trunk is overflowing with white, white light and I wake up still screaming, and hours after I have calmed myself I still sit awake, still in New Orleans, still wondering.

Wondering if it thought me familiar in the side of its eye.

Wondering if it had recognized me, then or after.

Wondering if it saw me on that sidewalk and mused: *Oh Wayne, my Wayne, oh you surely have grown.*

SIFTING THROUGH STATIC
ACT ONE, SCENE ONE:
(OR, CLEAVE AS AN AUTO-ANTONYM)

It will be seventeen years before my father introduces me to his specific dissatisfaction. The audience will occur in a room where we've curdled the paint from the walls, where we've warped the joists and spidered the glass, and in tatters he'll turn to leave. He'll pause at the door, left hand on doorframe, right hand on knob. He'll shake us our hands without looking back.

I wish I could've known you in my twenties, he'll say, I think we would've been great friends.

Wayne will shuffle away. His dissatisfaction and I remain to talk amongst ourselves.

Where did I leave off before I wasted all that air?

Inpatient thing. Classes.

Okay, yeah. Classes.

So I started classes through some foundation that had a subsidized housing dealie, too, and I took to all that pretty well, but I think—I don't know. I think at that point I saw it more as me cleaning myself up than me really making something of myself, if that makes sense. It was still just something I had to do for my program—or at least was something the powers that be very much encouraged me to do to prevent my recidivism, and I acquiesced mostly because I felt so worthless that I didn't care enough to object—but that was the extent of my investment, really.

But so I had this calendar and I'd cross an X for every clean day like I was supposed to, but I also had a big red circle around the date way out ahead where I'd be done, and when that date came I dropped out of classes and hit the road. They advised against it, of course, but I'd done the minimum they'd required of me to dodge them billing me retroactively, and I'd decided I was done with Los Angeles.

Where'd you go?

The City of Brotherly Love.

Philadelphia?

Philly? No, San Francisco.

Wait, is San Francisco not the City of Brotherly Love?

Last I heard that was Philly.

Oh. I thought it was San Francisco. Wouldn't that make more sense?

I don't really have much pull when it comes to these sorts of things.

Well whatever. So anyway, through whatever small jobs and stuff, I'd saved enough for bus fare and maybe a month's worth of shitty motel, maybe a bit longer of sleeping on some classified ad's closet floor, but I didn't really have a plan. So I hobbled myself on over to the Greyhound terminal and took a hard look at the board. Most cinematic thing I've ever done, I bet, standing there staring up with just the clothes on my back, a tiny bag, some cash in my pocket and trying to decide where I was gonna try to live.

And how'd the board look?

Decidedly uninteresting but for San Francisco, which I'd heard about but always meant to go to, and what the hell, Summer of Love hadn't been *that* far back, and it seemed like Frisco'd had a pretty good time with that. And I could get there on the cheap, too, which was another plus.

So San Francisco, then. Onwards.

And how was the bus?

Just like any other—too hot and you always get stuck next to the guy that smells like soup or the baby with the ear infection needs to scream about it for seven hours. Or, hey, you ever sat next to a too-fat person on a plane? Or maybe some old crone who likes your shoulder for a pillow?

I guess.

Yeah, well my bus to San Francisco had me sitting next to both of those in the same person. In spades. She's pouring over onto me the whole time and making me like some washer cinched between her lugginess and the window that I swear must've been bowing out into traffic, how hard she had me smooshed. Two hours of that before we stopped for snacks and a piss and I never before nor since have gotten up so fast over the chance to stretch my legs.

But actually an interesting thing then happened.

Oh?

Yeah, so I'm walking around outside and I spot this phone booth, right? And I don't know, maybe it was me feeling like even though I was running away from fixing myself, sort of, it was still something like turning over a new leaf, right, that I was making some sort of change. Something like that, I felt— and maybe it's fueled along by feeling free and alive out in the world after my incarceration on that bus, I don't know—but I just felt really good, right? Like things were good and good things were happening?

I mean I guess.

Yeah, I know it doesn't make much sense to've been thinking that now that I've got some distance from that day, right? Now that I've got some perspective on just who I was at that moment. But yeah, in that moment that's what I was thinking for some reason, and in that moment of weakness or whatever, I saw this phone and I thought Oh, what the fuck. So I dug for some change and got myself over there.

Calling Mom?

Nope. First number was Con, because I knew he was living in the Bay Area the last time I'd talked to him on the phone, but that had to've been a couple years b—

Wait, when did you talk to him on the phone?

His birthday or mine, I can't remember. I was in another dimension, but I remember having him on the phone, and I remember he gave me a phone number and told me not to forget it, so I didn't because I'm good with numbers. But anyway I was pretty sure I had his number clocked, but then a woman answered the phone in Spanish and I hung up.

Not so good with the memory after all, I guess.

Yeah, well, I took a big breath and a think before I picked up the receiver again, because I had another number I knew, but I don't know quite how I had it, but it was in my head and I knew it was right. Probly Con planted it in there or something sometime, because there were some times when we talked over those years, me and Con, some little calls here and there and I was pretty constantly fucked up but there were bits of them that stuck. But I knew this other number, and I dialed, and your dad picked up on the third ring.

—You called him? You actually called him?

Sure did. He picked up and the guts fell out of me and I gasped, and then I went like a wind-up toy—one of those little plastic ones that waddle and spit sparks.

What'd you say?

Everything, I don't know. Just like, Wayne? Wayne it's me. It's your brother it's Roy. Hey how are you it's good to hear your voice I'm good. Better. I'm better now, I've been a lot better. I had some run-ins and some stuff but it's all behind me now and I'm square. I've been going to classes and stuff and I'm moving, because I was in Los Angeles but I wanted to get out of there so I'm moving. San Francisco. I'm going to San Francisco and I think Con's up there? He's out of the Army now you know. I haven't talked to him in a while. Have you talked to him? How are you? I miss you.

Like that. I went on like that for I don't know how long, spewing into a pay phone at a gas station in the middle of California, and it went on, and on, and on until I realized he hadn't said anything. So the last thing I said just sort of hung there, somewhere on the wire between us, and I was just. Waiting.

Waiting—.

You don't even know what that's like, do you?

What what's like?

I mean everyone's got these stupid cellphones these days, and you don't know what it's like to be tied to a phone in place anymore, I bet. It's a visceral thing's been lost upon folks if you ask me, how it was magical in how it's been able to make that memory something tangible for me, standing there at a graffitied-up booth in the desert and how most folks'd have no idea what I'm talking about, really, if I tried to explain. No, now your pocket *boops* at you anywhere and a call is so commonplace that it's lost that magic, that ritual, and it's become banal. Routine. But an open line on a corded phone? That's one thing I'm gonna miss when the world digs up its last payphone—the sound of an open line. The impossibly soft sound like a faraway wave that never stops breaking, and then the ghostlike conversations you hear in that gape if you crush your eyes and cock your head, and they're so quiet you wonder if they're even there at all or if it's your head's the one that's hearing it. Just the sense of, I don't know, space about it all—.

And I waited horrified in that space. Endless, that wait.

And then he hung up. Without a word.

Click.

[—.]

—That must've been hard.

Mm.

How'd you take it?

[—.]

—Roy?

You ever been wrecked by something? I mean completely and truly wrecked.

Sure.

Sure, you say. Sure. Well, maybe you have or maybe you haven't, I don't know, but wrecked doesn't even begin to cover it. When he hung up on me I knew that it'd all sunk too deep to salvage, him and me, and then what'm I supposed to do from there? What do you do when you've spoilt something so bad it can't be fixed?

What do you do?

Move on? I don't know.

It was a rhetorical question, but thanks.

But was it, though?

Well—.

[—.]

Well what?

[—.]

—**Roy?**

—Hm?

What then, Roy?

Oh. I dunno. Everything since then has been a what-then of one sort or another, so to be honest I don't know what then. I'm here, I mean. I'm still puttering and I still have bills and I still can't stand the Dodgers. Sorer than I used to be, maybe, and I'm not getting any stronger, but I'm still here.

I meant more like what happened next? Up in San Francisco.

Who cares. Wayne was the last interesting thing that happened to me and he's been gone going on forty years now.

But your kids? Your wife?

What about them?

They're not interesting?

I mean call me a monster but they're not all that interesting, no. They're wonderful, don't get me wrong. They're wonderful and I love them, but nothing really interests me. I'm interested in them, I mean, and I was there for every first day of school and I don't step out, no, and not just because the wheelchair isn't sexy enough, and I love them dearly and sincerely, I do. But nothing really much interests me like it used to.

Nothing? Not Conrad? Not Wayne?

Nothing worth my time, anyway. Nothing I haven't worn down to the nub. And Con? Con's Con. He'll be exactly how he is until he dies, and that's fine. He still calls me on my birthday and he loves talking about the old days when we talk, and that's fine. But talking to Conrad's like pissing into an ocean of piss. Pointless.

And Wayne? Wayne and I have never really spoken since he left, not really. He mailed me things over the years, little bits of things, records, pictures, postcards with nothing written on the back. But that's not really speaking I don't think, and sure, sometimes they'd be something nice or something I'd recognize but there were pictures of some things so out of focus or so up close that I never did figure out what they were. I've got them all somewhere with the rest of the things worth keeping. Maybe you can take a gander and know what some of them are, I don't know. I don't know why he did that, but it never did much but make me feel bad. Or maybe that's what his plan was, I don't know.

But you never tried?

To reach out to him?

Yeah.

I mean of course I did. I've told you how I did, how I've tried to call or how I've left him messages or that I showed up to his wedding. Shit like that. I've been trying that sort of shit for forever, now, just that I'm pretty much done deluding myself into thinking that I'll ever again speak with him.

There's different kinds of speaking, you know.

Yeah, well, maybe you still talk to him I don't know, and whether or not you do's no business of mine. Just that I hope that he's well and I hope somewhere between then and now he came to peace with me, with what I've done to him, to myself. Knows that I'm sorry, that I'm still towing a lot of—I don't know if regret is the right word, or maybe it's still anger, I don't know. But it's a lot of something I'd rather not have, I guess is the point, and I know that all of it's mine, and I hope that he knows that I know that, but.

But—.

But?

But no. Maybe. Maybe I take it back. Maybe there's still something interests me, maybe.

[—.]

—No, but I'm too weary anymore.

What?

She had plenty of reasons to leave, shit. We all had plenty and maybe her most of all, but the way she left? I don't know. I mean she had her problems, yeah, her own and with Dad, and maybe it's just that one or both of those gobbled her up in the end. But then maybe she's still out there somewhere. Somewhere warm. Somewhere warm and away from what sour old men are still left behind.

Who? Harr—

Or but maybe not, though. Maybe not. I don't know.

All I know's that maybe Wayne knew something we didn't, or maybe he's just the only one had the balls to make that statement, right? To extend both middle fingers back at us and back at Dad and then get on with it? Or maybe he's just an asshole, likes to twist the knife but for just to twist it.

What are you talking about?

The picture, right? C'mon, you must've seen it.

Which picture?

Sunny day up a hill outside of Parker? Big oak? Squarish little headstone? You must've. He must've said something, no? About planting that stone on the ten-year of the night she left us and then how he sent me that picture with no return address, no note? Maybe even sent it to Con, too, I don't know.

—No? No bells are ringing?

I'd have to see it.

Well I've got it here somewhere, and fucking—you can have it. Let me find it before you leave and it's yours.

It's your copy. I don't need it.

No—.

No, you should take it. Take it and frame it, toss it, burn it, give it back to him or whatever. Just so long as you take it with you when you go, I don't care what happens with it.

But—

No.

No, it needs to go with you, and I'm done.

R—

I said I'm done, goddammit, I'm done. In me I'm done.

But why?

—Roy?

[—.]

Roy—?

CONRAD/YUMA, CA/2008-10-19
23:02:39—23:11:57

—**Conrad?**

—Hey hand me that other pack? Over behind your head. On the—yeah. Thanks.

And—.

And of course. Of course this fuckin' lighter's dead. Hey, you don't have a light, do you?

No.

Wait, waitwaitw—hah. Matches, motherfucker. Good thing I don't wash these jeans.

Good thing.

So let me ask you somethin'.

But I just asked you a question.

Yeah yeah, whatever. But let me ask you somethin'.

Shoot.

Actually, first—can I see your keys?

Why?

Can you just lemme see 'em? Just for a second.

They're in my bag.

I know they are. Heard 'em last time you moved your chair, bumped the bag—can I see 'em?

They're way down at the bottom, probably. Why?

[—.]

—Conrad?

Hnh—.

Something funny?

—Conrad?

You know a lot of sounds, right? Everyone knows a lot of sounds.

What do you mean?

I mean sounds you know inside of you. Sounds that mean somethin'.

Like, what—voices?

No. Well I mean, yeah, those I guess are close to what I'm saying how you can come to know someone's voice, and it's their voice and nobody else's and even if you ran into that person forty years later and they're sittin' behind you at a bus stop but now they speak French, and you don't speak French, but when they start speakin' French—that voice, right, that voice of theirs is still gonna kick you right in the head. No, I mean other sounds that do that same thing.

So sounds that someone is familiar with, you mean?

Yeah. Sound of your alarm clock, sound of your front door. Think about it for a second and you can pull up just about any one of those things and each person's gonna have a different set, right?

Sure.

And you know there's some of those that'll get a gut reaction out of you, like it or not, right? Like, the sound of your dog yippin' when someone's stepped on its paw, how if you've ever had a dog, how you can pull that sound up in your head and it gets you racin', instantly, or if you're out in the world and someone's got an entirely different dog and it's thirty years later, but for whatever reason you hear someone step on this other dog and it yips like your dog used to yip and for a half a second, before you even know what's going on, you're snapping your head around for your dog, even if after that half-second you remember that that dog's been dead since you were ten.

Okay—?

Do you know that? What I'm sayin'? How a dog or an alarm, or the sound of a shower turning on, or the sound of, whatever—of a specific blue car? The selfsame jingle of a particular clip of keys?

Sure.

—You weren't listenin' to me at all, just then, were you?

What are you talking about, Conrad?

I'm talkin' about hearing somethin'—fucking, somethin' I know that can't possibly be, but how you can hear a car and hear the tires and suspension squeak exactly how they should over a bump and being fuckin' paralyzed. I'm talking about hearin' boots I know exactly clompin' up and then hearin' a set of keys jingle in the way that you come to know how a certain set of keys will jingle, how it's a sound as distinctive as your own voice, one voice and no other, and I know because I still know that sound from anywhere, and—.

—And?

[—.]

Conrad—?

Y'know—.

Y'know let's talk about somethin' else.

Wait, you can'—

I can do whatever the fuck I want, so let's talk about somethin' else, I said.

But you were drunk, though. Not fifteen minutes ago you said you were drunk, and you were in a house you weren't supposed to be in because you'd broken in, and you were drunk. You were drunk and you heard something, and then—?

And then.

And then you asked me for your smokes. Great. Now you've got 'em. What happened next?

—Conrad?

[—.]

Conrad—?

Somethin' else, I said. Or there's the door. Either's fine.

[—.]

What the fuck happened to you, Conrad?

Look, if you're not gonna listen to me I really don't want you here, I said I don't wanna talk about it.

That's not what I meant.

The fuck'd you mean, then?

I mean how you became—*this*. What happened? —Conrad?

[—.]

Conrad what happened to you?

[—.]

Are you happy, Conrad?

—What?

Are you happy?

Happy? Who's happy, really.

Some people purport to be.

Well—.

Eh, I mean yeah, things've been worse, but whatever. That's all just—stuff. Just stuff, all out and about, and it bothers me about as much as it can bother anyone at a minimum I suppose. The minimum amount of bother, that. But it doesn't matter, really. I'm at peace.

I find that hard to believe, listening to you.

Believe what you want. My brothers do. Why shouldn't I?

So you disagree, then?

With you? Or with them? Them, I'll always disagree with them I think, because I've learned we're just not wired the same way, no. Not anymore.

And you? Long's we're bein' honest I don't much care about what you think or why, but don't take that personal. Just, you don't know me and I don't know you, is all—we're strangers. We're strangers and that's fine. Past that, you're the only thing I've heard from Wayne in near thirty years, and not that that counts for much, but it's somethin'. I see him in you, and I hear him too. But that's not fair to him, to you. To me. So that doesn't really count for anythin', now, does it?

I guess not.

How is he, anyway?

How is who?

Gandhi.

Wayne, idiot—who'd you think I meant?

I mean I could tell you, but then again I doubt it'd really count for anything.

—*Hnh.*

Sounds about right. Y'know I always figgered you'd come around because'a him. That's what I reckoned. That he's bad or that maybe you don't know, and that that's why you're here, and why you don't say. But I don't think it's gonna work out if you've come lookin' for shelter. I like you just fine, okay, but I don't need a kid and I owe him no favors. And actually—.

Actually, I think we're done talkin' about him.

Are we?

Are *you*? I don't remember bringin' him up in the first place so how 'bout you lay the fuck off. I don't 'member comin' to your house, go diggin' through your closet and try on all your old clothes. So we're finished, him—done. I'm done. *Finito.* In fact I'm done for today. How's about on your way out you take all that shit of his I've got, I'm done with that, too. Letters, junk, books I took from his storage.

And what am I supposed to do with them?

Wipe your inconsiderate ass for all I care.

Conr—

But I read them, you know. Tried to go through all the shit he'd left and learn because I care—I cared, I guess. Past tense. Cared to figure him out like a detective and try to get to the ass of that stack of shit so I'd know my brother because my brother never knew me, I don't think.

I mean who does that? Who never really tries and then just leaves like that? Who just up and leaves without a word—without ever another word? Nobody leaves like that.

I thought you had a sister.

You shut your fucking mouth or I'll shut it for you you *fuck*, you don't get to talk on her. Everybody talks on her but you don't fuckin' get to 'cause nobody gets to, you. You and them, the fuckin' same. You don't know anything but you think you do but I was there. I know. I was there and I know, you.

You.

You with your shitfaced little smirk, shakin' yer head like you've got the faintest fuckin' idea, I could tell you lotsa things. I could clear it all up in a second but that'd dignify you, the people like you, how you give up on her like how you give up on people like how they gave up on me and that's not me 'cause I don't give up on people, no, never, not once, and fuckin' maybe you'd not give up either if you took time to think, time to dig. You just gotta dig and you'll find her, and—.

Oh. Oh you're grinning, now, are you. Well grin about this—get the fuck out. Get. The fuck. *Out*. And take all this shit with you, out, get out with you, you fucking—.

You fucking—.

[—.]

Which box was it, Conrad?

[—.]

That one? Or I can fill one, just tell me which things. —Conrad.

[—.]

Conrad tell me now because I won't be coming back. Just—.

Just what? Just what, Conrad?

Just—. I'm sorry.

For what?

[—.]

For what, Conrad? What are you sorry for?

It's that box. No, the one with the—. No. The blue tape. Yeah, not the green tape. The one numbered nine, there. Toward the bottom.

Conrad—?

[—.]

Take care, Conrad.

TWO HUNDRED NINE

It was the right choice, I think, to leave the way I did. To go, and to go fully, but there were times—of course there were times—when something would happen, some joke or some bad day would happen that I would find myself wanting to call them, wanting to share with them, wanting to hear them say the things that I would expect they would say. How even sometimes I would turn around—I would turn to start talking to them and sometimes the words would almost come out before I remembered where I was and where they were and how large the distance.

So many stories they might have liked.

Like, one of my trips across the country, I took it in a Volkswagen Beetle that I had purchased for next to nothing because the radiator was shot and that car—that poor car, it needed more water than my plants, and even still you had to run the heater all the time just to keep it from boiling over. But so I was in the middle of the desert with Gordon, somewhere in Arizona, and I had the heater going, with the windows down, because it had to be over a hundred out there and the last thing we needed was to get stranded, so I was nursing the Beetle along.

But then Gordon asked me how hot I thought we could get the inside of the car if we rolled up the windows, and I told him I bet one-fifty, one-sixty.

First to roll a window down buys lunch? he asked.

And dinner, I said, as I cranked mine up.

So it began. And at first it was funny. At first we were joking and carrying on with pantomimed face-fanning and brow-wiping but then, slowly, it became less funny—not *not* funny, but less funny, slowly—until some miles later, when our contest stopped being funny at all.

The heat—.

You have never known heat like that heat. A heat like that is something you have never experienced, and I can say that with conviction.

Imagine a dry sauna but with all of your clothes on, but bright, too bright. The river down my back could do nothing for me and my head felt empty. Ten minutes and I could feel the moisture leaving my eyeballs and I could not stop blinking. Twenty minutes and my vision started to go. Twenty-five and each of us was whimpering like old hinges.

Up ahead came a sign for a rest area, and Gordon said: I—.

And that was all he had to say.

I whipped in. There were no parking spots in the shade of this solitary, beautiful oak tree in the middle of the lawn next to the bathrooms, so I drove over the curb and we had the doors open before the car had even stopped moving. I fell out of the car face-first onto that grass because my legs would not work and I just lied there, trying to stay conscious, with my feet still in the car's footwell, and Gordon was coughing and he was crying, I think, I could hear him in a similar position on the far side of the car—but then his crying became laughing, and I laughed with him, and even the car started laughing as it choked, and sputtered, and died. We agreed to split lunch and dinner, and we did. And that car never ran the same again.

See, that little story, so small of consequence, is something that I remember wanting to tell them about, wanting to share with them, but I have never shared it with anyone, and had I not shared it just now, it likely would have died with me. Not that I ever had good reason to not share it, I just. Well—. You know how I tend to be.

[—.]

—A relevant curio, previously known only to me:

Harriet wrote a note to my brothers and me about a week before she died, and she entrusted it to me to distribute among us, but I never did. I meant to. Really, I did. But my brothers— in the aftermath of Harriet's exit, I felt so strongly that they would think the note false, would think it some cruelty I had manufactured to coerce them toward closure, that I withheld it entirely and resolved to tuck it away until such time as they accepted her loss holistically, independent of influence. And then I could show them. And then peace would come.

Or at least that is what I told myself. What I used to be able to tell myself, I have—. I have never been—.

[—.]

I cannot remember an instance in which I willingly ceded agency. Not meaningfully. Not with them. Your grandfather stripped us of ours for so many years growing up that, as soon as I was able, I constructed my own and hoisted it high above reach—high enough to never again be compromised. Like how he broke my left hand once with a hammer, so I taught myself to write with my right so he could never again silence me in that way, so, too my brothers tried to suffocate me—Roy with his selfishness, and Conrad, his blindness, I—. I could not stay.

I tried to return, though. In my long loneliness, I tried to fumble after them, tried to reconcile my own obstinacies:

How many times did I call and sit silent until they hung up?

How many early mornings did I make it all the way to one of their doorsteps, only to find myself unable ring the bell?

I tried so hard until, eventually, the sum of my frustration cast me or them—I do not know which—into some solitary place from which there seems no reliable path, and now—? Now, I worry that this senescent *thing* that I became while I was not looking—I worry that it is not substantial enough to even suffer such a trail, because to make such a journey would be trepidatious, yes, but to attempt it and to be unable to find their hearts? Or to worse, to be turned away—? No. No—.

—The note.

The note—it was a simple, sweet little epitaph that was part goodbye, part instruction, and I carried it in my wallet until the day you were born, because I knew I could not bear to carry both it and you at the same time, so I put it into the orange cigar box along with the rest of my anchors as soon as your mother and I brought you home from the hospital.

For years—.

For years, I would take it out to read it on her birthday and consider, while rubbing its yellow and its fade between my fingertips, whether enough time had passed—whether enough time had passed that my brothers might see the note for all that it was, and I tried. I tried to imagine the sea that had swollen between us; how the note was a raft. Was the only raft, now, but that sea—. It had been once a pond, perhaps, but now—? Now a void of dozing water. Now a starless gulf of languid wind, and the horizon, yawning—.

I could not.

I could not embark across such a sea.

I mean, what could I say?

Hey Conrad, she died, and in all my fury I withheld her goodbye because nothing about you back then instilled any faith in me—any faith in the hope that you would see such a note and not swell up with rage over some presumed fraud.

Or hey, Roy, she is not coming back, and I know so because I held her last will in my hand, all but written in her own blood, and I waited so long for you to come up for air so that you might see it, and see her, and see me with clear eyes—but you never did rise.

And how could I ever broach with them the subject of the life for her that I built for them? For her. For myself. How many postcards have I mailed? What difference have they made, good or bad?

If but only I could have found the words, or the strength, or some amalgamation of both enough to write something on the back of even one card, would that I could have filled their mailboxes with me, with an affable honesty I never—.

I never—.

[—.]

Why am I like this?

Why do I keep things from people?

Why did I keep things from you?

[—.]

You know, I wonder, often, about these tapes and what purpose they will serve. I wonder, I wonder. I wonder, too, over what I will do if they never are needed.

Like, what if I outlive you?

Or worse, what if I show you? What if I lash these tapes together and embark across our own, widening sea? What if I risk that odyssey just to show you this raft, but then you shrug, insouciant?

What then?

What do I do then—?

Do I mail them? But to whom?

Do I burn them? But where? Surely these *things* must deserve some greater send-off, I—.

[—.]

Or—.

[—.]

—Or do they?

A whole life on tape—how much is that worth?

What worth could exist for a story unheard?

The act of creation does not also create value, and every library is burdened by books never read. Would that I might nudge the scales toward some better balance if I stopped this tape, heaped everything together in a box, and threw the lot behind some dumpster, I—.

[—.]

Tired—.

I am so tired.

SIFTING THROUGH STATIC
ACT ONE, SCENE TWO:
(OR, DISPATCHES FROM AN ABSENT PRESENCE)

This is a page from his journal:

Dear Wayne, This pen is almost out of ink. That is all.

This is a grocery list, dated 9 September 2000:

Frzn vgtbls, chkn, 6cn prk/bns, grps? wtrmln?

This is a postcard, blank on the back:

A tiny island. A palm tree's sway. || [—.]

These are some of the photographs:

Him, asleep with his boots up on a laboratory bench, a book splayed across his chest, two oranges next to his crossed ankles.

Him, beneath an oak tree, clean-shaven, mortarboard and gowned atop a hilltop I've made pilgrimage to before. He is so far from the camera that you have to squint to see his face.

Him, midair, hair twisting behind him on a 1951 Indian Warrior with green paint so faded it is almost white.

This is a worn-out copy of Debussy's *Prélude à l'après-midi d'unfaune* on cassette:

[—.]

These are the years that these things and others appear in my mailbox:

1998-2007

These are the years that I spend speaking to his dissatisfaction:

1998-2007

These are the years that we go without speaking:

ROY/LONGMONT, CO/2007-07-24
11:15:14—11:24:01

Nah. Nah I'm done talking about that. Regret—I'm done talking about it like I'm anything special, like I've dealt with anything that anyone else's never dealt with before. Really, I'm not that special.

You don't think so?

Well I mean mostly I'm done talking about it because I've spent my whole life thinking about it, talking about it or not talking about it. That's what I'm saying. So I'm done, is what I'm saying. I'm done.

When did you make this decision?

Oh, I dunno. 'Bout twelve seconds ago?

Well there's nothing in particular we have to talk about, you know. We could talk about baseball. Or cars. Or whatever.

Yeah, ho hum.

That's not why you're here and we both know that. You don't care, really, about me or about baseball or about cars. Not really.

What makes you say that?

Just a feeling. But it's fine, really. I don't know why you're here, nor do I need to. It's fine.

I—

But you're just gonna bug me about it, aren't you? So fine, we'll go through it one more time and then let's be done, yes? Yes. It'll be quick.

Roy—

So my whole life, you know it's been nothing but regret, and it's just that regret just doesn't fucking get you anywhere after a point. It's not that it's a bad thing, regret, but rather that the cup can only get so full before it starts overflowing and spilling all over you if nobody's gonna take it from you, and my brothers, they aren't interested in my cups. That's the gist.

You don't think so?

What, about my brothers?

Mm.

—Seriously?

Well but I mean it, though. You don't think they're interested anymore?

I mean Conrad plays nice, sure, but I know him to the bones. I know how he feels and I know he's plenty tired of my shit—been tired, even, since roundabout 1971, '72.

And Wayne?

Hmp.

At least Wayne's honest.

[—.]

So, Roy?

Hm?

What's something you still regret?

What?

We're talking about regret, right? So what's something that's still bothering you? Something that you wish you could change.

Out of everything?

Yeah.

Shit, I dunno. Take your pick.

From what?

Well—.

I mean H. missed everything. Missed me and all my shit, missed Conrad. Missed out on your pops like I missed out on him. That's one.

Why's that so bad?

You saying it's not?

I'm not saying anything.

I've noticed.

But I mean I dunno, my brothers? Who gives a shit. We— all of us—we broke each other in ways that I don't think'll ever really mend even if we tried, and I suppose there's some good finality in that. It's not what I would've wanted, but it is what it is, and I spent a lot of time thinking it wasn't fair. But then, what's fair, really? What does it mean for something to be fair?

Did I learn from my mistakes? Sure, so maybe all of this is fair.

Am I a better, stronger person after having done most everything without my family around bearing in mind, of course, what it was that I did to send them away? Fuck if I know, but maybe.

Either way I'm still here.

And do you think that's unfair?

What's unfair?

That you're still here. That things went they way they did.

Well I mean I guess the only thing that's really unfair about this whole hand I've been dealt's that things were never broken with H., right, but that things with her were the most unresolved.

Why's that the hardest?

It's in how she was something different, I think.

How so?

—It's hard to explain.

Try?

I dunno. It's partly she's different because things were never bad with her far as the three of us were concerned, right? And I know you could make the argument that she's the reason I am the way I am today, sure, that I'd've never gotten into any of the junk without her nudge, but I mean she got me started with the best of intentions. She gave me a hand when nobody would and that speaks to her character, I think, and that character's got nothing wrong with it in relation to the three of us, is what I'm saying.

What happened, really?

To her? I don't know what happened to her.

I mean with her and you. With the drugs.

I told you already.

I don't think you did.

But I did, though.

—When?

I did when I gave you the story I give to people about how I got hooked. That's the story I can bear to tell.

So there's another story?

There's always another story.

What do you mean?

Well I mean if I were to tell you that she was herself an addict, what would you think of her? Or if she was an addict and Gordon was, too, and that that's why she dated him. What would that change of your perception of her, hm?

Would it color her differently? Would she seem fouler to you if I told you that she and Gordon, that's one reason—not the only reason, no, but one reason—that they got together and they stayed together? That their slinging made them the kind of money people could run away on?

Or what if I told you that she mentioned more than once on the worst days how she'd fantasized on faking her death, and how she'd written up a whole plan if need be, and how there weren't that many loose ends to tie up, really, if she wanted to never be found? How she never told me who, but that she knew just the person to cinch that knot once she split? Hm?

You don't think the lie colors her worse?

But is it a lie, though?

Yes?

But I mean part of what I told you was true, though. It's not all made up.

Which part?

The part where the doctors couldn't figure out what was wrong with me so they stopped giving me meds. But the rest of it—

Why?

Why what?

Why lie, though? What's the point?

I don't know. Because it's something I can control, I suppose, and because she dealt with enough and did enough good that I can let that hammer fall on me. I *should* let that hammer fall on me.

Is that the only reason?

Well—.

Well also maybe the lie's how I would've liked my life to turn out, I figure. Maybe that's why, too.

What's wrong with your life?

I don't really like my life.

That seems unfair.

What, to you? What do you care? I don't owe you shit.

To you, I mean. It's sad.

Sad? Sad's a stretch. Sad's a lot of things but I don't think it's unfair.

What's unfair, then?

Unfair?

Unfair's a history full of holes. Unfair's being alone, even when you're around your family that you've made for yourself, because you've got no roots and you know that they've got nothing they can look back on and cling to after you're someday gone. That's unfair.

And fair would be—?

Fair's a full life. Fair's second chances, mended fences. Fair's certainty in knowing whether someone matters to you's still somewhere out there or whether they're in the ground. Fair's a story with a beginning a middle and an end and a clean thread you can pull between those three, front to back, and fair's found in the knowing that the story you've got's probly the right one.

So what do you think, then—have things been fair?

For me?

Mm.

[—.]

I was born feeble and still my father beat me. He beat my mother and my brothers both—one of them nearly to death on more occasions than I can count for you on one hand, and neither the other brother nor my mother never stood up for him or for us. My—I don't know what you want to call her, but H.—she's been gone since 1968, and I'm an addict in recovery living a painfully, painfully normal life now. I've got one brother's got problems enough of his own to where I'm ever just an ulcer for him anymore, and I salted the earth beneath us a long time ago besides. I've got a mother's been dead a long time, and dead long before that day, too, just no one ever got 'round to burying her. And my other brother—? I poisoned that well about forty years ago, now, and here I am still sitting on its edge, still biding the time, still watching the road.

So.

Fair?

You tell me whether things've ever been fair.

OCTOBER 19, 1989

Wayne there was a big earthquake a few days ago. I do not know if you saw it but I was watching when it happened on the T.V. live because it happened right before Game 3. I think you are in California but I do not know of course but if you are in California I hope you are alright and you did not get squished.

It has been a while since I have written again but I was watching the T.V. when it happened and it got me thinking about you and what would happen if you got squished and then I would not ever get a chance to talk to you again or you would not ever read all this shit I have been writing. So here I am again. I hope you did not get squished or anyone else that you care about.

Also I have been thinking brother and I have been thinking that I should have been better to you. For us and for her. You two needed me to be better than I was and I was not better. I was not even good enough for myself but I cannot go back and change that now.

I wonder about her a lot and why she left. I mean who knows why anyone leaves right? But she is gone and I know at least part of it was our family and then I am left thinking about that and what I could have done better you know? When I think back I think about all the good times we had growing up but then I think about the other stuff like the other times that I needed to be there for you or for Roy and I was not there for you and how that made things worse for us around the house and worse for our family. And if that is the contribution I can think of when I am thinking about what is wrong with our family then that is something I could have done better to fix. Maybe things would have been better and she would have stayed. Who knows. It does not make much sense even after I type all that out.

I guess I am just upset. I am upset she has been gone for so long and we have got nothing from her and I am upset how everyone has given up on her and how I am the only one holding out hope. Well brother let me tell you it sucks. It sucks being the only one who is still even talking.

And I know you wonder why I hold on. I know that. And for the longest time I have never told anyone but I have been getting postcards for years and they come from all sorts of places and those postcards are why I hold on. There is never anything written on the back of them sure but they are postcards of warm places and nice scenes and happy stuff. And that is just like her you know? That she would send me postcards of stuff I would like but keep me at a distance because she has her own life now. That is what she wanted. You know that. Her own life after her way out.

Giving up has always been easy for you I know that. And also I know that that was not always a bad thing like how you gave up on Roy and how that was probably the smarter decision when you wrote him off and wrote him out of your life. Good on you for that. He was better for quite a while but now he is in a bad way again lately and he has got the hook in deep with me and I cannot bring myself to just leave him. I should have just let him go like you did and maybe he would have gotten help a ways back and then things would be better now or maybe not and maybe he would have just died instead and we all three of us I think might be relieved but I do not really mean that. I hope too much. All that hope I lassoed him with it or he lassoed me I do not know but now he is thrashing and thrashing and I cannot get it to let go.

One of the things I do not regret though is holding my grudge on you. Holding out for you to come around and look at me straight so we can square up and move on. Not to say a bit of the blame does not fall on me or that your plans did not work out good for you or anything but you do not just do that to people. You do not just leave. You gave up hope and I cannot just let that go.

Other things I regret as long as I am here. The drugs. I regret those. Not that they were ever a problem for me like Roy but it is just that they were such a waste of money when I had none and of time back when I had all the time in the world and of people like how they can bend whatever you love right over the barrel while you are not even looking.

What else. I regretted the drinking. I did. I mean it. I am not sure how I feel about it today but I know that I regretted it there for a while. Today I am feeling more like how I should not regret anything I do with myself because I am kind of alone here so who gives a shit. Nothing is reciprocated to me anymore. No family. No love. I might as well be dead so why bother worrying.

You know maybe dead is best fitting for me considering how alone it is around here. And considering my track record I would probably be doing some strangers a favor so big and they will never know that they owe me everything since they will keep breathing longer than they would have if I kept puttering around. Something to think about. Something for you to sit with too I suppose.

Anyways I hope you are not dead. Last I checked you are a Giants fan since Dad was all about the Dodgers. So I will be rooting for Oakland.

Bye.
c

FOUR HUNDRED EIGHTY-EIGHT

There are things that I talk around, I know. Too many things, probably, and I know. I know it was never easy with me. Talking to me and getting to know me. I was not the easiest father to have, and I wish I could apologize for that. Was capable of apologizing, I mean, because I have regrets but I fear it is too late for me to address them with you directly, because you are not who you used to be and those grievances were levied against a *you* that no longer exists.

But insofar as how we have changed, how we hardly speak—these tapes, I think, have changed. Have grown. I started them so long ago for reasons I hardly recall—equal parts record and insurance, an outlet for rage and haven from it, maybe, or maybe just to tell a story I could only ever recount in solitude. Or an exercise in exploitation, maybe. Yes, maybe that. An exercise in exploiting myself for your sake, someday. To give to you what I have withheld.

The box for these things has gotten larger as the old ones have overflowed or fallen apart beneath the floorboards. This tape will go in a new box today, along with its brothers, and I finally got a plastic one. A tub, I mean. A blue tub with a lid, as you know by now. Blue because blue was your favorite color when you were small. Maybe it still is. I hope it still is.

But the point I was going to make was that as I was packing the new blue box, something compelled me to go back and listen to some of the old tapes, and this has never happened before. I grabbed a few and skipped through them to listened to some bits I have recorded over these many years. Most tapes I can remember recording, but some I cannot. And some stories—some little bits of stories and thoughts that I came across were sometimes things that I had forgotten entirely, or other things that I was surprised I had ever committed to tape.

But—.

But then other things surfaced during my time in the archives. The more I listened, the more I realized that I had not been honest. Honest with you, honest with myself. That there are things that I said that were half-truths, and that there are other things that I said that were outright lies, but lies I only realized in retrospect, because I would never lie to you intentionally. I never have. You have to believe that. But there were some things that I said, some things that happened to me that I so badly wanted to remember a certain way or wanted to not remember at all—. And that is how they came out. Out of my mouth and onto the tape. Omissions. Lies.

And now—?

And now I wonder what to do. What do I do with those? Do I throw those away? Do I leave them? Do I attach a note or append them? How would I append them, even, because some of these things happened so long ago—how certain am I that the things I am sure of are the things that happened at all? And what if I have changed? What if the things I remember as true now are just my head wanting those things to be true?

I ask, but that does not mean that I have the answer. All I can do, I guess, is fill in the holes that I have noticed during this impromptu review, but there are so many that I doubt I will be able to fill them all, and further—. Further, I doubt that the things I would fill them with would be any better, any more solid or true. Sometimes, I suppose, a hole is better. A hole is its own explanation, I think, in a way.

So—.

So, there are things that I talk around, I know. I am sure that you have had questions about so many things. Some, I know, you have asked, and I have evaded, and not least of these are those questions you have asked about the person you have long assumed to be my sister.

Even that. Even that label——.

Her name was Harriet, and she was five years older than me, and nobody speaks of her. Nobody. That silence wells up from the not knowing, and some days it is so profound that it seems as though she never existed at all.

That silence.

My silence.

The different kinds of silence.

I think of those silences and I think of her, of what happened to her, and I think of my brothers and the stories they must tell themselves.

That she could come back.

That she is out there, somewhere, escaped from us and living well, and someday she will call us all and set us free.

And I can understand their hope, I can, because nobody knows what happened to her. Not anymore. Not for sure. There are opinions, of course, and I have mine, and theirs are theirs and a person is free to hold out whatever hope for whichever thing—nobody could ever argue that.

But——.

But what can I say?

What can I say but that we each have our opinions, yes, but that I never expect that the phone will ring?

SIFTING THROUGH STATIC
ACT ONE, SCENE THREE:
(OR, BUILDING A BEACON OF RECALLED DEBRIS)

1998-2007

Nine years of frustrated grunts and attritive gestures before Wayne's dissatisfaction and I will find our common tongue.

This was the watershed:

The things I remember, I say. The things that seem so nothing. The things that rise from the carpet to latch to my ankle while I'm reading, or watching baseball, or anything else.

How in forty years I'll be seventy-one at a rummage sale when being nine will reach up from a trunk, will grab my wrist and say: Remember being nine and finding an orange cigar box of things that look cared-for. A brutal buckle. A yellowed letter. An ancient lighter. A clip of keys. Remember placing them back exactly, and still, how you asked if I'd been going through your things.

Mm, my father's dissatisfaction says.

And other things: how you spent an entire afternoon searching for a record before telling me that someone must have borrowed it or sold it, so you called a radio station.

Can you play something from *Rigoletto*? Anything from the version with Pavarotti and Gruberová, my kid needs to hear it.

And we ran to the car and idled there for almost an hour, you filling time by asking what I thought about everything and anything until, the hour gone, the radio acquiesced. I remember your surprise when Verdi interrupted our conversation, you having forgotten why we were in the car.

Mmph, it says.

Or how you drove us for half a day just to watch the Giants lose at Dodger Stadium, and how I fell asleep in the front seat and slept for a hundred miles or two hundred miles, who knows exactly how far. But how I woke to find you shading my eyes, your right arm outstretched, your palm blocking the sun, and how I asked you how long I'd been asleep. How you said, A while, and rolled your shoulder.

Wwhhtt llsse, it asks.

How Mom smoked Parliaments in our garage from the day you divorced and how I'd ask her to quit, and how she'd say, *Nothing lives forever Babe*, and then she'd ask about my day. How the first time I asked you to make her quit you said it wasn't your place to tell her what to do, but how on the twelfth time I asked, you said, *Fine, I'll take care of it*, and you went into the garage, and seventeen seconds later she came inside and told me she was done. How you never told me what was said.

A prsn alwys hs a chce, it explains.

And how you picked me up after school on the day my grandmother died.

Which one? I asked.

Mine, you said.

Was it sudden?

No.

Was she suffering?

How you said: Depends, but yes.

222

ROY/LONGMONT, CO/2007-07-24
12:02:11—12:07:41

The thing about it is that she wasn't really our sister. Not fully, anyway, and we didn't even know what she was until sometime later growing up. Before that we figured she was a cousin that was staying with us because her parents traveled a lot or had died and it was better for her to stay in one school. At least that's what I thought.

So what do you think she was, exactly?

Half-sister, I think.

Whose kid?

That's the thing of it. I don't know. Probly she was from Dad, but I don't know. They never told us.

You never thought to ask her directly?

Of course I did, but just she wouldn't elaborate, but it's clear when I asked her that she knew something she wasn't saying.

Seems like an odd thing to hide.

Yeah I thought so too. We all did. But we weren't about to ask Dad, and Mom was never any use for fear of him, and the only thing I could think of, the only explanation that I could come up with was that maybe—maybe she didn't know either.

Not fully, at least. That's the only thing I can think of. So if Mom didn't know, it had to be Dad's doing.

Why didn't you ask her after he died?

Tried that, too, but toss in the fact Mom's a vegetable for months after the wreck and I'm starting my sink right around then, too—you don't end up with the most fruitful of conversations. By the time I'm a human being again, shit with her's so fractured and it's been so long and Harriet's—. Well, she's been gone since before Dad, and—. And I dunno. I guess it just never really came up again.

But aren't there records?

For her?

Mm.

Maybe there are. Probly there are, but I don't even know where I'd look. Where I'd start to look to find her.

Records aren't that hard to dig up, though.

Sure. But they're harder when you don't know who you're looking for. Because we call her Harriet, because everyone called her Harriet, but that wasn't her name.

—What?

Her name. Her name wasn't Harriet. Either that or someone did a grade-A job of destroying all her paper, but I can't think of a single reason anyone'd do such a thing. And I looked. Believe me, I looked. Libraries, police, hospitals, D.M.V., everywhere. Even paid a P.I. some years back to find out what he could but he came up with nothing. Nothing at all.

So what's more likely, that she went missing and someone did a G-Man job of removing any evidence that she was ever here? Or that this person, who for years we were lied to about, wasn't named the name we called her? Which do you think, *Occam?*

But why?

Why's a fabulous goddamned question. And I don't know. I don't know and I don't think I even care anymore.

Why not?

Because it's all wasted air's why.

So you're fine with it, then.

With what—with her?

Yeah.

Well there's shades of fine. If you haven't realized this by now then you still have some growing up to do because everything's a compromise. Everything, even the best things, got dissatisfaction salted through and you've just gotta figure out how much you can take, is how it is. Or how to eat around it. But it's hard to eat around salt.

But are you?

Am I what?

Fine.

I mean if I had to answer you, then no. No I'm not fine. I've never been fine with this and I doubt I ever will be. The not knowing. The wondering. The frustration that somewhere, sometime, someone has had the answers you'd like.

But it's like that everywhere with everything, kid. So do yourself a favor and get used to it. Get acquainted with not being fine.

OCTOBER 10, 1990

Wayne last time I saw you do you remember how we drove way back up into the hills and you showed me constellations? Set a fire and laid out until I fell asleep to you talking and going on and on about all this cool stuff like the old stories like the things that happened before there were books and people had to pass the stories down by mouth. Or how did you say it. You said they had to pass shit down by carving or by carving up the sky star by star to reason out the parts of the world that they could not explain. To feel less alone I remember you said. I remember you saying that. That they did that to feel less alone beneath the vast and the cold. A sort of nightlight sort of you said. I remember you said that.

And I remember I tried to tell you that when I still had you on the phone that night when you called me after the truck I was driving got hijacked and I could not figure out how you even got my number. I remember I asked you if you saw me on the news and that was how and if you saw me on the news then were you in California and if you were in California then please come over Wayne please we will go for waffles and I am buying Wayne it is all on me whatever you want. I remember trying to tell you about it but I guess I was just excited to have you on the phone so I just sort of blurted it all out in one breath and then it was quiet again and then I said we should go again. Do you remember I said maybe there are some good hills out here in California who knows? Are you in California? What cities show S.F. or L.A. news? Who knows which you saw me on but a bunch I bet but how far from Burbank are you come on we should eat brother whatever you want. Whatever you want. On me.

But then you hung up. That is when you left me forever and became a ghost.

See I figured it out a long time ago what I want and what I would say if you ever wrote me back or if you ever called or if you Lord forgive actually rang my doorbell.

I want to call you that to your face. Ghost. I want to call you that and have you look at me while I called you that and know why.

Why because it is honest and you called me dishonest that last time we spoke and why because that is what you are. Why because I want you to know I am here and for you to give a shit that I am here but you are still somewhere out there and I am still just here but I do not know for how long and I need to look at my brother straight and say I was wrong to look at him and call him what he is and for him to hear me say that and for him to say I am right about the rest of what I say that he was wrong but that he can hear me say to him also that he was right that you are right that you were right and I was wronger Wayne you were right you were right you were right all along I know you were right you ghost just look at me Jesus just look at me and see how crooked but I am here I am here I am still here I have always been here but where the fuck did you go?

C.

SIX HUNDRED SIXTY-FIVE

Your grandfather was three people. There was the sober version of him, the drunk version, and then the something else. They did not share equal time.

The sober was a strange object to deal with in that it was such a rare beast, so when it came by we had an impenetrable trouble in interacting with it. I cannot speak any other languages, but I feel like it must be what it must feel like when a Spaniard speaks with a Portuguese how it seems the languages would be just compatible enough to where you might think you should be able to speak, that maybe there are some words that you both understand, but still. It is difficult to explain.

When I qualify the sober-him, this different from the third thing, the something else that I will get to. The sober-him was the one that would take you to ice cream, and the whole time you would be wondering what sort of game this was, what sort of pain you were due because of the ice cream. Maybe the flavors are traps, that he has some expectation of what flavor your cone should be and dire consequences could follow. But then he rests his hand on your head while they scoop your cone, plays with your hair and maybe jostles your head a little, and then he pays, and then he takes it and hands it to you, and then you eat it, and then you go home, and then it was just ice cream after all. That was the sober. He was rare.

The drunk was everywhere most of the time. The drunk was a claustrophobia. A brutality. The drunk would disappear for days and then catch you up on the beatings you missed while he was gone. The drunk may have made you—you, specifically—some aunts and some uncles that are still floating around out there somewhere. Hooray.

But then—.

Then there was this other. This something worse. This something else that only emerged a few times.

Harriet was well acquainted with all three of these—*things*. Perhaps more than any of us ever were.

The sober told her to break it off with Gordon. Insisted, even. Told her that he was bad news and he forbade the relationship. I remember overhearing it when it happened. I was reading in my room and she came in late, and he was up waiting as he often did. I heard her keys fall into the dish near the door and he laid it out for her, that she would end it or he would end it.

Okay, she said.

He did not believe her. When he asked if she was serious, she said No, and she laughed. I remember she called him by name. None of us ever dared to, but she always and only called him by name.

The same situation happened some weeks later, more or less, but this time it was the drunk. He had been up waiting, but this time with a bottle, and the same interaction followed almost verbatim. But this time it ended differently. This time she said, No, and she laughed, and he reminded her. He reminded her how he had trained us all to dig holes, how fast they could be dug and how they were the perfect size. How smooth the ground was after the filling.

She said nothing.

I caught her packing two days later. I skipped out on work because I was tired of that job and I had decided to see how long it took me to get fired. She was filling a duffel bag when I walked in, and I asked her what she was doing. She said she and Gordon were planning on leaving, and that they just needed a few more days.

I asked her how I could help.

She kissed me on the forehead and told me to take care of myself. Above all else, she said, just take care of yourself. Everything else is secondary. She hid her packed bags beneath the floorboards in her closet, and I expected that that would be that.

The day after that it was late, and I was getting ready for my other job because I owed some shifts, and she came in late again, and he was drunk. He had been drunk since work. She came in and he asked her if she had been packing.

Who told you? she yelled, and he asked her why it mattered how he knew, but he knew, and he never told her she could leave. Then there was yelling, and some throwing of things. And I considered the knuckledusters I kept beneath the mattress, the knuckles from Gordon. I considered them, and I fisted them, and I almost went out. Almost.

This is one of my many regrets. That I did not leave my room. I was big enough, finally. I had been big enough for months, and I was waiting—had been waiting. But in that moment, I froze. I did nothing.

He stormed off and I heard his car start. I heard it jump the curb as he left, and I heard the tires squeal around the corner.

I went out and she was crying. It was the only time I ever saw her cry.

I might leave earlier, she said, I might have to leave early.

I told her I would stay home, that I did not need the job and I would stay with her until Gordon came, until they could leave and things would be okay.

No, she told me, no. Go, she told me.

I protested but ten minutes later she was walking me to my car. She promised me that she would call Gordon just as soon as she got back inside, and he would come as soon as he was able, and then they would leave.

I drove off in the dark. She stood in the street, barefoot in her white dress. I can still see its faded floral print, lit up red by my taillights, her silhouette shrinking as I drive until her features are impossible to make out, her hands clasped at her waist, her sandy-redblonde braid a rope to touch her collarbone. I round the corner and she is gone.

[—.]

That shift was the longest shift of my life. I watched the clock and it seemed to move backward. I could hear every tick.

Six hours in, and Gordon shows up.

Where is she? he asks, and I know.

We ran out the door while my boss called something after me, but he was already too far behind to distinguish what he was saying. Probably he was firing me. But we sped home and everything is how it was left—except. Except his truck is gone. When he left earlier he had taken your grandmother's Chrysler, but now the Chrysler was there and his truck was gone.

Gordon went to go check some other places she might be, he said. He left, and I felt lost. I sat on the front step. I did not know what else to do.

Your grandfather returned as the sun was coming up, his tires muddy. After he had finished angling the truck into the driveway, front corner lodged in the hedges, he turned the ignition off and he sat there and he stared straight ahead for a while. He did not know I was there. He got out and he almost fell, but he grabbed the side mirror in time. He shut the door and as he staggered around the front of the car I saw how muddy he was.

Where is she? I asked him, and he startled. He looked at me, and looked at me, and looked at me. And then he walked the other way toward the side door to the garage.

Where is she? I asked again, but he said nothing.

Gordon returned after the sun was long up and found me still sitting on the step.

I looked everywhere, he said. I looked everywhere.

Breakfast, I told him, we need to talk.

I started toward my car, and Gordon followed.

SIFTING THROUGH STATIC
ACT TWO, SCENE ONE:
(OR, EASTWARD BOUND AT FIVE BY FIVE)

Hello, I say, and admire Wayne's dissatisfaction. It is a thin man. Fibrous. A mass of muscle spun tight like radio wire. It wears boots you could use to hammer nails. It keeps a beard you could keep pencils in. It doesn't wear glasses, and it doesn't say hello.

Instead it says that in 1969 my father's jaw is still a drawbridge down and his shoulders are yet broader than his shadow. It says his hair is a thicket falling past his shoulders, and it says that his hands are a construction of scabs, and it says that he still sings.

You should really visit us, it says.

So I do. I visit them often.

In 1969 I hitchhike to his house because I'm too afraid to hitchhike today. A 1942 Ford pickup, blue with a wooden bed, stops at his curb, and I wave thanks as it sputters off into predawn. He's always waiting barefoot on the bumper of a car he owns in 1969 and totals in 1981. I approach, and he never says Hello, or How are you? or Whatchya feel like doing? No, he always asks me if I want to drive to Vermont.

Why?

I've never been to Vermont. How much cash you got?

I'm broke, but the summer of 1987, that impossibly hot, hide-a-bed summer that crushed Mom straight into the St. Louis concrete is as east as I know, so—.

Typical, he says. So east it is, then.

We get into a 1956 Porsche 356A with green paint so faded it is almost white, and I think, Man, this car. I wish I could have driven this car.

He says I wish you could have driven it too.

And I don't even care that he knows what I'm thinking.

In 1969 he lives outside of Denver, but here, in 1969, he lives south of San Francisco. He drives us north toward the bridge, but we stop for oysters on the wharf. The sun stops rising while we eat.

It can wait, he says, for us to eat our oysters.

When we finish, he starts the car and so starts the sun, and it's on the lower deck of the bridge where he remembers the footage that'll flood the television in twenty years.

What day is it today? he asks.

Whatever day you want it to be. How about October?

Yes. October. Remember the earthquake?

Yes, I remember. I was almost nine.

I was thirty-eight. Are you going to be okay?

I'll be fine. I'll be outside when you mow the hedges with your bumper, when you rip the screen from its hinges, shouting.

Tell me you're going to be okay. I'm going to worry about you. I'm going to wish I had this car when I can't get to you fast enough, when nobody has a cellphone and I don't know if you're okay.

I wasn't hurt.

But the fish tank flipped and the carpet drank it up.

That's the first thing you're going to see, yes, but don't panic.

But you always read beneath the fish tank.

I wasn't hurt. You and me, we buy new goldfish the next afternoon. Remember?

But there was so much glass and you weren't there.

236

You and me, we ate only at restaurants for six days, remember? Until the power was back? You and me.

But you were outside. You were finding shapes in the clouds.

Yes. Remember how you came to lie with me and the sirens went for hours.

You weren't hurt?

I wasn't hurt.

You weren't hurt.

I wasn't hurt.

The wind fingers his long hair and John Fogerty wails through the hiss of amplitude modulation.

ROY/LONGMONT, CO/2007-07-24
12:41:17—12:48:48

The worst one—the worst one I'm in Denver, downtown somewhere I don't recognize, but I know for sure it's Denver. Mom has sent me to collect Wayne and bring him to Dad's funeral but I can't find him anywhere but somehow she knows he's downtown. So I go. I search. I search but I can't find him anywhere, but I look and look and look through all of the streets and past all of the people but I can't find him but I'm searching, searching.

Then, slowly, I realize that there are fewer and fewer people out on the streets, but it's not like they don't all disappear at once but it's like, I don't know—it's like watching a pot boil in reverse if you can picture the bubbles, until eventually they're all gone and it's just me, alone, and I can't find him anywhere.

Then I feel something, something behind me sort of, but distant. I don't know how to describe it. Like a fingernail sliding up nape of your neck, but not really, but just, like, the feeling of that fingernail if you were to try to imagine it, how like if you think about that happening—how your brain can try to imagine what that might feel like, I mean. I don't know.

But I turn around to look but there's nothing there but downtown and parked cars and the breeze between buildings pushing trash through the gutters, but I'm feeling that something's, I don't know—present. Maybe present's the right word but far away. But slowly it gets closer but I don't know how I know and I get this feeling that I need to find Wayne before this whatever gets to me, like, maybe I need to find him to keep him safe.

Or maybe it's the other way around.

Either way I start moving faster and faster until I can't move any faster because my legs get tangled beneath me and my arms can't move my crutches fast enough. Then I hear Wayne up ahead, around the corner, and I get around the corner and the something is so close now but I round the corner and I can hear Wayne's voice coming from inside the next door and it's a laundromat. It's always a laundromat. I duck in and I can feel the thing is right behind me and I'm out of breath and I'm in the laundromat and all of the machines are running and they're those machines that open from the front with the glass windows and I can see inside them and there are pieces of people. There are pieces of people in all of the machines and I start screaming and something hits me in the back of the neck and it's so visceral I can feel it on the back of my actual neck and the black and white checkerboard linoleum rushes up toward my face as I fall forward and I wake up screaming.

Are there others?

Others? Of course there are others. There's always others but they can't be that much different from anyone else's weirdness. No, dreams are weird for everyone I think. I don't think I'm special.

Do you think they dream about you?

Fuck if I know. Maybe. Hopefully.

But then what would they dream about? What, pushing me around the block? Finding me in a ditch? Watching me fuck with an engine for a whole night because I can't sleep but getting nowhere with it? None of those sound much like dreams worth having. And even if they did, what then?

What do you mean?

Well, are they good dreams or are they bad dreams if I'm in them? And are they good or bad just because I'm there no matter what else happens? Do I ruin things just because I have a presence in them, I'm asking.

That sounds unlikely.

Maybe to you, maybe. Maybe to you because you don't know me and I don't know you and you never had to put up with me and all of my shit, y'know—to put up with the let down. That's me. That's the me you don't know so maybe they're different.

But okay, but so what if they were to dream about you, and it was a good dream—what do you think that'd look like?

Rainbows and candy. Enchiladas. Some good blow. I don't know.

No but really. I'm asking.

I dunno—.

[—.]

Have you made enchiladas from scratch before?

No.

You should. That's something you should do. It's medicine, that process, and everyone should do it at least once.

Why?

Just, you know, just the making of the tortillas and feeling the meal between your fingers, beneath your fingernails, pressing them and balancing the sauces, red and green, until it's all just right. Grating the good cheese that you went to buy special. The all-day simmering of the meat that drives you mad because it smells better than anything you've smelled since a happier time, and then the process of assembling. The wrapping, the lining-up and the smothering. The sipping tequila that you pour carefully, that slides like water while the aromas mature, fill the kitchen. That'll get its hands inside you'n press out some crinkles.

Sounds nice.

Yeah, that—. That's what I want, I think. That'd be my good dream.

Who's in it?

All four of us are, but no kids, no parents. The four of us in a kitchen and it's close to sundown and there's candles and a Leo Kottke LP spinning soft in the other room, but just the four of us are there but we're all, I don't know, better. Better than we are.

Better how?

Better like my legs—.

My legs are stout and my arms, they're girthy. I'm grating the cheese, running it over and over the box grater and it's building up inside the box on a plate until the box is filled, and then I lean back in my chair and balance on the back legs and I look around the kitchen.

I look around and I see that Wayne, he's got no need for glasses and he's stirring the sauce with a wooden spoon and his hair's tied back and you can see the slow torsion. You can see that, what do you wanna call it—that choir? That choir of muscles all making up his forearms, all singing songs beneath his skin.

And Conrad, he doesn't look so used up. He's sober. He's a sculpture again and he's rolling out tortillas with the heels of his hands and the dough, it's working with him, it's wanting to become something, too, and it knows it's an honor to be kneaded by those beautiful hands.

And H., she's there. She's humming and setting the table by candlelight and by the dusk pouring in and her hair's braided like it's always braided but there's strands, just a few strands of it that hang wispy by the sides of her face but she doesn't brush them away.

All of us. All of us there in a kitchen preparing a dinner. We don't even need to eat.

APRIL 12, 1994

Wayne:

I have been doing a lot of thinking lately. Lots of stuff I have been putting together about us and our family and some of it that I never figured out until now but stuff that makes sense. And I have been thinking about all this stuff too that I never talked to you about even though I wanted to. I would have told you this in person but that is difficult to do on account of I have no idea where the fuck you are.

But I have come to a good place with myself and with all our shit. Took the day off of work today. Went out to breakfast and ate too much. Went to the park and walked around cleared my head and came back to write you.

It is about Harriet and it is about stuff that I am sure you are still convinced of but I hope you are not. It is about our father about what happened to her really.

I know you think it is his fault or that he did something and that you and me have never found a footing on that notion. And I understand. Really I do. I know that you probably had it hardest out of all of us and that you and he never got along and I know that that was not entirely your fault. He had a hard life. He had a hard life and he took that out on us sometimes because he was just so frustrated with how things panned out for him you know? This is all true. I will concede that much. But he was not the monster you think he is. He had a lot of shit swirling up inside him but he would never do something like that.

And here is where I start telling you stuff you might not know. I think that you probably know that she and Gordon were planning on running away. But there is more that she told me that I do not think you know. Like how she was planning on leaving Gordon. Like how she had more money saved up than anyone could imagine and she was looking for an out some moment she could cut and go. Someplace warm she said.

And then there are the postcards. I have been getting postcards for years and they come from all sorts of places. There is never anything written on the back of them sure but they are postcards of warm places nice scenes happy stuff. And that is just like her you know? That she would send me postcards of stuff I would like but keep things at a distance because she has her own life now. That is what she wanted. You know that. Her own life after her way out.

Kind of funny I think. That you have got your idea of what happened and you are so locked in on it that we cannot even talk about it. And this over someone that does not want to be found someone we have not seen in going on thirty? Thirty years? She could be anywhere. She could be anywhere with her life. She could have done anything and we have no idea.

I fantasize about the things she might have done. Maybe she went to school and maybe she is a professor now with a different name. Maybe she got married had kids. Maybe she has got grandkids even. Dogs. Or maybe a horse ranch. I still remember that she loved horses.

And to think of all those possibilities from where she started. Growing up in Who-Cares Colorado. Tough life under a tougher man who had a tough story of his own. Graduated all that to wander off and do whatever she wanted with no real punishment. From there into selling drugs and from selling drugs to strangers to giving drugs to our brother and then selling them to him. Sticking around just long enough to get things stirred up and then drop off into nothing.

Where does someone go from there? With a life all laid out before you and you do not want any part of where you come from. That is a funny thing. Not wanting an anchor means you can do anything you want and you are not accountable to your past. Shit situation like that would mean that you could make up your past as you go and who would know? Nobody. Nobody would ever know.

I still remember the last thing she said to me. She was heading out of the house a few days before she took off and I was walking in. It was late and she hugged me which was weird because she was never a huggy person but she hugged me and when we let go she told me to take care Conrad. I asked her why and that's all she said. Take care. Take care. Take care. She drove off in a Lincoln I had never seen before. A green one.

I have not seen her since that day but I know she is fine. I think thoughts to her and something always comes back.

c

SIX HUNDRED SEVENTY

This is tape six hundred seventy. Today is 14 September 2006.

What things are best buried with me, do you think, and what things should stay alive after I die? This is something that struggles me.

My previous lives, my childhood—of course these things have never left me, but so much of it all seems so far away on most days. Some days it feels much closer, of course, but most days it feels foreign enough that I wonder whether I am remembering scenes from my life or scenes from a movie that I have not seen in forty years and then, when mulling that perplexion, I am left to puzzle over what the relation of those stories could possibly do for you when I cannot even settle their place in my canon—or whether if, even, those things are canonical at all.

And then the very nature of those stories. Their content. Why—?

I mean, what would you say if I told you that your grandfather once burned the bottoms of my feet with his lighter, made me put my shoes on, and then forbade me to take them off until my soles had healed? Assured me he would do it even worse if I told anyone or if I cried?

What if I told you he did this because I had been doing something as egregious as poking through his toolbox, and then what if he was too drunk to remember his actions, and then what if nobody believed me?

What if, in fact, the next morning he beat me for playing with his lighter, he having found that, somehow, I had managed to scorch the soles of my feet so badly that I needed to go to the hospital?

And what, if anything, would it change if I was seven when this may have happened? What would you say?

What *could* you say, even?

Hm?

What could anyone say?

All I know is that yes, I kept things like this from you because it is I who is fettered to that burden, not you, and I thought that keeping such things secret might be a gift you would never even know that I gave you. That was my choice. Maybe it was the right thing to do, or maybe not. Either way, this was, and remains, my struggle.

That said, I know that my struggle has been hard on you, I know. History knows no innocent bystanders and my struggle—I know that its existence changes everything, and I know that its substance is made of holes, and that these holes, sometimes I feel that they have played perhaps the most significant role in leaving us as we are today: as partialities; as sieves. And then these holes, they seem only to allow more holes to form around them, to allow more history to fall through. Holes begetting holes begetting holes. Watch as my struggle grows.

But sometimes, though—.

Sometimes I wonder if we could maybe have patched us if we—if I—had tried. I was not strong enough, I know, but then I wonder—. I wonder what might have made me strong enough to try.

Like, what if I had run away with the family? What if we had run from him and made new lives together?

What if she had not died, or what if she had died much younger, when life was less brittle?

What if the dynamic had been different—if Roy had not been sick, or if Conrad had been a girl, or if your grandmother died while we were small and he was left alone to care for us, or not?

Him—.

What if I had killed him? Before.

Of course I am unsure what, if any, effect these options might have had, but I do think that I could have been stronger had she lived to see us through, but—.

But she died.

She died, and everything started its spread, and the already-cracked foundation crumbled, and then, a second later it seems, I am sitting in a darkened room, speaking into a microphone, and you are gone, and she is dead, and your mother—. And my brothers are broken, and your grandmother is little more than a stunted idea—was maybe never more than an idea that nobody really entertained.

But then, is that not the genesis of my struggle? The slow snapping of many tensions, each catalyzed by the same absence? Or do you think my struggle is as reflexive as it is inescapable? That is: should her absence be or have been somehow rescinded—would that negate my struggle, or do you think something else would have instigated its life, its maturation, its catastrophic collapse?

Hm?

Hm.

Hft.

[—.]

You know—.

You know, they say that if sun—.

[—.]

They say that if the sun ceased to exist—. Because the speed of light is inviolate, and because gravity, too, is but a function of that form—.

They say that if the sun was *there*, and then the sun was just *gone*—just evanesced from this plane in a blink, that all of the planets would carry on orbiting, being, conversing with the sun until the light died upon them. How Mercury would go blind in one hundred ninety-three seconds, and on that mark, its four-and-a-half billion year gyre would become a vector, and how exactly two minutes forty-eight after Mercury, Venus would find itself on its own lonely and uncharted trajectory, forever launched and linear away from the instant that the darkness came. How on Earth, the light would last until eight minutes, nineteen seconds after death began its throttle across that empty sea.

Eight minutes, nineteen.

For four hundred ninety-nine seconds the sun would keep shining upon us, and we would have no way of knowing that it was over, that the first two of the family were already leaving and we would soon be falling in line and falling away, and that in the minutes and hours to follow, every other body would exhale in ever-distal turn to slouch off alone into the black, each being fated then to float, forever apart, in the dark.

SIFTING THROUGH STATIC
ACT TWO, SCENE TWO:
(OR, DETOURING THROUGH A CUL-DE-SAC)

Across California, east, we speak, across the valley and up the other side.

These mountains, my father says, are much like the ones I used to know. I would disappear for days, he says, and nobody would know where I was, and I would not speak, and up in those mountains, once, I hiked off-trail for hours in a killing heat until I found a tarn with a waterfall. I stripped naked and dove from a low cliff that hung out almost to the middle, but I didn't think about that the water must be snowmelt until between when I jumped and when I struck the surface.

Oh, I thought midair.

Oh no.

And my body went beneath, and an impossible cold coiled itself about me and I broke the surface flailing, sucking air, sucking cold water into my throat and thrashing back against death's gelid grasp.

Oh no oh no, and I whipped my head in search of shore, but my glasses were in my left boot, over there, or over there, or wherever it was that my boots were basking.

Oh no no no and my mind went a great, rabid animal, but part of it didn't go, no, part of it stayed clear, and soft, and quiet, and there, in the thrashing, we spoke, myself and I, and myself asked me how long I thought it would be before the body was found.

Will it be found?

Will something eat our blue body?

That would be nice, we thought. To be used. To go unwasted.

But I didn't die that day, Wayne says. I found the shore or the shore found me, I don't know, but I didn't die. I seized on twigs and mud in a violence of shivers beside the jeans that I'd folded so neatly, clutching my clean shirt to my muddy chest crying, feeling small.

But we're not going through Reno, my father says, We'll take 659 South before Sparks and hook into 395. 395 can get us to 431 and then 267 can get us back to 80.

I assume we're bound for Lake Tahoe, but he doesn't even stop for gas in Tahoe and he won't tell me why we've wasted half a day.

ROY/LONGMONT, CO/2007-07-24
13:03:08—13:10:49

She dated a lot. Lots of guys coming through, sometimes three in a week and even a girl or two thrown in for good measure. Dad never liked them, any of them, so he avoided them, scowled over the top of his newspaper, stayed mean. But some of them were decent.

How'd that go?

Lots of guys'd be peeved by that but in that quiet, fearful sort of way that first-visit boyfriends tend to be, but some of them would just keep talking at him being either oblivious or unafraid, I still can't decide which. I do wonder if he respected those ones for that.

That doesn't sound much his style.

You'd think not, but he was a small man inside. Inside he was small which was why the outside was so vicious—to protect the delicate bits. Small men are all reverence and fear when confronted with confidence, real or assumed, and then after that it's all how prickly their barbs are, how it'll go from there. A few of those boys were confident, and there's no way that didn't resonate with him. Somewhere in there it had to.

You think?

Well but I mean it's like that for everyone, right? How you meet someone and they're everything how you'd like to be when they're talking to folks they don't know. No bashfulness, no cocking around, just, *Hey I like that painting, reminds me of Montauk*, or, *Dude, looks like you banged up your hand pretty good, how'd that happen?* That sort of stuff all before the coat's even come off, and none of it ever rubbing you like prying nor invasive or nothing, just genuine, friendly curiosity. Makes it so much harder to dislike a new boyfriend on principle. And that, I think, is something you've gotta respect.

How'd that affect you?

What?

I mean him being unsettled by a boyfriend. I can't imagine that'd go over well.

Well on that you'd be right. Mostly it didn't. Mostly he'd sit there and steam and then he'd take it out on us later but I don't think he'd ever admit to that directly, because, of course, he was never wrong. But yeah, you could tell. You could always tell.

How?

Like there'd be little things that'd set him off that were already there, but now, after the new guy, those infractions'd become some new kinda treason.

I don't follow.

I mean like he'd see a painting hanging crooked, or he'd see a hamper that'd gotten all the way full before someone started a load. You know. Important, pound-your-family type shit.

What'd Harriet think of this?

Of the beatings?

Of his attitude over these boyfriends.

Oh. Well you know—.

You know I go back and forth on that.

Part of me thinks that she brought these guys in out of spite—the smarter, confidenter ones, just to see how he'd handle it and what he'd do, and then she'd get bored with them or whatever and there'd be someone new there a few days later and he'd mock the new one because he'd be dumb and weak, and then she'd be bored with that one too, and then there'd be another. And those boring ones went off without a hitch and life would continue on as it does. But then I suppose she'd be bored with the boring and she'd pull in someone unsettling just to watch how his muscles tense. Sort of a dance if you think about it. But it's hard to not be irked when everyone knows that those two were dancing and meanwhile we're the fucking floor. Still, it was fun to watch him squirm.

But she never kept anyone around? Just these flings?

Oh, she was just bored a lot. One of the things I remember about her was she was always looking for something better to do. You could see it on her face, how she was half here, half somewhere else. So for most of the time, yeah, it was just these flings or whatever you want to call them. But then, of course, there was Gordon.

You know him, right?

You've told me stories about him yourself.

Mm.

Well, yes. Gordon. She had this long string of guys coming and going but then when Gordon slipped into town she took interest, but that sort of distant interest you keep with someone while you're still trampolining around with lesser fodder. Something to look forward to, someday, maybe. And I don't know much about him or what he was doing before or since, but you could tell he was into her, too, and that it was only a matter of time before they got together. An inevitability, not a possibility.

Anyway, they got together later. Toward the end. And it didn't go over well.

Meaning?

Meaning Dad was less than pleased and he took it out on us, on all of us, but where it'd usually just be a one-and-done sort of deal with the boring boyfriends, this time it was unending. To the point where we were all afraid, I remember. For the first time really, truly afraid of the man and what he might do.

And the drinking. Jesus, the drinking—.

He was drinking more and more and she was never around, but when she was it was a special kinda war.

So what happened?

Hm?

What happened? With the war?

What about it?

I don't know. Anything. How'd it end?

Oh.

One day she was gone. No note, no phone call—just gone. And six weeks later, Dad was dead.

MAY 17, 1987

Hey Wayne so I am driving again. Nobody else was hiring and my old boss moved companies but he remembered me so I am driving again even though I cannot stand it but I need the money. But I do not need money from you or anything. I have no idea why I wrote that.

Man I really wish I had your number right about now but these letters are still the best I can do, and I have no idea why I am writing them after the last bundle came back R.T.S. Makes me think that the other bundles never got to you either. But whatever. I wish I had your number.

Strangest thing. Yesterday I was pulling out of Fresno and just off of 5 there is this diner I love and whenever I am running through the area I always try to stop there because the owner is Millie and Millie is the kind of lady who makes you want to eat at her restaurant. Anyways I walk in and I go sit at my spot at the counter and I am chomping my burger and shoving fries and I am just sort of zoned out you know how you zone out after a long day and I hear this voice next to me and it is a voice that I recognize and he orders a coffee and a short-stack. Voice snaps me out and I am trying to figure where I know it from as I look over and it takes me a second but fuck me if it is Gordon. I swear. Gordon in the flesh.

He looked worse Wayne. So much worse than I remember and he had so many tattoos and I do not remember him having any before but maybe he did. My jaw drops and my mouth is still full but I cannot help from saying holy shit man Gordon? He did not hear me or something so I said his name again but he still did not hear me so I tap him on the arm and he looks over at me and he looks so tired.

He says who are you? but in a bad way like they do in the movies and so I try to swallow and I try to explain. So I get my bite down and I tell him Gordon man Colorado and I am Conrad and you and my brother Wayne man you guys were pals remember me? He looks at me for that extra beat before he says oh hey and that beat makes me think he did not remember me at all.

Whether he did or not I play along and I give him the highlights from the last what fifteen years? And I guess he is sort of interested or at least seems it but when I ask him what he has been up to it gets weird. He waits so long before he speaks that his pancakes come and he has already gotten a coffee refill and I have gone back to my burger because it is so awkward and he has cutting his pancakes and he says L.A. Been so long it startles me but I ask him about what he has been doing in L.A. and he says jobs. What kind of jobs? I ask him but he just goes back to his food and does not answer. I said a few more little things small questions but he just sort of grunted at them or answered with a yes or a no and after a couple minutes I got the message. I told him it was good to see him when I got up to pay my tab but he did not say anything to that either.

I do not really know what to make of this. I wonder if he would have acted any different if you were there with me or instead of me because I am still not convinced that he actually remembered who I was. But Wayne he looked so used up. He looked like how guys used to look like back in the shit when they been out for too long that tired around their eyes that looks like it will not ever sleep off. And the tattoos. Jesus his arms and his hands and letters on his fingers and I saw one creeping up his neck and I can only imagine what is going on across his back and his chest. They were not fancy tattoos.

Anyway I just felt like I wanted to talk to you and I have not written in I do not know how long. Too long. And I thought you would like to know that he is alive but maybe you still talk to him but I know he left and I certainly did not see him ever coming back. I guess seeing him just sort of got me thinking about shit how people come and go how even some of the really good ones that you want to stay how sometimes they still end up going and sometimes you never see them again. But sometimes you do see them again. Sometimes it just takes a while but they come back one day or maybe they plop down next to you at a diner and you pick it up like old times like they never left like they were always there the whole time.

Something to think about. Wherever you are.

Conrad

SIX HUNDRED SEVENTY-FOUR

I wonder what you remember.

Do you remember my apartments? My many apartments? If I asked you, I wonder how many you would tell me you think we lived in.

Three?

Five?

More?

What if I told you that it was nine, and what if even that was a lie? This is something that I spend time thinking about.

There are other things I wonder. Like, who do you remember from those early years? My friend Victor? Victor, if you remember, we spent a great deal of time with. He and his wife would make you spaghetti and you would play with their dogs, German shepherds, and after dinner they would give the plates to the dogs to lick clean before putting in the dishwasher and you thought this was the funniest thing. Victor was a good man but his wife, she turned out to be too Christian—or rather, you and I were not Christian enough or at all—and she compelled him to stop seeing us, and he did. I think I told you that he moved, and I think I did that because I thought that seemed an easier explanation for a kindergartner or however old you were. But I regret this decision.

And then I wonder if you remember Gordon. Or, I know that you remember him, but I wonder what of him you still recall, what things you may have deduced and what other things you still do not know. I know that I have told you stories but those stories have always been attenuated, for better or worse, how even the things we did with him I spun, and now—. Now I find myself regretting this, too.

Like the time we had to pick him up from the big gym, I told you. You were three. Maybe you figured it out or maybe this is something you never remembered at all, but the truth is that he had been drunk, and I had to pick him up in front of the jail after he had slept it off. But he was happy to see you, Gordon was, and we went for waffles on the way home.

Or maybe you remember the day when we dropped by his apartment because we were in the neighborhood, and we saw his Harley on the curb but he would not answer the door, so I pushed you through a window to unlock the door, and we found him on the couch, and I told you to try your hardest to wake him up while I called the doctor because Gordon took some bad medicine and he was very sleepy. Maybe you put that one together on your own, but maybe I should have told you later just how close he came.

Gordon—.

How I told you that he was always away for work, popping in for a few weeks or a few months but then he would have to leave, and how that went on and on until he left on a Sunday and he never came back—. How that was only partly a lie.

Gordon—.

How he had a hard life and was often in a bad way, and how his problems started young. At fifteen he got drunk, stole a pickup truck, crashed it, and paralyzed another boy, and he served three years in juvenile prison in Canada for that, I think.

How other things happened during the first stretch that I knew him, and then he went away, and how we would then go months or even years, sometimes, without so much as a call. And then how he showed up unannounced on a Tuesday to apply for a job at a factory I was managing, and I hired him, no questions, though the years had been gnashing on him hard. But how he was never late, not once, while we worked there.

And how we went fishing on a Saturday in May of 1985 and caught nothing, and how his call woke me the next day before dawn. How he just wanted to say thanks for all the times we went fishing. How we both understood his tacit goodbye.

Gordon—.

How I never asked him about Harriet, really, because I was afraid of what he would say, so I said nothing. And how I regret that. Or how I wish so much that I could just talk to him now, but—.

I may never be able to tell you directly, but I saw someone today, a man I have worked with sporadically for twenty years but whom I had not seen in five, and we were catching up, and on a whim I asked if he had lately heard anything about Gordon, where he was, how he was doing, because I knew that Gordon and his heavies had once operated as something like a collections agency for the man's business, and, crestfallen, the man furrowed and informed me of what he assumed I had heard: that Gordon's body was found in an alley in 1999.

Gordon—.

How hundreds of dollars were left in his pockets to show that the theft of him was no robbery. How his switchblade was missing and how not all of the blood there was his, but how there must have been enough men leftover to duct tape his wrists. How they took off his boots and then laced them up empty, and how neatly they placed them beside where he knelt, and how he remarked to me once how unearthly it felt to feel perfectly certain that what weapon would kill him had already been made like a child, he went on, how for most of your life it will subsume your life, but you never will meet it until it arrives, but that weapon, Wayne, wanders toward me today, as we sit here, as we speak, and there will be no after, but before is right here and before is right now, and after comes later, comes after today, and how I sobbed in the restroom after I was told, and how I wish I could have told you that I wept and why but why are these the things that I never say?

SIFTING THROUGH STATIC
ACT TWO, SCENE THREE:
(OR, THE CAUSAL DESPONDENCE
OF PRESUMED CONNECTION)

Our Nevada is the roads that were paved and forgotten, where things slither their sleep across rocks and greasewood spreads to stretch for sky.

Wayne stops the car at high noon and tells me to get out, and we get out. The doors still open, he walks to the road's center and takes off his shirt and bunches it for a pillow and makes to lie across the yellow paint that splits the road and I take off my shirt and bunch it and lie next to him and the asphalt is warm, awake, and warm but not hot like it should be and we'll watch clouds until we're done watching clouds, and he points to the clouds and finds shapes in the clouds and breathes stories enough to score the full firmament and nobody knows that this ever happened. He stands and returns, and I stand and return, and my father and I drive on without needing to speak.

Our map does all the speaking at a hundred miles an hour. Blue highways vein themselves to show we're heading back, heading east, heading back to the center. I hold up the map to see his face through the paper.

This is the face of a different man.

This man knows nothing of the three-job years, or the ninety-hour weeks, or the months when dinner will be a bag of oranges because oranges are six cents cheaper than apples. This man's hair is long. This man still sings.

Your brothers are alive.

He nods, and he half-smiles, and I think for a moment that we might have an understanding.

They haven't been buried yet, either.

He nods, and he half-smiles, and I know at that moment that we've no understanding at all.

They're no better than you. They're alive and you're alive and they're no better than you and I know.

I know what happened. I know.

But nothing comes back, and I'm done speaking. And miles always pass, here.

ROY/LONGMONT, CO/2007-07-24
14:02:31—14:12:40

We did a lot of stupid shit as kids. More than most, probly, and some of the stuff—Jesus. Even thinking about some of it gets my palms a bit sweaty.

Like what?

Well there's the obvious stuff, right, the kid stuff that everyone enjoys at least once. There's that.

Like what?

You know. The dabbling in arson. The treehouses that you have to get into by standing one foot in a bucket with a rope tossed over a branch and your brothers have to hoist you up thirty feet. Sensible shit.

Did you guys ever get caught?

For what, the arson?

For any of it.

What kid doesn't?

You get into much trouble?

Well sometimes, sure. Most times not, but sometimes, yes. But it wasn't always a bad thing.

Meaning?

Meaning sometimes getting caught was a blessing, I think, thinking back on some of the shit we were up to. Sometimes getting caught and punished was better than the consequences that might've come had some of that shit gone bad.

Example?

Well like so I know I don't have much on record when it comes to Harriet, but I'll always remember there was this one afternoon she took all three of us way out of town, way past asphalt in this beat up Buick that barely ran.

She had a car?

Had? Or owned?

What's the difference?

Well the Buick was stolen's the difference. I don't know from where.

Oh.

Plus she was only fourteen, maybe, to boot.

And none of you minded?

Didn't seem to bother her, so why should I worry?

But anyway, she took us way into the boonies and stopped the car near an old cattle fence and we got out, and she went back to the trunk and pulled out this bundled-up something about as tall as I was but thin enough it could've been a broom, and we followed her under the fence and into the field and she dropped it at no particularly important or special looking spot and started unwrapping it and we all stood and watched.

What was it?

I think it was Wayne who said what it was first, but he did it by asking where she got it, not asking what it was.

Where'd you get a longbow? Wayne asks her. But she never was good at answering questions.

A bow?

Mm. Coupla seconds and she had it levered behind her leg and strung up like it was something she'd done a thousand times before and then she'd stabbed maybe half a dozen arrows into the dirt and she was palming the bow by the top nock and twirling it on the ground, stood up between her palm and the ground, and she was chewing her lip and scanning the horizon for something to shoot, but there was nothing to shoot.

It was Wayne said he could set up some targets from some of the old hunks of fence lying around, and she agreed, and so he and Con set up the world's crudest range, marked out at maybe fifteen and thirty yards, give or take. And then the lesson began.

She'd stand with us, each of us, behind us in turn and we'd draw back as best as we were able and she'd help us hold it steady and she'd help me draw it back on account of my arms. One guy'd shoot until he's out of arrows, and then the other two would go hunt and fetch for the most of them that'd miss the target entirely, and then it'd be someone else's turn.

How'd you do?

Couldn't even work the thing on my own, but miserable. We must have been out there an hour or two but there wasn't one of us was any good. At least not compared to her.

Oh?

Yeah, when all of our forearms were tore up good from the string and we'd lost interest, that's when she took the thing up, and Jesus—as far away as we'd been standing, she could've been hammering nails into that fencewood from half again the distance, I think.

Thock.

Thock.

Thock.

Arrow after arrow, and we just sat there in awe.

So this was a hobby of hers.

If it was, she never told us about it. But it wouldn't surprise me, how much about her we don't really know.

But anyway, we sat out there and watched her until the magic wore off and we started getting bored, and I suppose she could tell that we were getting bored because she asked us if we wanted to see something cool, and we said yeah, and she told us to sit and she walked from us with all of the arrows to maybe fifteen, twenty yards away from the targets.

So then we're sitting, waiting, wondering what's next. She picks a tuft of grass and tosses it to mark the wind. Then she nocks one, aims it almost straight up ninety and pulls back full.

Thwip.

And we watch it go up until we can't even see it anymore and she's just standing there looking straight up with the bow dropped by her side. Just watching, watching. I can't see it anymore, but then I hear it, a hiss quicker than you could believe and then a subtle thud. Arrow's buried halfway up the shaft not fifty feet from where she stands. And before I can even register the shock she's got another one loaded up.

Thwip.

Watch. Watch—.

Hissthud, but this one's closer, maybe thirty feet. I remember saying: Um. But then she's got another one gone just as fast as she can nock and loose. This one's maybe twelve, fifteen feet. And then she's aiming again, but this time with purpose, right, like she's actually got a bead on a cloud, and I say Hey?—and as I speak, she lets fly.

I've still got a picture of her in my head just then, head back and the wind's caught her hair and her dress just a bit, and her eyes are closed, and she's not smiling but she's not frowning and her arms are relaxed and her heels are together, and her eyes are closed—.

—And?

Five feet. If that.

The fiberglass quivers until it deadens and the fletching—I remember the fletching. It's two yellows and a red on the fins. And we're sitting there, and we don't know what to make of this, and we don't say anything.

She opens her eyes, tugs it out of the ground and starts off for the other arrows and it's time to go. She drops us back at home and drives off, and she walks through the front door some hours after that. Dad tells her she's late for dinner but she sits quiet and she pays him no mind.

NOVEMBER 11, 1980

Dear Wayne:

So you got married. Wonderful. I know you did not want me at your wedding. I could tell. I know I wasn't invited and I know that that was no accident but I had to go. I had to. Sorry. Thanks for not being mad.

You were not mad were you? It was hard to tell with how little it seemed like you actually saw me. I was worried you were mad because I know your face and it seemed like you were when we made eye contact that once. But then it was like you saw right past me like I was glass and then you were shaking hands with other people and you never looked at me again. So I hope you were not mad.

Your wife is pretty. Someone told me her name but it turned into kind of an embarrassing situation for me when they followed up by asking me how I know you two. I thought about lying but I did not. Maybe I should have. Oh well. I am happy you found someone.

Ceremony was nice. I did not expect that you'd have it done up Catholic but then maybe it is her family calling the shots on that one. Unless you came back to the church? More surprising things have happened I suppose. But it was a nice ceremony and more people there than I was expecting. I looked for Roy but I didn't see him. Cake was good.

I am having trouble writing today. I know what I feel like saying but the words are coming out sort of dead on the page here as I type. Do you ever feel like that? Like there is no juice in your words? That is how I feel. Like my fingers are running on fumes. Maybe I am just distracted.

Aside from wanting to tell you how nice it was to see you there and how nice the ceremony was I guess I just wished that there could have been more of our family there you know? Roy. Mom. You know the rest. I noticed them gone like there were all these holes that I saw there but not exactly like that. It is hard to describe. I guess I just miss them.

I pretended like they were there. I closed my eyes while I was there and tried to imagine what it would have been like to see them there at the reception.

Roy would be in the back sitting in his chair or leaning up against the wall depending on his legs that day with a drink in one hand and a Camel hanging off his lip. He would be there with strangers and they would be bullshitting about something cool and I would wave and he would lift his glass at me.

Mom would buzzing around in the back somewhere asking if anyone needed food or napkins or a new drink. Keeping herself too busy. You know how she keeps too busy to really see what was going on but that's just her you know how she enjoys things. Would have been one less caterer to hire too.

I will not talk about Dad and what he looks like there. I will not bother you with that.

And I guess most of all I missed H. It has been so long though. I cannot help but think that she would have given a badass speech though you know? Something badass. Something that really sums you up in all that you are. Blasts away the dirt. She would have talked about the kind of person you are how you are creative and how you are stubborn but she would have painted that in a good way. Maybe not the same way that I would have. But good. Faithful. Maybe she would have called you faithful past reason. I do not know.

I guess at the end of this I just wanted to take the time to tell you that I am proud of you and I love you and I am happy for you and your life and I hope it is better. I hope it is better now than it was when we were young. I have been thinking more about that lately and I guess the hindsight thing is picking up more and more pieces of just why you left and why you stayed gone but maybe I am just lonely.

Anyway I am proud of you and I am happy for you and I miss you and I love you. I wish you two long and happy lives and a bunch of kids if you want them and none if you do not want them.

Also I got you a dog but I did not name it. It is a beagle. I left it under the gift table the crate labeled BEAGLE.

Conrad

SIX HUNDRED SEVENTY-NINE

I wished him dead for what he did to her. To us. For all the years of torment, for all the ways he broke me inside. For all of the things that I was never able to do for you as a father because I never knew how, and for the fact that she never had a chance. For being the kind of person he was, I wished him dead every. Single. Day.

And then it happened. Then he was gone, and it was over. The police came by in the morning, early, because it happened at night. They pulled your grandmother outside on the porch and told her, and she said, Oh, and then she said nothing while the policeman stood there holding his cap, and then she said, But I just made breakfast. He always calls before he misses breakfast and I already cooked the eggs.

I had been awake, and I came out of my room and smelled the coffee and ham, and I heard the officer say: Miss? as she shuffled back inside looking vacant, wringing her hands.

The officer saw me and asked me if I had overheard them, and I told him I knew. He apologized and asked if I would like him to come in and sit for a while. No, I told him, we are fine.

The accident—.

The accident had been horrific, but from the outset, it seemed like the sort of accident that, if you wanted to, you could call less than an accident. Certain aspects of it, certain things—it was like trying to use a metric socket on an imperial bolt how things were so very close to connecting, but never quite could.

The story was, as best as the police could figure, that he was drunk and he veered off the road, plowed through a fence and smashed into a telephone pole at better than sixty. There was no seatbelt in his car, but he was not the sort that would have worn one even if it had been an option, and when he hit the pole, several things happened in synchrony.

First, his body shot forward and his hairline, more or less, broke mostly through the windshield and his face was birthed partly through that glass until its sharp halo came to rest where the bridge of his nose used to be. Both of his eyeballs ruptured and dribbled their juices down onto the dashboard. The crown of his head had lost its curve.

Second, the steering column, non-collapsible, was forced into the passenger compartment at the moment of impact, and the steering wheel pinned his torso to the roof of the car, bowing the roof up cartoonishly in the shape of his form. His ribs and his lungs were slurried. His heart was spread back across the inside of his spine.

He might have lived just long enough to feel it, they say. Maybe—.

Nobody knows for sure, but I will admit that I often fantasize about how it could have been done. He was a drunk, and the story where he accidentally runs into a telephone pole is plausible, but also, anyone can see that that would have been a great cover if someone wanted him dead, and this want was not an uncommon sentiment amongst the populous. Everyone had reasons.

An example: as I have said, I spent most of my childhood looking through things that I was told not to look through, and I knew every stash that your grandfather kept, even the ones he was sure nobody could ever find. I found money. I found letters and folders full of documents he probably should have burned, and when I was nine I found an orange cigar box filled with photographs beneath the spare tire in Edsel's trunk, perhaps a dozen pictures. All of them were photographs of nude women, but eight of them were of the same woman. She had dark hair. She had kind eyes. She wore a wedding band.

I think it plausible that maybe this woman was the wife of someone important, because after he died, the accident file was closed within a day, and his car, I heard, was crushed within two. And this was strange. Then, like today, it was strange for a death's case to be closed so quickly when there were parts of the story that never quite added up—how some of his possessions were missing from the scene, and how unusually private the investigation seemed, how the police maintained that the investigation was sensitive and there was only a small blurb about the crash in the paper. Then they called it an accident, closed the case, and destroyed all of the evidence.

Was she the wife of a police officer? Perhaps. That picture would fit the frame. Or maybe this woman had some other relationship with law enforcement, or maybe the cops thought that he had done enough damage to our family and, charitably, wanted to help us get past it without any other difficult questions or painful discoveries. Or maybe something else. Who knows.

All I know is that the wishing part of me often fantasized about his final night, assembled a story about how it would have had to have happened if it was not accidental after all.

One angry cop, I thought, never seemed like it would have been enough. The road home was dark, yes, but it was entirely straight where he wrecked, and in all the years he had been driving home from bars, he never once so much as scratched the paint on his vehicle or anyone else's. He was a kind of drunk-driving savant—even better, it seemed, behind the wheel when he was hardly able to stand. But so a straight road like that, and the size of that car, I figured that you would probably need two guys and two cars to get it done.

These two guys would have had to have stalked him to Pawnee's, the bar where he spent the latest nights, and they would have had to sit outside and wait for them to kick him out at closing. From there he would have gotten into his car and commenced the lurching home, and the two cars would have followed him in line, the front one riding his bumper, aggravating him and keeping his speed up. He would have tried to pull over to let them pass, but they could sit behind him as he tried, swerving when he swerved, accelerating when he tried to brake until, eventually, he would anger and floor it, resolve to leave the hooligans safely behind, and this is when the second car would swing out into the empty, oncoming lane.

That driver would pull up next to him to look him in the eye. His face would be twisted up with anger and his eyes would dart back and forth between the driver's and the road in front of him.

The driver on his side spots the telephone pole and pulls the gun.

He sees the gun and the anger drains from his face at the sight of the iron through the dark. His eyes widen. He whips the wheel over to the right, not realizing in his drunkenness that there is no road remaining beside him. He grips the wheel and braces as the tires leave the asphalt.

The noise sounds like a washing machine dropped from the tenth floor, and then the cloud of dust, and then the quiet.

The two cars stop, then reverse down the shoulder, then stop again near the ruin.

One driver approaches on foot, finds him gurgling. Maybe that driver says some words to him as he takes a few valuables—takes his clip of keys, his belt buckle, maybe takes his lighter and his flask—just enough missing so as not to pique the interest of the police, just enough to pawn without drawing too much attention. Or maybe just to keep. To remember.

Then that driver returns to his idling car, and the other driver looks out the window to the first, but says nothing. The first shuts his drivers' door and purrs off, and the second car slips behind to follow.

And no one is there when he goes.

SIFTING THROUGH STATIC
ACT TWO, SCENE FOUR:
(OR, THE INDELIBLE AFFECT
OF WEEK-TO-WEEK WALLS)

My father speaks just before Utah.

He says, Remember, remember when we would drive around the block until you fell asleep? Remember, remember.

Remember when Gordon moved apartments and the lowlives he loved came to help him, too, and you threw couch cushions down to them from the balcony while a wraith named Rodney rattled apart at the stove. How Rodney was a week sober and slipping, but how Gordon gave him small jobs, like making hot dogs for the kid, and don't fuck it up, man, you're done fucking up, remember? Remember that you'll forget that this ever happened until May of '03, when you'll happen past that balcony on a sunny day and you'll see yourself throwing couch cushions down to casehardened men. You'll remember Gordon and how he was kind. You'll remember how much I miss him.

I remember, I remember.

Do you?

I do.

What do you remember?

I remember your twelfth apartment, the one with more windowbars than furniture. I remember how a troupe of dusty children would ask if I could come play in the dirt. I remember you'd tell them I couldn't play. I remember your shame.

I was ashamed.

It's okay.

Was it?

It's okay. It was nobody's fault, and it's okay.

It was my father's fault.

Why?

My father gave me shame.

You're wrong. He never knew any better or he wasn't as strong as you were, who cares, but either way, you're wrong. He gave you nothing.

Certain things must be given.

You're wrong.

ROY/LONGMONT, CO/2007-07-24
16:42:18—16:49:44

To be perfectly honest I don't remember her much. Bits and pieces. Stuff that doesn't really matter, I don't think.

Like what?

What—what I remember?

Yeah.

Well I dunno. Little stuff. Like how she wore her hair. How she'd braid it. Her dresses that she wore with the flower prints she liked, and how she wouldn't care when she got paint on them. How I only remember her reading one book over and over, so much that the cover was smudged up where she'd hold it and the edges of the pages were mushed and there's so many dog-ears that they couldn't possibly be useful.

What book was it?

Why's it matter?

Why shouldn't it?

I dunno. What if it doesn't?

What, you don't think it does?

I don't know.

Well what, then?

—It was Homer. *The Iliad.* But just it seems so useless, you know? Those details? Doesn't it?

Why? What makes you think so?

Because it's just debris. It's just debris and there's other stuff I'd rather have taking up the headspace, I think.

Like what?

Like anything.

Anything? But you have something. A few things, even. Seems to me that that's something, at least, and there's lots of people that've got none of that at all.

Yeah but I don't care about lots of people, though.

No?

No. Well—I mean I'm as selfless as the next guy when it comes to my time, my money, all of that, right? But this is different. My memory—my memories of her, of my brothers, of that life I used to have—.

No, I won't apologize for my attitude regarding any of that.

But what about those details, though? You're saying they don't matter?

But why should they? is what I'm asking you. What's it matter what dresses she wore or what book she read?

You don't think you're, I don't know, losing her? By forsaking those things?

Who's saying she's lost?

Well you, sort of. If you really mean what you're saying right now.

How's that?

That, what'd you call it—debris? Those details? That's all a person is, really. A person's just a construction of details.

But is that really so surprising?

Is what so surprising?

That I feel this way.

I mean—yeah.

Well what about—.

Well I mean, shit, I remember, vaguely, Thanksgiving dinner in 1971, and the next clear memory that I can definitely pin down to a definitely specific date isn't 'til '73. And there's tons of that scatter goin' all the way back as far as I can remember—some small, some bigger. Like how our dog lived to be sixteen but I can't remember his name—Peanut? Peaches? Pee-something. Or Wayne's eyes. Are they green? I'm pretty sure they're green, but, I mean, what's that say about me that I'm only pretty sure about something like that, now?

Conrad's are green.

Well—. Well whatever, I guess. But see?

See what?

That it's not like it's entirely by choice, right, is what I'm saying—how I tend to feel about the details, I mean. Because part of it's that my head's probly a bit scrambled after so long on the bottom, I think, right? But so put yourself in this chair. Put yourself on this side of the table and try to tell me if you didn't keep distance from your wanting of those details that it wouldn't get unbearable, is what I'm saying.

Do you have a photo?

Of who? Of her?

Mm.

Not anymore. But I don't want one, either. I don't want to deal with things not lining up, my head and some photo.

I might be able to dig one up if you— .

No. Don't do that. Don't ever do that to me. I couldn't take that. She looks just how I remember her from what little pieces I've got and that's fine. Really, it's fine.

Why?

Why?

Why?

Well so let's put it this way—what if you woke up tomorrow and your parents said you were adopted, hm? How would that feel, do you think? To have something broke from the way you've known it all along.

I don't know. I don't know that I'd feel particularly strongly about it.

Bullshit.

Well I don't know that I wouldn't, either.

Well but so what I'm saying's that at a certain point it's better just to leave things as they are, to hush the wonder and let it all be, I mean—.

Y'know, I see you're confused, but that's okay, it's fine. It's okay for this to all to sound foreign. You don't know what it's like to have someone leave without saying goodbye, to be there and then to, just—not. You don't know what that's like at all and it's fine.

Says who? And either way, why couldn't I know what that's like?

Because it's something can't be taught. And I don't really know you, so maybe you already know what I'm talking about. Or your own version. But basically you're asking why it matters, and if you're asking, then you don't know.

I never asked why it mattered.

Are you so sure about that?

Well what would you ask her if you could?

—What?

If she were sitting right here. What would you ask her?

Nothing I'd feel like sharing with you, I can tell you that much.

Okay. Well what do you remember of her, then? Just of her.

Didn't we just go over that? And why the fuck do you care?

It's something I've been thinking about.

What, memory? What people remember?

Well that, but more I meant if they were to appear across the table from you as they were, as they are, whichever—if that happened and if you could speak to them again—what would you tell them you remembered?

Well—.

Well I dunno.

I dunno, I guess I'd say I remember, like, some of the little things like I've already told you.

What else?

And other shit I won't tell you.

Why?

Because those things are mine. Those things are not for you.

Okay. So what else, then? That you can share.

Well, how she wasn't around much even before she got old enough that she could make it on her own. There's that. Or how once she could hold down a job and could buy her own groceries and could buy—. Well, could buy anything else that she'd need. But how once that happened she cut a lot of ties, but she never got estranged from us, I remember that very clearly, that she never felt estranged.

But she was distant.

It was more like she was around, but almost like a roommate is around but never like a sister, like how there's a space around a roommate that never quite gets breached no matter how long they're around, and then once you someday move, or maybe they do, then that person's gone after a handshake or a hug. Forever. Goodbye.

What else?

I dunno.

[—.]

There's the way she left. There's that. I'd tell her how I remembered that.

What about it?

The jolt of it. The doubt. The doubt that still hangs over the whole mess.

What do you mean?

The wonder of where she went. The wonder of whether she went anywhere at all.

FEBRUARY 12, 1991

Wayne:

So I was thinking today about what happened when you left that day on that day that you left town and did not come back.

Mom must have gotten home as you were leaving and she must have seen you with that big rucksack and asked what you were doing and in my version you say that you are going away and I say my version because she never told me how it started and Roy is fuzzy on the whole thing but I am smart enough to put it together. Mom told me you two argued and she started slapping you when you walked right by her but the slapping did not stop you so she started hitting but you kept walking. My version says you kept telling her was that you were going away away away away you were going away and she could not make you stay because that sounds just like you.

So she keeps telling you that you had to stay because your brothers needed you and she needed you and where the fuck were you going she was worried and all this while she is hitting you and hitting you. Then you tell her you're going away and that you are tired and not to worry about you because you had made it this far and she never kept you safe anyway. That part she did tell me so I know that that part happened.

Then maybe she is saying what the fuck do you mean who do you think you are where the fuck are you going? All while she is hitting you and hitting you. Slap slap punch punch punch and you just take it and take it and keep walking through her. Punch. Punch. Punch. Punch. Until you finally get fed up because I guess anyone would or maybe you just needed to exclamation point your point who knows. But either case you stop walking and she keeps at it punch punch punch punch and then that is when the magic happens. That is when you finally hit her back. Hard. Laid her out right there in the driveway and you just got in your car and leave. Leave both of them each in their own little pile and drive off like fucking Eastwood into the sunset.

Brother I admire you. I cannot help but think anyone would admire you. I have no idea what it was that Roy did to set you off but you certainly made your point. You certainly stuck it to them and took off on your own like you always wanted to do. I wish I could do that. See something that I want and just take it like that. Ball it up in a fist and then go.

But anyway here I am and there you are. Wherever you are. And I no longer blame you. Some days I do but today I do not. Hell I would have liked to leave too but someone had to stay.

Mom is worse. She is slower and she is getting old. Someday she will be gone and I wonder if you will come back when we bury her. Roy is gone too but I still hear from him sometimes but who knows if he is ever really going to come back or if he will even make it at all. I hope he does but who knows. Maybe I will call you when they find him someday. Oh wait! Ha Ha!

You know people ask me why I stuck around and why I blow paychecks on plane tickets back here when there is nothing really here for me at all anymore. It is easy enough for me to tell them that it is for Mom because someone has got to look out for her and come keep her company from time to time. But that is not why I come back.

You know I still remember the last thing she said to me. Not Mom. I still remember she was heading out of the house a few days before she took off and I was walking in. It was late and she hugged me which was weird because she was never a huggy person but she hugged me and when we let go she told me take care Conrad. I asked her why and that is all she said. Take care. Then she drove off in a Lincoln I never seen before. A green one.

So truth be told I come back hoping to find a note on the back door. I hope that I will get in late one night after Mom's asleep and I will come to the back and when I go to unlock the door there will be a note on the door from Harriet and it will say where she is staying and I will drive over there and we will go out for waffles. Stupid as it sounds that is part of the reason I keep going back because I don't really have much else to hope for. There's so much uncertainty out there and so much that seems so already decided but I mean I just think there is a few things out there that could still surprise me and she's one of them. She is why I go back.

I thought about ending the letter right there but I went to bed before I took it out of the typewriter. I got up this morning and it was still in there and I reread it and I would like to add something.

You. If I came back one night late and I found a note on the door and it was in your handwriting I would go meet you for waffles. I would go meet you in a second and I would buy you waffles. I was so angry at you last night but then I had a dream and I do not know if it was just because I wrote about eating with our sister right before bed but in my dream you were at the diner I go to some mornings when I am back here but I did not recognize you from the back because you were sitting at the counter. I went to my usual seat which was next to where you were sitting and there you were sipping coffee and reading one of those old cowboy novels and you just said oh hey and then you waved for the waiter and you told him to bring another plate of waffles for me.

I am not sure what all of this means but I'm going for breakfast.

Maybe I will see you there.

C.

SIX HUNDRED NINETY-FOUR

This is tape six hundred ninety-four. Today is 19 August 2006.

[| |]

[—.]

[| |]

[—.]

—There are days that I wish I had died before I could disappoint you.

SIFTING THROUGH STATIC
ACT THREE, SCENE ONE:
(OR, SHADE'S FORAGE, SHADE'S SHADOW)

More miles until my father and I stop at a highway diner lifted up from dust. A gravel parking lot, empty. A sun-bleached sign and a candy-stripe awning. How the engine clicks after it's killed.

Inside, the light spreads through in sheets while a jukebox petrifies unplugged. A radio mumbles classical music from the shelf above the malt blenders. Split vinyl and chipped Formica form the bones of this place. A ceiling fan turns too slowly to matter.

We sit at the booth in the corner. I reach for the menus wedged behind the napkin dispenser.

Cheeseburgers, Wayne says before I touch them.

With fries.

We wait for the waitress and my father closes his eyes. His head sways, faintly, to the radio.

Do you know this tune? he asks me, blind, swaying.

Debussy.

Prélude à l'après-midi d'un faune.

I close my eyes.

It ends, and the waitress arrives.

Cheeseburgers, he says.

With fries, she adds, and she is gone.

So what have you been reading? he asks.

Nothing, really. Mythology.

Any favorites?

No.

Do you know Phaethon?

Son of Helios?

Son of Helios. Do you think he was at fault?

Phaethon?

Helios.

For what?

For the damage. For the cities and the crops that burned with the people. For the darkness that followed. For the shatter he became after Zeus cut his boy down.

I've never thought about it.

Mm, he says, and the food arrives. We eat our fill and return to the road, but I am preoccupied.

Phaethon's headstone reads: *greatly he failed; yet did he dare greatly*, and I wonder, often, about my father's life and who he might have been had things gone differently.

ROY/LONGMONT, CO/2007-07-24
16:41:36—16:50:50

But there's not much to say about it, really, unless you really want it spelled out. But you're smarter than that. You don't need me to spoon-feed you everything.

Humor me.

Why? Why should I?

Because it's important.

Why?

It's stuff I want to know.

So go ask your dad, then.

You don't think I would've done that if I could?

Why can't you?

He's impossible to talk to.

Yeah, well—I hear you there.

And further, how am I supposed to know that I'm getting the real story if there's no corroboration?

But hearing what I say changes things—how? So I talk, and then you have two stories, and probly they don't line up exactly or maybe not even close. What then?

Then I find a way through.

But you're no better off, is what I'm saying.

No, I think you might could make more sense out of everything if you tell me what you think, I think. Maybe that. Maybe do that and I'll tell you how right you are, hm?

And how would that be any different?

I dunno. It'd be more interesting for me, at least. That's for sure.

Probably.

So how 'bout it, then? Whatcha think?

Do you really want to know what I think?

Ayuh, sure.

Really?

No, I'm lying and my feelings are fragile don't tell me oh please, oh please.

Come on. Out with it.

I think there's a lot about her that you're not telling me, for starters. That nobody's telling me. And part of it's, I think, that you don't know what happened—not really. And then I think if you really wanted to know what happened, you could've found out, but you didn't find out, so my guess is that you don't want to know, and my guess is you're content with that complacency, and my guess is you're afraid.

Ha! Look at you! I like this side of you.

Well?

Well what.

You tell me.

Well—.

Well you're right. You're right on all counts. Except on how content I am.

So you'd want to know, then. You'd want to know what happened to her?

I mean, sure, I guess. But I don't know that I much care anymore.

I mean I do, I mean. Care.

But not really.

Why not?

Wouldn't change a goddamned thing, how things went. The way things are.

What if I could tell you what happened, though? Definitively. If I could open my mouth and tell you a story that was true, and then you'd know.

Even if that was something you could do, I don't think I'd believe you.

Why?

Because it's all subjective. Your story, mine. Every story. And that's not even counting the fact that whatever your story is, I like mine better.

Well?

Well what?

Well what's your story?

Well in my story, since you're so interested, she's a liar. In my story she's everything you've heard about her and none of it at the same time and in my story she was the only one that was there for me when nobody else was there for me, took me out of the pain I was in and ruined my next nineteen years all in the same go. In my story she tells me she's grown tired of Gordon and she's thinking about leaving him, but the next day she says that nobody's ever gonna make her has happy as he does and she'd die if they weren't together. In my story she's a smiling tornado, a flaming puppy, an island of mess.

Island had some nice beaches, though.

So sh—

And in my story she fights with Dad all the time. She tells him he's got no right to her life and she'll do whatever she wants, and he tells her he'll kill her if she doesn't listen, so she plans on running away, but then he finds out and gets scary. Gets dark. Gets the kind of dark you run from if you can run at all.

In my story he comes home early from work and finds her packing and I'm the only one home, but neither knows I'm there. They have it out. They have it out bad. He wants to know where the Buick's from, the one in the driveway, and she says it doesn't matter. Things are thrown. Glass breaks. I hear

301

the wet thump of fist on face. There's silence. A door opens and then slams. A car starts and fades away. There's silence, and then a door opens, slams. Then a car starts, then fades. It's hours before a car comes back, but only one comes back. I hear the faucets run for a long time. I hear the shower run for longer. The sun comes up.

How's that?

Is that what happened?

Hmp.

Something funny?

Do you have any idea how long ago that was?

Thirty-nine years.

Thirty. Nine.

Even thirty years is a long time. What's your earliest memory?

What?

Humor me.

But—

Just do it.

Well—.

Well I'm probably two. It's Christmas. I open a present on the carpet and it's a plastic bell. Red. I stand and turn. I take two steps. I ring it at my parents and my mother claps and my father reaches for the next present. The bell doesn't make a sound.

And that was what, thirty years ago? More?

Sure.

I'm realizing now that I don't even know how old you are, but so thirty years. Thirty years, right? Thirty's a long time.

It can be.

How sure are you that that bell was red?

What?

The bell. How sure are you that it was red?

I'm sure.

How sure?

I'm sure.

And what if it was orange?

It was red.

But what if it was orange? What I'm asking you's what if someone showed you a picture from that exact moment and in that picture the bell is orange, and you're standing and you're ringing it, and the bell's a blur in your hand because you're too fast for the shutter, and your mother is smiling, and your father is reaching, but the bell—the bell's orange.

What would that change?

It was red.

Answer's nothing. It wouldn't change a fucking thing for you because your bell is red. So who gives a shit what color it was, really.

JULY 10, 2008

W:

I have no idea why I still write these. Seems an awful waste most of the time how we never talk and lots of days I wonder if this is just salting the cuts for me. But fuck me I guess. Here I am again but I am not drunk today.

I had a bad phone call with Roy. We are not getting along like we did before. Not that we ever got along really great like you and me but I am having a hard time. I guess it is going to be that way sometimes when it comes to brothers and their lives and their problems and how they figure it out. Sometimes it is going to be bad and you are just sort of along for the ride.

Anyways that bad phone call got me thinking about how I wish I could call you because I think you are the only other one that really understands what it's like to have Roy for a brother. Clearly that is not happening so this is kind of my backup plan. As long as I am here I thought I would take the opportunity to tell you about the other bad calls and stuff I have had to deal with to keep Roy alive over all these the years that you have so conveniently missed out on.

One time who knows how long ago it was but maybe ten years ago I had to drive Roy to the hospital because I found him so bad. I got pulled over for speeding and I just waved and waved for the cop to hurry up to my window once I got on the shoulder and he took his fucking time. He gets up there and I yell at him I need to get to the hospital my brother is dying but the balls on this guy he looks at Roy and asks him if he is okay and then just sort of stands there thumbs in his belt loops waiting for a response while Roy is all pale and slumped and clammy. I say come the fuck on man I am going to just go and you can chase me there and arrest me in the E.R. and I turn the car on and Roy picks up his head and looks out the window at the officer and Roy squints hard like he might know the guy and then he asks the cop do you need anything from the store? Hand to God that is what he said exactly. And then the pig gasps a little and sprints back to his prowler once he really seen Roy and we are lights and sirens all the way there. Roy does not remember any of this.

Another year Roy called me almost every day in the first half of February to wish me a happy birthday and every time I picked up I would remind him how he called me yesterday and come on man you know my birthday is in March. I would tell him remember my birthday cakes they were always green because I am in March man like shamrocks remember? But eventually I just stopped picking up the phone and eventually he stopped calling.

Would you believe I actually fixed him up once? But only once because I felt so dirty about it after. I remember how Roy used to pester you for a fix sometimes and you would say you would help but you would give him something else entirely like something he never asked for and how he would be so mad. He would be so fucking mad at you he would break things remember?

I remember once you handed him a huge basket of strawberries you had nabbed from somewhere but you never told us where you got them probably because you got them from somewhere you were not supposed to be but I remember how he just threw them down on the driveway where he had been waiting for you just threw them down and stomped them and stomped them until he slipped and fell but you did not help him up.

He kept me up nights between the hospitals and lockup. Few years there I kept my keys on an envelope with three or four or five hundred in cash on my nightstand next to the phone so either I would have cash to wire the bondsman or I would have the money handy in case I would need to buy a plane ticket and a suit.

So I do not really know what the point of all of this was with this letter aside to tell you that I am angry at you. I am angry at you for leaving him with me like this. You took the easy way out because you are selfish. You took the easy way out because you are not strong enough to do what is hard.

And I guess there is more too it is not just to be mad at you. I know you probably had your reasons to go and I have tried to understand them but I am still coming up short. But I guess the other reason I am writing is because I am pretty sure she called me yesterday. It rang and I picked up but there was no one there but I said hello a few times and I swear she was on the line. There was some breathing I could barely hear and then way faint like it was a voice in the other room it was her voice like she was sitting in the room and she told someone else to call the number to see if I picked up and then she told the person something or asked them something while she was sitting there but she was trying to be quiet but I could hear her. I could hear her I swear. I was so sure of it that I called Roy but that is why I started writing this letter because the call was so bad with him and then I felt frustrated because I wish you were here.

Wayne I am still writing like I have been writing as long as I can remember since way back even when I do not remember so good about what I was doing or who I was. I can go back and I have still got letters from the Conrad back then. Whoever that guy was. But that guy was writing you and both that guy and this guy don't think you know how hard that is. To keep writing. To keep going when there is nothing coming back at you from the other side. It is hell. No it is worse than hell it is purgatory. Hell would be nice I think sometimes if you would just write me back something even if it's just a letter I open and it just has the word NO typed small in the middle. That would be fine. Or just a picture of you giving me the finger that would be fine too. But to keep writing like this. To stay all coffined up with a phone that has no earpiece. You have no idea what that is like Wayne and I wish I could tell you. I am telling you here. I am here. Jesus Christ Wayne I am here and I have no idea where you are.

I do not know why I even wrote this. I do not know why I still write but every day I try to. Not every day I manage to get something down and sometimes it is a week or more or a month or two before I am able to load up my typewriter but I try. Every day I talk to you. I think about you and what you are doing how you are. Sometimes things happen to me and I still think man Wayne would like that but then there is this fraction of a second before I remember the way things are. Every day. Every day there is something to say and when I can I try to get it down on paper. But these letters all of them they just pile up and up while I wait for an address and when I have an address I send them and when I send them they come back in a brick with a tag that says Return To Sender or No Longer At This Address or sometimes with no note or sometimes they do not come back at all. Shame. It is a real shame.

I cannot help thinking about the things we have missed of us. All these years all this growing up and changing and of things happening good and bad. All of you is dark to me and me to you and that's sad but somehow. Somefuckinghow I still have hope and it is there every day. Every. Single. Day. And it is something so incredible Wayne. It is what I am most proud of and it is something you have never seen something you will never know. You could have known it because I offered it but you spent your life slapping my hand away. That is not to say that we are out of time. There is always time always for something to get better. For all of these plans and possibilities for you and me and Roy and for the family to start over and get straight again and bury the bad deep. I just hope you have some hope too. I hope I find a way in.

On the bad days I feel like I would tell you to be ashamed if we could talk but then I think what is the point? Who gives a shit really. Nobody is keeping score and it does not matter what anyone or anything else says about it. We are here now and that is all that matters and if we only end up with one good afternoon together after all of this one chance then I would be happy. I would be content with that that we were able to get it all straight and get back to living even if the living only went until the sun went down.

I feel good today Wayne. I feel really good today for the first time in longer than I can remember so maybe this will be the last letter. Maybe not but it will be the last for a while at least. Not because I do not like writing no because this is my favorite thing to do because it is my way to talk to you and I feel like I can talk to you like I cannot talk to anyone else. It is sometimes hard to explain.

Your kid called me out of the blue and asked where I lived and if I was free for a visit on two weeks from today. On your birthday. I have no idea why. I have never before spoken to your kid and I have no idea why that would ever change now but maybe I will go along with it. Who knows what could happen. Unless.

I hope there is no bad news. I mean I don't know what is going on with you but I have no idea why your kid would be visiting me and not you on your birthday and I guess that is one reason I would get a visit if there was some bad news about you or about something. You had better be okay. I hope I am not going to agree to this just to find out that you are dead that that is why this is being arranged. That would kill me if you died. I have lost I don't know how many people dozens of people but I could not stand it if one of my family died. There was enough of that with Roy all those years of wondering and waiting for a call. It never came of course but it sure did wear me out all that wondering and the dreading. And now I am dealing with a bit of it again. Idiot me forgot to even get a phone number from your kid I just agreed to Thursday morning early. Maybe I will make breakfast. Your kid is not a vegetarian or anything right? Whatever.

I have a job again. I guess if I end up sending this or getting it to you or something that is something good that you should know that I am working. It does not pay very good but my boss is a reasonable man. A fair man. Nice change of pace. He is a vet too. He was Marines but we still seem to get along. He was three tours and his old man was in Korea like ours but his dad did not come home. I am driving a forklift for starters but they say that if I do good they have got a warehouse manager that is due to retire soon and if I do good then they like to hire from within for that kind of gig so that is a goal I have. I am trying hard.

You know I figured out something that I never really had before and it is going to sound stupid but hear me out. It is goals. Real ones. I have never really had many of them but it is amazing how well they work for things you know? When you decide you are going to do something and then you do it because fuck that thing and anything else in the way it is going to happen. And Jesus Christ does that make me sound stupid but well I have been doing that now. One of them is that I read the newspaper every day now cover to cover except for the advertising and obituaries. I am trying to drink less also too. That and a few other things and I will be the best fucking candidate for that promotion they have ever seen because who does not want to have a manager that knows what is going on in the world and is not such a loser. I am betting nobody.

I do not know what else to say really. I guess I can just say that I am feeling good and I am trying hard at something really really trying for the first time that I can remember in a long time and I hope it works out for me but even if it does not work out it is okay. I will just find something else and try for that. I just thought you would like to know.

I wonder about you you know. All the time I wonder about you and I talk to you every day. I talk to you every day about wondering what you are doing and where you are and what

you are doing for work and if you like it and how you are. I
hope it is good. All of it. That is what I want most even though
I know it is hard to see and I know that maybe sometimes I did
not do the best job of showing it even back before but brother
I really just hope for life to be good to you. I do.

God knows you have earned it.

Goodbye for now.
Conrad

SEVEN HUNDRED ONE

What do they weigh, do you think? Their truths. Do you think they weigh something?

Most days I feel that they must because when I think of my family and their thoughts, they feel heavy inside my head. And maybe that is just me, right—that is always a possibility, that, perhaps, it is just I who is odd, is different, and that what I feel is something nobody else feels.

But maybe not, though. Maybe I have something by the toe here and I have latched onto a question much larger than me and my comparative pettinesses.

I mean, name me something more cumbersome than truth. Show me a person who does not know how difficult it is to be honest about the way things are, about the completeness of however things are. Find me a person that does not see the comprehensive truth as anything but a box made of all corners and no edges, unwieldy and uncomfortable to hold but you hold it because you have to, because nobody else will hold your box for you and to drop it is to die.

Everyone has a box. I feel I know what yours must be, but what is mine, you maybe are wondering?

I would think it obvious. For the sake of avoiding misunderstanding, though, I will say that at some point growing up you must have noticed that there are no pictures of me like there were of you. There were so many snaps of you on the walls—so many that I ran out of room. You playing. You growing up. Maybe you spent time looking at them. Maybe you looked at them and noticed, once, that for a man as old as I am, there are hardly any pictures of me save for the few that your mother kept.

My silhouette on a fishing trail, tackle box and pole.

My hair blowing back on a motorcycle, some four feet off the ground.

My ankles crossed on a laboratory bench, a book on my chest, asleep.

And this is the most of them.

I can tell you of a few others that exist. Maybe they still exist somewhere, but they still exist in my head for as long as I still have it, and you should know about them for after I am gone.

The first is of Harriet, and it is perhaps the only picture that I ever saw of her. She is young, maybe two. She is standing in black cowboy boots, a man's boots, that come up almost to her hip beneath a frilly white dress. Her right hand is gripping the seat of a chair in our kitchen and her hair is in pigtails. She is looking up in surprise, mouth open in an O and eyes above the camera, looking, looking, looking at the person taking the picture, probably your grandfather. And her eyes have this look of such—how can I put it? Not betrayal. Not surprise, though, either. Shock? Or disbelief. Perhaps disbelief. Disbelief that she has been seen. That someone could see her.

The second is of my brothers and I and your grandfather, the three of us in the yard and him with his back turned. Roy is sitting and Conrad has a baseball bat. I have something in my hand, in my closed hand, and for the life of me I cannot remember what it was. Something I did not want seen. All of us are looking at the camera because your grandmother was taking the picture and told us: Boys? and we turned. I was probably eight or ten. This is, I think, the last picture to have all three of us in the same frame.

Pictures are funny things. Pictures are a corner of my box or maybe just a heaviness inside it, I cannot decide, but their fettle hides inside their objectivity—that they are objective in a way that memory is not, I mean, but also that, intrinsically, they are devoid of grander context. A picture has elements of focus and obstruction, light and shadow. A picture has a frame—an edge of the scene, that is to say. And a person looking at a picture of themselves will always be to some degree left wondering how the picture itself or some element of it contradicts, complicates or obfuscates their memory of that moment, that day, that year of their life. Like, what was in my hand? I know I had something, but that thing is gone from me. Only that it was something, and it was in my hand, and that I had it in my hand at that moment and I did not want it to be seen. That is where that little story ends, and nobody else knows that this story even *is*, let alone about whatever I had hidden, and had I never seen this picture I would never have wondered this at all.

Pictures—.

Pictures are an aggravation.

What was in my hand?

I know that pictures mean different things to people, and I regret that I had none to show you, none that might give you more than the few, singular snippets of me that tell you almost nothing.

My feet on a laboratory bench. When?

Midair on a motorcycle. Where?

What was in my hand?

If but I could go back with a different life, how I would take pictures my way, with all of the things that a picture needs, with good people and with a story. I dream of pictures that are little more than membranes, of context blowing through them that means something to me, to you, to anyone looking at them who, but for that image, would never know that I was even here at all but could look, and could see, and could know.

One of these pictures that I want, it looks like this: an oak tree and a lake. Me at twenty-four, Conrad twenty-six, Roy is twenty-three. Conrad and I are two sides of similar coins, fibrous and thick-armed with wild hair that touches the shoulders, my beard the way it was, wide and impenetrable and his mustache a broad blonde beam to curve about the mouth. His Army dress shirt. My stolen plaid. His arms crossed beneath his chest and my left hand braceleting my right wrist behind my belt.

We stand abreast of Roy, sitting cross-legged between us because he wants to, not because he has to. His cropped hair. His fleshy neck between his balanced shoulders. His legs, whole and deep. His white shirt smudged with the same grease that smudges his thewy arms, his blocky, leathered hands. His hands, pulling grass.

We are all looking straight into the lens. It does not matter if we are smiling. We can be smiling, if you like, or not if you think that suits us better.

In front of us, on the ground, with her back on the ground, and her head back, and her chin up, and her hair spread about her, and her dress spread about her, and her feet in black cowboy boots with her heels on the ground, and her toes up, and her palms on the ground, and her fingers spread. Her eyes are closed. She is smiling. The breeze catches strands of her hair to writhe them up alive, and her lungs are taut with air, and sh—

•••
•••

SIFTING THROUGH STATIC
ACT THREE, SCENE TWO:
(OR, TO BREATHE SALT AND SLEEP)

What are your favorites?

The things that nobody considers, Wayne says, the things that seem so nothing. That Perseus is remembered for his deeds, but that death follows him long after he's left the stage. How nobody remembers Phineas, Andromeda's betrothed, murdered into stone by Perseus' casual hand, or the giant Chrysaor, all gold and fury, who sprung from the Gorgon's neck alongside Pegasus and was abandoned on that rock when Perseus rode his brother into the sky.

Chrysaor, a grandson of Poseidon.

Chrysaor, a child of death.

Chrysaor who himself would father the abominate Geyron, a many-featured, eldritch thing that was evasive of description, yes, but was a thing spawned all the same, and a thing spawned already-fated to fall to the poisoned bolt of Heracles, son of Alcmene, grandson of the selfsame, cancerous Perseus and Phineas' stolen Andromeda. Or even—how about this—or even just setting Perseus' malignancy aside. Even just excising him to see that, in relief, none are ever the least bit troubled by

Poseidon's perpetual gelding, hm? Or that that trope's engine rests always, in part, at Man's incomparable feet?

Such pain in the wake, my father says, such anguish. So many stories of vying for remembrance, yet so many are forgotten but to those who dig. How plutocratic! he laughs.

There are other stories. Stories just as forgotten.

Like what? asks his dissatisfaction.

Like your father, for example. How he once caught you and Conrad smoking cigarettes behind the shed when you were seven and nine. How he read the newspaper while you knelt and ate the rest of the pack.

I—

Or like how you killed a dog once that ran through your legs while you were logging the Rockies. You had two, three hundred pounds on your shoulder and this dog, the foreman's, it wouldn't stop running through your legs and nipping at your heels, wagging its tail.

It—

How the hill was double-pitched enough that to drop that log was to crush your leg or maybe to die, and how you strained. How you waited until you couldn't. How it was quick, yes, but it was far from painless.

[—.]

Or there.

[—.]

Right there.

[—.]

Like how your silences have sickened me.

[—.]

How they spun me up. How they've salted my lungs.

[—.]

Like how you and yours, you taciturns, how you've charged me to speak, hm? You and your brothers? How from silence I spoke to delimit that silence, and how your brothers—how I spoke not with them, no, but *as* them? How I *became* them? To write for you? Hm?

[—.]

Hm?

[—.]

How I wrote for you?

[—.]

About you?

[—.]

As you?

[—.]

How I saved everything that I wrote for the someday again when we'd speak, and then how the call came, and how I came, and how I gave it all to you to remember.

How you said *Thank you* as you placed it all, gingerly, into a box. How you lid me up like sleep.

How you straightened the box atop the table, aligning its edges to the table's edges and how you stroked its lid and stroked its lid as I watched me ripple from your eye.

Then how you looked up, and how you smiled.

Oh I'm Wayne, you said, and I shook your shaking hand.

So see? Everything is a death of some kind, everything. So Phineas? Chrysaor? Let them go. Let them be as they are. Watch the road.

He adjusts the wheel. He says nothing.

ROY/LONGMONT, CO/2007-07-24
17:22:24—17:28:02

One thing. If I had to name one thing—.

I guess if I had to name one thing my life's taught me it's that fractured families make for lonely children, but I don't mean that in the obvious way. Obviously if your family's shitty, you're gonna have a shitty life, no, I don't mean that. I mean it gets passed down in ways you wouldn't guess. Or at least in ways I never guessed.

Example?

Well take you—I don't know you. You don't know me. My kids know you exist, but to my knowledge you've never spoken. And me? Well. I doubt you even know my middle name or if I have one.

You could make a list of the holes in your history, in my kids' history. And whose fault is that? Not my kids. Not yours.

Whose, then?

Isn't it clear?

I wouldn't be asking if it was.

Yeah, well—.

Well what have you done to mend your end?

Not enough, I suppose, but then that's taking the position that it was ever fixable at all. And maybe there was a time I thought differently, but I think now that there's plenty shit you just can't fix.

So you never even tried, then.

Well first of all, fuck you. Second, after you and my kids were born I tried making some calls to your pops. I was hoping that he'd pick up and we'd be able to talk, that we'd be able to come together and bury our dead, you know, take you kids to the park, maybe. Start over fresh.

I didn't know.

I know. I mean, I didn't know that you didn't know, but somehow I knew.

How'd you know?

Your dad's smart enough to hit play on an answering machine. So I knew. I knew I was running into a wall.

[—.]

What—?

—It's more than that, though.

Meaning?

I mean he's—. I don't know when you last tried calling him, but he's—. For a long time he's been—

He's been gone, yeah, I know he's been gone. I know he's dead. Or if not dead, then I know he's been gone somewhere past where you could follow.

[—.]

How did—?

I'm not stupid.

—How long have you known?

Oh, seven—? What time is it? Maybe seven, eight hours ago.

—While I've been sitting here?

I mean I've kinda always known, kinda. That that's the picture if I'm the frame. But like I said: I'm not stupid. You don't live so long as I did on the bottom without learning how to read a person, so yeah, seven, eight hours ago, you blinked.

Thirty-odd years you've been staring me down, but you blinked first. And you didn't even notice.

Besides, I know what today is. I don't forget birthdays. I'm not stupid, and you're not that clever.

[—.]

—And you're not upset?

Upset—?

[—.]

—*Hmp.*

There's this phenomenon—*semantic satiation*—that I read about in a waiting room, once. Shrink's office. Some journal. Skimmed the article, but the gist's that it's naming that thing where how if you repeat a word over and over again for long enough, how that word will then lose all its meaning.

Upset.

Upset.

Upset.

Upset—.

[—.]

—Roy?

You wonder whether I'm upset. Fine. I'm aware how I sound, I'm aware what I say, so fine—if you're asking if I'm upset, then fine. I can fathom your diffidence. But if you're asking if I'm grieving—?

If you're asking if I'm grieving, then *fuck*—you haven't even been listening.

JANUARY 9, 1974

Dear Wayne:

I had a few minutes before heading to bed so I thought I would write you and tell you about my day. Of course I do not know where you are living right now but I felt like writing you today and then maybe when I have an address for you I can mail this. Sort of it can be like a time capsule for my day today. I think you would like that. Maybe I will keep writing you as an experiment whenever I am thinking about you.

The landlady did not knock today. She usually comes over for coffee or tea when I get home because she always hears when I get home and it is time to get up for most people anyway. Most days she knocks about ten minutes after I close the door and we talk for a little while. Maybe she just did not hear me today or maybe she is out for breakfast or out of town. Or I suppose she maybe could have died. I just thought of that. I will check after I finish this to make sure she is not dead. But she is a nice old lady and it is nice to have someone to talk to but I think she is just lonely and I do not think she has much to do. She never has much to say except for what she watched on T.V. that afternoon but that is okay I suppose. She is nice enough. I do not mind. Anyways there is no company this morning and I felt like talking to someone so I guess this will have to do.

This new job is a bitch Wayne. They have me managing a whole warehouse and the boss is a hassle. I am never late but his watch is fast so I am always late. It does not matter how many times I tell him to check his watch either because it is always all on me. Get here earlier he says but I cannot make the bus drive any faster and I am not about to catch the 10:26 and show up to that hellhole an hour early. Get a car he says. Fuck him I say. But I never really say that.

Some nights are slower than others. The worst nights are Mondays and Thursdays because that is when we usually get bigger shipments coming in. Today is Wednesday though and a slower one than usual because part of the load for today got stuck in customs or something so it will be coming in tomorrow which means tomorrow might be a double. I do not think I will be staying at this job long but I need to save up a little money first.

My New Year was a drag. A few weeks ago I broke up with a girl mostly because I did not want to buy her a Christmas present and things were not going well anyways. I was just being practical but she still called me an asshole. Anyways I thought I would just hang out alone but then at the last minute I guess I got lonely and I called one of my other exes but I do not think you remember her. I cannot remember if you even met her but I do not think you did. Whatever. Her mom picked up the phone and I asked for her but her mom told me that a few months ago she got sick and she died. I was very sad. I thought about calling other people but I could not really get ahold of anyone who was around and everyone else was out of town. I ended up at a bar by myself and there were some other old guys there and we watched the ball drop but it was not very fun. I drank too much and I woke up on my doorstep with my keys in my hand. I guess one of them called me a cab.

You Know Who has a birthday coming up. I have no idea if you are planning on doing anything for her but I will most likely get her a card. I would get her something else like maybe a book or two but I do not have much money right now. Maybe I will make her something or maybe I will write her a letter too. That sounds nice actually. I think she would like that too. I will have to hold onto it for now of course but then I am doing the same thing for you right here. I am very much looking forward to the day when I can mail this to you and the other one to her that I think I am going to write next.

I hope you are doing well Wayne-o. I miss you. I know things were not great how we left them but I miss you and I hope I can catch up with you soon. I wonder a lot about what you are doing and how you are doing. I bet you are doing some great things wherever you are. You always had great things in you. I hope you are doing something great. I know you are.

I still remember when you called me a while back and how we were going to catch a football game. I still have the tickets but we will need new ones by now. That is fine though. Whenever you have the time you let me know and I will get my hands on some good ones down near the fifty and we will drink beers and eat hot dogs and we will have a good time.

I miss how things used to be back before all the mess came through. Do you miss it too? Sometimes I wish I could go back you know? Go back and fix a lot of things. I know we fight but that is what brothers do sometimes they fight. But fights should not end things. Fights should bring people together I think and we can fix everything I know we can. We can fix everything before we are old.

I hope we never grow old.

Your brother Conrad

SIFTING THROUGH STATIC
ACT THREE, SCENE THREE:
(OR, SELVAGE HAS NO SYNONYM)

From the driver's seat, my father breaks his silence: I tried hard, you know.

I know.

I tried hard but I failed. It all fell apart in my hands.

No it didn't. But both of us can hear those words come out empty.

How I admired the things they had inside, he says. The things I could never find.

Like what?

How my brothers could forget. How I wish I could forget.

But you did, though. You did forget.

But I tried, he says. I tried to be there for the things that mattered, and how I tried to ward them from afar.

How I loosed Gordon beneath Los Angeles and he dredged Roy up in under a week. How Gordon heaped him near the hospital, and how he watched them rush him in.

And oh, how substantial Roy looked in his mortarboard and gown. How he scanned the crowd, I think, for me and how I almost waved from the back but I couldn't because I couldn't bear his scanning eyes and how they scanned, and scanned, and scanned, I think, for me. I was there, though, I was there. In the back I was there.

And Conrad, how I kept his letters, how they piled up and how on some days I could almost open them and oh, if but I could have opened one. If only I could have opened one and seen him, could have read his words. What might that have meant for us? What might he have said?

It doesn't matter.

But I was afraid! I was so afraid. I don't even know why.

It's okay. It doesn't matter and it's okay.

I killed it in us, though.

Killed what? Everything is a kind of death, yes, but everything is also alive.

No.

Yes.

No.

Yes. Yes it is.

—Is it, though?

Consider Roy's flailing. Consider how he thrashed for your ankle and missed. How his drowning drifted you on.

I—

And Conrad? Revel in how he never breached your door.

But—

Revel in how he stuffed himself through the mail slot but that his impositions came in vain. He's panacea, yes, but also he's poison, and always both at the same time. You've known this. You've always known this and you've never needed it.

But you. I was never fit enough for you. I tried, I tried, but I succumbed to myself. I failed you in my silence.

I am alive. I am alive, and we are alive, and here we are, heading east. The sun is rising and setting and the wind is with us. There is nothing now but that we are alive, and here, and the sun upon us so your shame, your dissatisfaction—I raise you from these and bid you speak. Speak to me while we are still alive.

ROY/LONGMONT, CO/2007-07-24
18:02:01—18:08:01

All I can do now is hope.

That wasn't the question, really.

I know, but I don't care.

What do you tell them, anyway?

My kids? About my family?

Or whatever.

I dunno. Not much.

[—.]

—I don't tell them much. I tried to when they were much younger, when they'd come home from school and ask about who their grandpas or their uncles or their cousins were when other kids would have those people pick them up from school, and I tried telling them then, I did, but it was always so awkward. I mean, try telling a kid they have two uncles and an aunt, sort of, but no, you couldn't talk to them, and also you've got a cousin, I think, or maybe more than one. I don't know that either.

How do you explain yourself to a six-year-old? I never did figure that out.

I don't think there's much to it, really.

Got kids, do you?

Would it matter if I did?

Oh I don't know, maybe you do. All's I know's that the childless are the ones always thinking that talking to a kid's as easy as opening your mouth.

Isn't it, though?

My point exactly.

But no, I'd try telling them things time to time, but then the telling always begat more questions I didn't have answers for, so then I started to fall back onto the old *we-just-can't* answer whenever they'd ask, and eventually they just stopped asking. Was that the best way to handle it? Fuck no. But it was all I could manage do.

Do you talk to them about it now?

They don't really come around much anymore. There were a couple of times when maybe one of 'em was over for a beer, late, after getting off a swing shift, and a couple of times I even started to speak. I'd open my mouth and, *Hey, listen*—but then: nothing. The words just wouldn't come out, and after a beat I'd end up saying something innocuous.

Hey, listen—don't forget that Mom's birthday's coming up.

Hey, listen—I wanna make it over to a Rockies game before September gets too cold with my joints, you know.

Hey, listen—I love you.

Something empty. And that'd be that.

What's stopping you from dialing a phone?

I dunno. Fear. Mostly fear. Mostly wondering what they'd say and being worried they'd be angry at how there's so much stuff I never told them, so much stuff they were boxed out of on account of my dark, and them being upset, and me ending up worse than when I started. Lonelier. Ending up lonelier than I am now.

But isn't there a chance that they'd just listen? That they'd pick up the phone and you could start talking and you'd get it all out?

I mean sure, there's always a chance for something else to happen. But I know how my luck goes. I know exactly what would happen and I don't think I could take it.

Well. Okay. So what do you hope for, then? Since life's so unkind.

Oh I hope for lots of stuff. Little stuff, big stuff. Stuff that's medium-sized.

Give me some sizes.

But everything's a different size depending on when you ask me, though. Something can be big one day and forgettable the next. Or the other way around.

That's not what I meant.

I know.

Roy—.

[—.]

Mostly I just hope everyone's okay, y'know? All the people I care about, even the people that I don't see that often or don't remember that I care about but I'd know everything about them in a second if you brought up their name. All the crucials. I hope they're okay, that they're happy and they're okay, all of them, wherever they are.

What else?

I dunno. I hope my life wasn't a waste. In the end, I mean. I hope I'm in the black when they burn me up, I mean to say.

And you don't think you already are?

Oh I don't know. Maybe. I hope I am, but I dug myself a hole for too long using people up, spitting 'em out. And that's no good, no good at all. Enough of that you do and there's no coming back.

But yeah, I don't know. It's been a long time I've been making up for it but I don't know if I'm there yet. Soon, I hope, if not already. Soon.

What else?

What else? I don't know. Typical father shit, I suppose. I hope my kids don't find me too much a drag. And I don't pray anymore, but Christ-in-a-waffle-iron, don't let them make the same mistakes I did. I made enough for a whole family so they deserve a pass, I think, and I hope they're happy and they do all the things that they wanna do, go all the places I'll never see, sing *Kumbaya* on the moon, whatever. All that. I hope for that.

Anything else?

I mean I hope I stay ahead of the pain meds for as long as I can, right, there's that, too. They're a tricky bitch to deal with these days and always have been, considering, but lately it's been trickier. Narcos I can't take anymore, but the docs've been good at swinging me around on different stuff, mix'n match, and every year they're inventing some newfangled wonder-something for the low, low price of eighty a shot. So whatever. Most days I wake up stiff and what's left of me hurts like you'll never know, but by lunch I'm typically tolerable.

Sorry.

Don't be. The pain's an interesting experience if you look at it from a Zen sort of way, that it's just another experience, just another way for the universe to be experiencing itself. I've been reading books about that lately and I don't know if I buy it, but I was sort of there in that headspace before I even read them, thinking that hey, at least I'm feeling something, and something beats dead nine times outta ten, yeah?

I suppose.

And I hope she's happy wherever she is. Or if she is. If she's not—I mean, if she's gone—.

If she's gone, then I hope she's at peace, that she was at peace at the end, whether it was forty years ago or forty minutes ago. I hope that maybe most of all.

—Is that it?

I don't know. Is that it? There isn't that much else out there that I really hope for.

There doesn't have to be more. I was just wondering.

Well I hope you're getting what you want out of this, whatever it is. Goes along with the same hope I've got for my kids, that they do the things they're interested in, and that those things give them the things that they want. It's about the most you can hope for out of life, really, I've found. That and lots of money.

[—.]

Well, for whatever it's worth, this has been helpful.

Has it?

In many ways, yes.

Mm.

Well that's good. That's good that with this—that you found at least a little of whatever it is that you're looking to get out of it. Out of me. I don't know what you'd want out of me.

Every person knows something that you don't.

I suppose you're right. I mean, I've led an interesting life I guess you could say, but it wasn't great. But I'm glad that you came by today.

Me too. I'd like to come back if you'd have me.

Mm—.

[—.]

—Roy?

Don't take this wrong, but no, I think this is it for us.

Why?

Because I feel that I'm done, and I think this is it.

Roy—

Yeah, no. No, this is good. This is good and I'm done. I'm done now. No more from me.

—Is it, though?

Is what?

Is this good?

Well dontcha think it needs to be? I think it needs to be so you don't keep looking too hard for whatever it is that you're trying to find, I mean, right? That's maybe the last thing for now that I hope for—that you don't look too hard and you learn to let go when it's time to let go. That when something's done, you learn to let it be done, and just be.

Just be, just be.

And then when it's time—when enough time has passed and it's time again—.

Well—.

That's when you just go and find yourself something better to hope for.

SIFTING THROUGH STATIC
ACT THREE, SCENE FOUR:
(OR, METONYMIES YOURS, REVENANTS MINE)

I am envoy to my dead. I speak because my dead do not speak as they should, as people should.

People should speak, but my dead are barely people. They transfix upon synecdoche, how this moment is all of history, this pain, all of future—how of course we are distillable into these. Single. Things.

My father and I, we drive. We speed always east, shortening the days, quickening the time while the sun spins about us day, then night, then day again, faster and faster until the sky goes a dim denim and the road unravels at impossible speed, faster and faster until the features about us shed their selfhoods to become the great grey that we hum across so fast, it feels, that we seem to stop moving at all.

CONRAD/BAKERSFIELD, CA/2014-07-24
05:32:30—05:39:59

Why what?

Fuckin', why are you back?

We're not finished.

With what? What could we possibly not be finished with, fuck. Fuckin', all you do—all you did with me was show up and rip off the Band-Aids, twirl the salt about, and get pissed at me for being me. So are we ever going to finish this thing, this whatever? 'Cause I'm pretty goddamned tired of it if after, what, six years—after six fuckin' years you're back and this is the same shit again, Jesus fuckin'—

Depends on you.

—The fuck does that mean?

Depends on you when we're finished.

Well isn't that a fuckin' riot.

Not really, no.

So let me ask you somethin', then.

Shoot.

Why don't you like me?

What makes you think I don't?

I mean what did I ever do to make you not like me as much as you don't like me?

You're just part of a problem that I've been trying to understand, is all.

Again, what the fuck does that even mean?

Means I don't not like you.

Well four fingers of bourbon, *garçon*, and find me a fuckin' party hat.

Conrad?

[—.]

—Conrad will you describe them to me?

—What?

Them. Will you describe them to me?

Who?

Your family. Tell them to me, each.

Why?

Will you?

But why?

Conrad.

Fuckin'—Roy. Roy's in a wheelchair, and he's prolly got his Twenty Year-Chip now, lest he limped off the wagon, and—

No.

No, I mean will you describe them to me as you see them. When you think of them how you'd like them to be, maybe, but when you think of them—how you see them. Tell me that.

Oh.

[—.]

—Conrad?

Conr—

Roy.

Roy's clean. Roy's strong. Roy's got short hair and he wears overalls because he's usually in the shop, but they're all smudged up and he's got some grease on his face from where he was touchin' his face when he didn't realize he had grease on his hands. His eyes are blue, pale blue. He's got bigger muscles than me and his back's straighter'n mine. He's not tall, though. Roy's never been tall and that's not how I see him. Short, and clean, and strong, and good.

His hands are torn up in the way that, you know—the way that old mechanics' hands are torn up. How they look just like stones. How they look like hands that get used the way most hands don't get used anymore.

His hands, I see 'em stuffin' a rag into the back of his overalls while he stands in front of his bookshelves full, full, full of books of all kinds. Books from different places and in different languages and old books and new books and books I never ever heard of, and he's stuffin' a rag in his back pocket and he's pickin' out a book for after dinner, by the fire, until he falls asleep with that book on his chest like he does until he wakes up.

Wayne—.

I dunno.

Wayne's got long hair. Long hair like it used to be. Is it long now? It's been so long. In my head it's long and he's got it held up out of his eyes with a rubberband but he yanks it out and runs his fingers back through it and he's lean, real lean like a mall mannequin, and he's wearin' those ratty clothes that he always wore, the ones I'm not even sure he bought because I don't know what place'd even sell clothes like that but he opens the fridge for beers, for me and for him, and he grabs two with one hand, both of them those old ones where the can's like a real can with the pull tab on top that you rip off, and he tosses me one, and I catch it, and I tap the top, and we sit, and we cheers after they're open. We sit somewhere nice. Up on a hill, maybe, beneath a old tree. We just sit, and I hope he talks to me, but I don't think he'll talk to me, but that's okay because it's nice to just sit. To just be.

Harriet's—.

I dunno.

I guess the way I'd see her's different.

How so?

I mean I've got the picture of her in my head much like whatever picture that you've prolly heard of how she looks, what she usually wore, all that shit. But when I think of her, I think more of how she was different than anyone I ever met, how she'd show up in the oddest places and say the strangest things just when you'd never expect her to and how she was never really there but somehow it felt like she was there the whole time, you know? So when I think of her—I dunno.

I think of my brothers, all of us standin' together for a picture but she's taking the picture. We fight about how we line up, how Wayne doesn't want to be in the picture but he plays along, and how I say we should line up by height but Roy doesn't like that, so he says we should go by age because that makes the most sense, even though that's the exact same fuckin' order. So we're reorganizin' and hittin' each other and carryin' on, because that's what you do even when you're almost thirty 'cause that's how old we are in this picture. And we're fightin' and laughin' and hollerin' and laughin' and then Harriet, she says Great, and we all look, and she's already taken the picture in the middle of all of that.

And then it's a polaroid, one of those first ones that you rip off the top sheet yourself, and when it's done we look, and sure enough, there's all of us all over each other but she caught us all laughin' but her finger's over the bottom corner of the picture, big enough it looks like a rock that's blurry out of focus in the corner but then when you look close you see that, no, it's her finger, and she's managed to make it into the frame after all.

And somehow—.

And somehow that's perfect. All of us all laughin', all of us caught up in a moment of life, alive. All of us. Together with her behind it, but also there in the corner, invisible 'til you see her, and then you wonder how you ever missed her at all—.

Good, Conrad. That's good.

—Is it?

It's good.

So—?

So what?

So what now?

So now we start again. At the beginning.

—Why?

Because that's how we move forward.

What's that supposed to mean?

[—.]

—He's gone, Conrad.

Who's gone?

Wayne. He's gone.

I know he's gone. I thought that's why we're here.

No, Conrad. He's *gone*.

I don't understand.

You know. You know, but you just can't bear to say it.

Say what? What are you saying? I don't understand.

[—.]

—He's dead, Conrad.

[—.]

He's been dead for a long time.

[—.]

I never understood him either, Conrad. I don't think anyone did. Not really.

[—.]

But Conrad—?

[—.]

Maybe together we can. Maybe it's not too late for that. For us to try.

[—.]

So, Conrad—?

[—.]

So now we start again, Conrad.

[—.]

At the beginning.

[| |]

SIFTING THROUGH STATIC
ACT THREE, SCENE FIVE:
(OR, THE SABOTS WE WERE ARE
THE ROUNDS WE WILL BE)

And here he's ever fibrous, wound tight like radio wire. Here his clothes are secondhand, stolen and traded-for and his boots could be used to hammer nails. Here his jaw's a drawbridge down, and here his shoulders spread far past his shadow.

His elbow in the wind, his left hand grips the wheel, and I can see that the scabs are healing. His right hand behind me on the seat, tapping off-time to the stereo—the stereo, crystalline.

He closes his eyes. The wind licks his long hair. And I fade.

My head turned toward him, my hair long like his. My hair going cellophane and my hands, brushing it back until it is gone. My hands becoming glass, and my arms becoming air. My chest, evaporating with each exhalation, and my legs— a sublimation slipping through the window in rivulets of fog.

Here is where I always leave him, just him, just as he was.

To his left: the grey blear of nothing but nothing. To his right: a void I will fill and refill beside the passenger window of a 1956 Porsche 356A, its green paint faded almost to white, the window framing road signs flipping past too fast to read:

Speed Limit 55. Colorado State Line 184mi.

COLOPHON

Buddy I know I'm dead. To you, I mean. But do not throw this away. You don't need to read it today or tomorrow. You don't need to read it next week or next year. But do not. Throw this. Away. We've still got some time. Go snub me awhile if that's what it takes or go have a good laugh at my cost with your pals. I'd understand. I'd expect those, even. But believe you me, the second you toss this you'll kill us for good.

I know now full well all the hell that I am. I was never a great dad and we both know it's way too late for me to start being your pops again anyway, but that's not why I wrote.

Truth is, I'm not doing okay. I'm not sick I don't think, but I've been real far from fine. In my head, I mean. In my heart. But I think all that's changing.

That's this bundle I'm mailing, buddy, what you're holding right now. All this paper. It's something that probably won't make tons of sense until you read the whole thing, each entry, each page, but it's straight flipped my whole head, and it's got me smoothing my old hurts to even—even the most of those I'm sure are part yours. It's been so long for us now that I can only guess at the size of those, but I don't want to. But this here thing in your hands, I know it's just what can shore us up,

351

fill us out whole enough to where we can just be, you know? Just us. Just as we were.

See, all these papers, they come from someone's lawyer. I'm only mostly sure I know whose, but I'll explain that in a minute. But last week this lawyer just shows up at my apartment, tells me he's sorry for my losses and hands me this exact same hodgepodge I'm sending, but uglier and thicker, so I bound it up nicer. But it came to me all two-hand heavy and slumpy and barely together beneath brown paper and twine, and the thing was old, no question. The thing looked like it came from some hacksaw butcher who didn't know that you're not supposed to bundle up a bunch of unalike cuts.

But this lawyer, he just holds the whole heap out at me, says sorry, and then he just stands there chewing on his lip and giving me a once-over or two and looking like he's wanting to say something but can't, so he just stands there all glassy and silent and sad.

But so I take up this package and I ask him what's in it? But he says he can't say. Package was in a trust, he says, and it's directed to me as the trustee to open.

Like a will? I ask.

Sort of, he says, but it's a trust. Trusts come with more options.

But someone's dead, though? I ask.

That's often how these things work, he says.

Who? I ask.

Can't say, lawyer says.

Fine. How long you had it then?

Can't say, he says again.

Well who else got stuff, then? Because isn't that how wills go? Because this is weird.

It's a trust, he says, not a will.

Right, I say, whatever. Who else got trusted?

Shouldn't say, he says, but nobody, and this delivery is the whole shebang, besides.

So I ask him what am I supposed to do with it? But he just shrugs and says that this delivery is it, and I'm the only one, and there is nothing else I can be told. Oh, and I'm sorry for your losses, he says. He says the trust says he has to say that.

And then just like that he's all turning to go. Hold on, I say, and I asked him if he wanted to come in while I opened it at least, maybe crack a beer? Beings that I'm pretty much all alone anymore any company is nice. But he just declines me politely and guns out this rainy little smile and says he hopes I have a better life.

Than who? I ask, and he turns for a sec, and he fiddles his jaw, and then lets out a sigh. Then he goes right on back to his walking away.

Hey mister, I say, and he turns back again.

This person, this whoever—(and I'm trying to think of a question he might answer, and I wish now I'd come out with anything else, but what came out was:) were they suffering?

And he waits a long second.

Depends, he says, but yes.

Then he was going again, his eyes back on the sky. I looked up at it too, it wild, white and blue. But there's never a cloud I'm quite able to name.

Buddy, do you remember at all from those times we would talk when we'd lay out for hours beneath all the clouds? You would make me up stories. There's a monster, there's a boy. I think on those times all the time. Or how we did all the ballgames, remember? And I'd yell at the Dodgers whatever you wanted? Your face looks like boogers, your hair smells like pee, and you'd laugh out so hard that you'd stop making sound. Or how we would outlast the sun on the south shore of Tahoe. How the whole beach was stones, all glossy for miles. How just it was us and that water, wet socks and Saltines. I remember you thinking we'd run out of stones. Do you? Remember?

There's lots I spend too much time remembering and more still that I know now I should've told you. Some of it's hard. Most of it's stuff that I don't know how to write. One of those things now is something I can talk on, though, because it's something makes sense to me after the package, finally, where it made none before.

I told you I was adopted. That wasn't a lie. What I never told no one's that when I was tiny I was left at a firehouse. No return address, no note. All I know of whoever left me is a clip of four keys that they set in my paw for a rattle, four totaled in all: one handcuff, two brass, one steel. These are the same keys that ended up hung round my neck or hooked on my belt each day of my life until the day I left town. You remember them maybe. I gave them to you in the driveway that day. I told you to hold onto them for a while.

I never told no one their story, not even your moms. I wanted no one to know how that scrappy old clip of four keys to nothing was my one lonely comfort I kept to remember. My only map to anywhere. I know I told you that they were important and that someday I would tell you why, but that was a mistake. I should've told you right then what they were. I hope you still have them, but I'd understand if you don't. The way I left, I would've thrown them away if I were you.

You know, whenever I think about my family I always first think about you. I mean it. It's only after that I then think about me and where I come from and how I always wished I knew more about all of that. I know a lot of orphans want that too. But I don't know. I somehow always seem to get more hung up on all my baggage on account of I know less about where I come from than most orphans I've known. Most of those kids got a picture, or maybe a story, or something meant something to someone even if the family they come from was nothing worth knowing, but I got nothing. Not until now, at least. But I think all that old lonesome and venom twisted me vicious inside, I think, and spread low and deep. I think that's the cancer that caught us, you me and Moms, and it wasn't but recent it made itself known. To me, anyway. I don't know. I'm off track.

Back to the package. To be honest, I thought about not opening it when I got it. (I'm sure you're maybe thinking the same thing right now.) I thought about waiting a while in case something else happened, like maybe the lawyer comes back, or maybe I get a phone call. Maybe something else strange. Who knows. So I watched the Giants suck for eight innings with that pile on my lap, and I clicked the tube off when they went down by twelve. No knock. No ring. No nothing. So I tore at the paper and tugged loose the twine. And buddy, I didn't know quite what to make of it all.

It's all a weird mess of stuff that seemed first so sideways, just tangled up lines. But then, I don't know. I sat there past sunrise, and the further I went in, the further it wasn't so sideways. Not quite. Not really. Not if you turn your head just right. From just the right angle you can see it's less a tangle and more a square, sort of. I don't know. It's hard for me to put, but like there's a long talk in here, right, that seems it ate a whole day, but there's other talks, too, but spread through six years. Those two, they're different pictures of the same pain.

Then also there's two kinds of letters, half sent and half not. Some, I think, were read by the intended, but all of them feel like they fell on deaf ears.

And between them in order, there's this, I don't know, this play or something. Something like a play. But it laces up lots of these stories, I think, and it's all about the same family but there are only a few names but I don't think the names are what's important because this family is the same as us but different. Different in the people but the same on the inside, I think. The same as us, I mean. I see us inside them so strong that there's no way they're not of our blood. No way. They're ours. It's three brothers in here, best as I can tell, and one of their kids, and they're all unalike but they're mostly the same. They all talk a lot about one certain someone, but something's off about her. I don't know. I can't dial that one in.

But the clip of four keys, two brass, one handcuff, one steel. My keys. That old clip of keys, wherever they are, they're the big golden bridge between what's in this bundle and here. They're what's selling me on all this big knot being written and sorted together by one of my parents because, see, those keys.

Those keys are in here everywhere, and everyone knows.

That's why they were given. That's what I think now. That's why they were left in my hand in the dark and the cold. I know it's her or it's him, whichever it is. It's them coming to me from fifty years back, right back to that firehouse. I know it. I don't know.

I don't know who's at fault for the disaster we are. Part of me wishes I could blame us on them, on these people in here, but then they never knew me at all. Seems strangely unfair.

All I know now for sure is that I'm sorry for taking myself far from you. I wish I was kept and not left at that station, but I'm trying to be more peaceful with what I can't change. And I know better now why I left you and Moms, but those reasons in hindsight are so fucking selfish and so goddamned small. But I'm here now, I'm here.

I'm here now but listen, before you read on there's two things I need. They're not things I want. They're important, I think, but they will not sound kind.

First, I need you to take whatever hopes maybe surfaced when this hit your doorstep, and I need you to bundle them up, all together and each, and I need you to trash them. I mean it. Gone. This chance in your hands, it's stronger than you and it's older than me and it'd tow all those hopes out way far past their depth. Trust.

Second, if you do hear me out like I'm hoping you will, I need you to know from the start: this bundle is nothing but suffer stacked sad, and low, and mean.

I love you. I'm not trying to be hurtful.

It's just that past here's the same dark that's rounded us always, but listen—hear me now, *listen.* You and me, we have a chance to get out from in it. It will not be quick. It will hurt more than anything. But I was handed our chance, our hard little chance, and now I'm here propping the door. Beers are on ice. Lights are on full.

Buddy please don't throw this away. You don't have to read it until you feel ready, but please. Do not throw this away. Please read it. Please call me.

I miss you, and I love you, and I am so sorry.

ACKNOWLEDGMENTS

I am indebted to those who have assisted me in completing
this long endeavor, be it by reading drafts, by listening,
or just by asking me how things were going.

As in life, I find that the most difficult aspect of writing is not
deciding what to include—it's knowing where to cut. As such,
I am beholden to those who have shown me how
to leave the unnecessary behind.

ABOUT THE AUTHOR

Ben Tyler Elliott holds a master's degree in English literature, and his research explored the symbiotic relationships between allegory, angst, and the subversive narrative. Whenever he isn't reading or writing, he can likely be found riding his bicycle, baking bread, or wallowing in Wikipedia's quieter corners. He's a lifelong fan of Major League Baseball's San Francisco Giants and, consequently, his second favorite team is whoever is playing the Los Angeles Dodgers today. This is his first novel.